"My summertime girl," he whispered, kissing her reverently on the forehead.

The softly uttered words and the caress of his hands on her back sent tingles of excitement racing through Summer. Her arms moved up to encircle his neck and she lifted her face.

"You want me, too!" Relief and surprise made his voice husky and transformed his anxious face. Slowly, almost haltingly, he lowered his mouth to hers.

The first gentle touch of his lips awakened a bittersweet ache of passion. Glowing waves of pleasure spread like quickfire through her body. They were two beings blended together in a whirling tide. . . .

Dear Reader:

We trust you will enjoy this Richard Gallen romance. We plan to bring you more of the best in both contemporary and historical romantic fiction with four exciting new titles each month.

We'd like your help.

We value your suggestions and opinions. They will help us to publish the kind of romances you want to read. Please send us your comments, or just let us know which Richard Gallen romances you have especially enjoyed. Write to the address below. We're looking forward to hearing from you!

Happy reading!

Judy Sullivan
Richard Gallen Books
8-10 West 36th St.
New York, N.Y. 10018

This Loving Land

DOROTHY GARLOCK

PUBLISHED BY RICHARD GALLEN BOOKS
Distributed by POCKET BOOKS

A RICHARD GALLEN BOOKS *Original* publication

Distributed by
POCKET BOOKS, a Simon & Schuster division of
GULF & WESTERN CORPORATION
1230 Avenue of the Americas, New York, N.Y. 10020

Copyright © 1981 by Dorothy Garlock

ISBN: 0-671-43563-9

First Pocket Books printing September, 1981

10 9 8 7 6 5 4 3 2 1

RICHARD GALLEN and colophon are trademarks
of Simon & Schuster and Richard Gallen & Co., Inc.

Printed in the U.S.A.

TO LINDY
Be proud of yourself. You are truly a beautiful person, with a special kind of courage.

Mom

TEXAS 1852

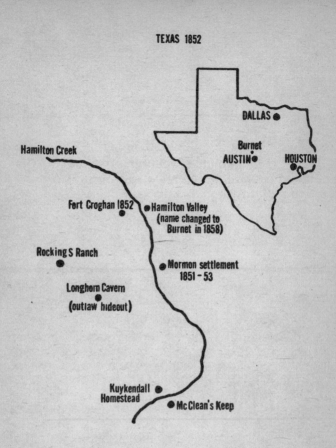

McLean's Keep, the Rocking S Ranch and all the characters in this book exist only in my imagination, with the exception of the Kuykendall family—my ancestors—who came to Texas with Stephen F. Austin in 1823 and helped establish San Felipe, the first Anglo-American settlement.

The town of Hamilton Valley, later named Burnet, is not to be confused with the present-day town of Hamilton, county seat of Hamilton County, which is to the north of Burnet County and was established in 1858.

Dorothy Garlock

Prologue

"Sam! Sam . . . !" The girl in the loose, homespun garment ran down the oak-shadowed path, jumped lightly over a fallen branch and threw herself into the man's arms. Closing her eyes tightly, she knew she was blushing with the thrill that leaped through her at the feel of his muscular, pulsing body pressed closely against hers.

"Ye looney lass!" He held her away from him. "And how many times must I be a tellin' ye not to run and leap like a frog? Ach, but ye'll be a fallin' and a hurtin' y'rself . . . or the bairn." The voice was rough and masculine and musical with its strong Scottish accent.

"Sam," she murmured urgently, "I'm so happy! I'm so happy I'm scared, Sam."

"Scared?" he murmured against her ear.

"I'm scared something terrible will happen. This has been the most wonderful summer of my life, Sam. It's been so wonderful, but it's so wrong. . . ." Her voice was muffled against his throat. "J.R. is fighting the

Mexicans, and I'm so gloriously happy. A wife should be sad when her husband is gone. Oh, Sam, I find myself, sometimes, hoping he don't come back!"

A growl of protest came from his throat. "Nye, sweet lass, ye don't be a wishin' that."

"Then I think, Sam, about Libby and the boy. Something terrible will happen to me for the wicked thing I've done to Libby."

"Hush, darlin' lass. Libby is safe in her dream world. She can never really be me wife, and I'll not fault her, for it's not of her own doin'. I love the laddie, and I'll be lovin' this bairn, too." He placed his big hand over her swollen abdomen. "If y'r man don't come for ye, my sweet lassie, I'll be a takin' care of ye and the bairn."

He gathered her against him, his hands stroking her back with long, slow caresses until she was molded so closely against him that she couldn't catch her breath for the excitement that beat through her.

"I want this summer to go on forever." It came out in a sort of gasping sigh, half-questioning, half-exulting, as suddenly, beyond her control, her body arched against his.

"It couldn't be wicked to love like this," he whispered breathlessly, suddenly lifting her and carrying her to where they could both lie in the soft grass, mouth to mouth, breast to breast. He kissed her tenderly, lovingly, again and again. "Don't be a thinkin' about the right or the wrong of it, think about now, and how I love ye."

All thoughts of being wicked retreated from Nannie's mind before the strength of the force throbbing through her in answer to his passion. And then it was as if a dam, which had been holding back wild, tempestuous waters, broke and washed over her. Her mouth was against his so that breathing was almost impossible, his weight held her pinned to the sweet-smelling grass and it was like drowning as she was swept along on the turbulence of their desire. Through the bursting darkness sudden joy, like a great flashing light, exploded within her. Afterwards, there was the warm, sensuous afterglow, as she curled up in his arms, the wetness of tears on her face and on his. She rested her cheek against the smooth silky hardness of his shoulder. Lying motionless in the kind of peace she knew only when she was with him, she fell asleep.

When she awoke, she felt quite different, and for a while she lay with her eyes closed, wondering why she was so tired, why she was alone. No arms held her comfortingly, no hard, muscled shoulder was beneath her cheek.

It was night-time. She could sense the brightness of the lamp through her closed lids. Gone was the sweet-smelling grass; she could feel coarse sheets on her bare skin. The only thing that was the same was her wet cheeks. Everything else was different. She was different. Feeling lighter than air, she floated like a feather, happy because soon she would be free. She knew what heaven would be like.

Nannie opened her eyes to find her daughter bending over her.

"Mama, you've been dreaming."

"Summer." She smiled a little. "My beautiful Summer."

"Can I get you something, Mama?" Gentle, anxious fingers touched the tears on her mother's face.

"No." It was a weary whisper. She couldn't help but be disappointed at finding herself in another time and another place. She closed her eyes again, hoping to feel the warmth, the ecstasy, to hear the passionate whispers. With a little groan of anguish, she knew the time was not yet. But soon . . . soon. Her eyes filled with anxiety and she lifted a hand to tug at her daughter's dress. "Soon," she whispered weakly. "Soon you'll be alone with John Austin. I want you to go to Sam

McLean. Find Sam, Summer, and tell him who you are. He'll help you. He'll take care of you and John Austin. In my little chest is a letter telling you where to find him."

"Mama. . . ." Tears brimmed in the violet eyes. "Mama . . . no—"

"Promise me, Summer. Promise me you'll go to Sam. Sam. . . ." The weak voice trailed away and Nannie Kuykendall closed her eyes, never to open them again.

Chapter One

It was unbearably hot in the closely-packed stagecoach, and remembering the deep coolness of home—the Piney Woods—Summer felt even hotter under her cape of blue-black hair. She was pretty, sitting there in her cotton dress, the sun shooting lights through her hair. Small, pretty and determined; she was nineteen years old and she was on her way west with an eight-year-old boy in tow.

The girl's face showed lines of tiredness, but the black-fringed violet eyes refused to close. She was determined to stay awake, using her hat to fan the flushed face of the child sleeping in her lap.

He was very dear to her, this small brother of hers. She had brought him up virtually alone. When he was three, their papa had been killed—a wheel of the wagon he was driving collapsed, throwing him and their mother down a steep incline. Their mother's back was injured, and after that she never left her bed until the day she died. The responsibility of raising the boy and caring for her invalid mother had pressed heavily on the shoulders of the fourteen-year-old girl.

Summer watched the perspiring face of the sleeping child with troubled, patient eyes, as the slight breeze created by the hat lifted the damp hair on his forehead. They had come a long way from the Piney Woods.

Across from her sat a ranch woman in her forties or fifties; it was hard to tell a woman's age in this country where the wind and dust ate into the skin, making it old and wrinkled after only a few years. The older woman sniffed and looked out the window. Summer knew what the gesture meant. She was piqued because she hadn't opened up and told her their family history. The woman had been explicit with her inquiries, and Summer had told her no more than that a family friend awaited them in Hamilton.

"It's a good thing. Hamilton's no place for a girl alone."

Summer didn't tell her about the letter she had received signed simply S. McLean, or that the letter had contained the startling news that she and her brother owned a plot of land with a cabin on it. The letter had been short and curt, without warmth or welcome, but it was a letter nevertheless, and Summer's hopes clung to the security of the written words.

They rode on in silence as still as the land they were passing through. The land looked lonely, Summer thought wistfully. She understood loneliness, because she had often been lonely herself—in between dilemmas, that is. And there had been dilemmas. Every day. What to do on a cold, windy night when she thought her mother was going to die? Should she run for help, leaving the five-year-old to watch his dying mother? Her mother, whose days were numbered, or the small boy with his life before him? It had not been an easy decision. She had stayed, and her mother had lived—to die three years later, under the very same circumstances. Her sweet, patient mother, who had suffered in silence, had left her and John Austin scarcely three months ago.

Summer smoothed the hair from the boy's face with long, slender fingers. He has no one but me, she thought sadly. Then her eyes widened and the sadness was replaced by hope. No one but me and Sam McLean.

A nagging recollection of the hill country where she had lived as a small child with her mother until her papa came back from the war tugged at her memory. She vaguely remembered someone squatting down in front of her and saying: "Don't cry, summertime girl. You go on with your ma and get all growed up and then I'll come. I'll come and fetch you home."

The shadows were longish across the road as the horses sped through their own dust cloud, and into the new town of Hamilton that had sprung to life in 1850, just two short years ago. One rider raced ahead of them down the rutted road, hallooing to announce the arrival of the stage. The big Concord creaked to a halt in front of a lean-to with a shiny tin roof. Grubbily-dressed men swarmed around the coach from all sides, craning their necks to see who was inside.

"This is Hamilton, John Austin," she whispered to the tousled boy.

He did not reply. He was watching the dust as it lifted and drifted away, and wondered why he couldn't see the wind that carried it. There must be a reason. He wished he had someone to ask. Summer was too busy taking care of them to think about the wind. He was so absorbed in his own thoughts that he didn't hear what his sister was saying. Her voice drifted over and about his head, like the wind, but he knew well enough what she said: "Stay close to me, give me your hand."

Summer stood beside the grimy coach and waited with the other passengers for the driver's helper to hand down her trunk. She held tightly to John Austin's hand, in case he saw something that interested him and tried to wander away. She glanced shyly at the people lined up to meet the stage: cowboys, drifters, soldiers from Fort Croghan. No one came forward to speak to her, but their interest was so embarrassing that she turned her eyes toward the stage driver and kept them there. In that brief look at the bystanders, she saw no one she would take for Sam McLean.

The driver climbed down, then reached up and swung their trunk to the boardwalk.

"Someone a meetin' you, miss?"

"I don't know. Ah . . . arrangements were made for us to stay at the hotel." Her voice, which had begun strongly, coolly, faltered to a near-stop under the steady gaze of the driver.

Summer let her eyelids drop over her eyes and failed to see the expression of softness come over the weathered face.

"Wait right here. I'll take you up there myself soon as I'm done. Ain't no call fer you and the kid to be a walkin' up there by yoreself."

Summer hadn't known how apprehensive she was until she realized how much his words relieved her. Pride made her cover up quickly.

"Thank you. Arrangements have been made for us," she repeated, lifting her chin, shaking her head a little.

Hamilton, Burnet County, Texas, was not much of a place from what she could see. The wind blew dust clouds through the early darkness and drove grit into her eyes, making it just that much more difficult to see it. But as they waited for the driver, she was able to take a quick look around and her face fell. She'd seen quite a few new towns on the journey west, but she'd not set eyes on one as primitive as this. It was a hodge-podge of unpainted buildings and lean-to's like the one used as the stage stop, and was strung out along a rutted track. Very few lights glowed in a street that swarmed with men, teams and wagons, saddle horses and soldiers.

The driver nodded to Summer and shouldered her trunk. She picked up her valise and, pulling John Austin along beside her, followed closely as he stepped off the boardwalk into the dusty street. It was all very new to her—this rawness, wildness, newness. Music, played on a twangy, out-of-tune piano drifted from one of the buildings they passed, a dance hall where men could have a rousing gallop around the plank floor with one of the girls employed there. There were only three or four horses tied in front of the building; but then, the night had just begun.

Her first look at the hotel told Summer why the driver had elected to escort them. One of the town's four or five wooden buildings, it was hard to distinguish from the saloon. Split log steps climbed to a board porch lined with benches, occupied by an assortment of men of all ages and, from their attire, all occupations.

A handsomely-dressed man in a dark frock-coat and ruffled white shirt lifted his bowler hat as she passed. His dark eyes roamed her figure boldly, and he showed even white teeth beneath a trim black mustache when he smiled, knowingly, at the crimson that flooded her face. He moved to approach her, bowing slightly, then whirled away, as if suddenly changing his mind.

There were two slatted, swinging doors leading off the porch into the saloon and a tall, narrow door that opened into the long, thin hotel lobby. A fat-faced man sat behind a counter eating a bowl of stew that reeked of chili powder. He wiped his mouth on his sleeve and got to his feet.

"Ya got lodgers, Bill?"

"You got room for 'em?"

"If'n they's the Kuykendall kids I do." He grinned at Summer, showing that most of his upper teeth had been removed.

"Well, one of 'em ain't a kid, so watch yore manners."

"Is them the Kuykendalls, Bill?" A short, bowleg-ged, graywhiskered man came puffing in through the saloon door. "Ain't ya in a mite soon?"

"No, I ain't a mite soon. And you ain't neither." Bill eased the trunk off his shoulder and lowered it to the floor. "You ain't never been on time in yore life, Bulldog!"

"Well . . . I . . ." Bulldog's expression was of sur-prise, then pleasure, as he stopped speaking and looked at Summer.

Summer looked back with interest, then shook her head, an unconscious habit of hers when confronted with curious eyes. The lamplight caught the movement, and her hair shone blue-black against the walls of the room. Dust clung to her face and dress and her hair was disheveled, but no one noticed, least of all the man called Bulldog. He thought she was the most beautiful woman he had ever seen.

"You were expecting children? Didn't Mr. McLean tell you about me and my brother?"

"Well, yes'm, he did. But he didn't say nothin' 'bout one of ya bein' so growed up."

"One of us is indeed growed up, as you can see." Pride added a touch of hauteur to her voice.

"Yes'm. He tol' me a boy and young lady. I jist never give it no thought you'd be so growed and purty."

"You got a room or don't ya?" The stage driver was impatient to be on his way.

"They got a room. Give me the key." Bulldog picked up the key, lifted the trunk, and started up the stairs.

"He'll look after you, miss. Don't pay no never mind to how he looks, but listen to what he says." The driver chuckled.

"Thank you," Summer called after the ambling form of their driver.

The room at the end of the upstairs hall was small,

but had a good-sized bed and a cot. A bureau and washstand with a blue-glazed pitcher and bowl were the only other furnishings.

Bulldog set the trunk at the foot of the bed, and John Austin went immediately to the window to look down on the busy street.

"Ma'am, I'm just plain old sorry I warn't thar to meet ya."

Summer smiled. Her heart was lighter than it had been in months. This man, this small, grizzled cowboy, was her first link with the Sam McLean who would take care of them. All she had to do, her mother said, was tell him who she was. He would take the responsibility for John Austin.

"It's all right. The driver looked after us." Her mouth curved in a lovely, sweet smile and her eyes sparkled with excitement. "Will Mr. McLean be coming for us?"

Bulldog looked uncomfortable. "No, ma'am."

It was the expression and not the words that affected her. She went quite still, as if she were suddenly depleted of all strength. Her hands pressed down the sides of her dress.

"You're taking us to him?"

"No, ma'am . . . yes'm . . . thar aint nothin' but a creek a'tween the two places. Yore place is fixed up real good fer ya, and ya can have a Mex woman to come and stay if ya wants." His hard hands twisted his hat. He sensed her disappointment and didn't know what to say.

Disappointment wasn't exactly the word for what Summer felt. Heartsick might have described her feelings better, or anger at herself for her impossible dreams. And dream she had, because she needed hope badly. She had built up an imagined figure; a tall, strong rancher, hard from life on the prairie, but kind. He would be someone of their own . . . a second father, a friend. Was it possible her mother had been mistaken? That Sam McLean didn't want to be responsible for them? How could she and John Austin make a living out on a homestead, even if it was just across the creek from Sam McLean's?

Summer swallowed the lump in her throat and blinked. Her small, round chin tilted, her dignity returned in the guise of very stiff, proud posture.

"It was kind of Mr. McLean to see us to our . . . ah . . . homestead. Please express our appreciation and tell him we'll try not to be a bother." Summer's lips pressed together, revealing more in silence than in words.

Bulldog scratched his head and looked down at his feet.

"Can I trouble you for one more thing?" Summer was sorry now, impatient with herself for her cool words. "My brother will be hungry, and I don't know if we should go down on the street alone."

"No, ma'am, ya ain't better. Anything happen to ya and I'd have my hide took right off." His faded blue eyes crinkled when he grinned. "I think it best to have some grub sent up fer ya and the boy. And—ma'am, I'll be here in the mornin' to take you all out to the Keep. Ain't no more than twenty-five or thirty miles out. McLean's Keep reaches way out to Spider Mountain. Now, that's a fer piece."

"McLean's Keep? Is that Mr. McLean's ranch?"

"Yup."

It was clear he was not giving out any more information about his employer than he had to.

"I'm sorry, Mr. Bulldog. It isn't your fault that Mr. McLean didn't choose to meet us. There must be a reason, and I'd rather he not know of my disappointment and think us ungrateful for what he's already done for us."

John Austin, leaning forward, elbows on the window sill and chin cupped in his hands, was not listening. He was watching the street, and particularly a fight in progress in front of the saloon. He always left everything to Summer. Summer would know how to handle things. She always did.

"The one with the whiskers will win," he announced suddenly.

"Win what, John Austin?" Summer was glad her brother had said something.

They moved to the window and looked over the boy's head to the street below. Bulldog chuckled.

"No, he won't, boy. That's ol' Cal Hardy down thar. He's a fightin' son-of-a-bitch. He can whip his weight in wild cats afore breakfast. Yup, that ol' Cal's a fightin' bastard."

Summer gritted her teeth to keep from saying the words that sprang to her lips. Nothing passed John Austin's ears and eyes!

"He won't win this time, Mr. Bulldog. The other man is not as strong, but when he hits he puts all his weight behind the blow, while that man, Cal, only uses his arms, and he's making himself tired, too, the way he struts around. The other man don't waste his strength a'tall. See, see how he comes up on one foot when he hits?"

"Dad-burnit! Ya just might have somethin' thar!" Bulldog slapped John Austin on the back. "It's 'bout time someone whupped that bastard's ass."

"Please. . . ."

Bulldog was so wrapped up in the excitement of the fight that he didn't hear the word that burst from Summer's lips.

"How do you know that Cal's mother didn't marry his father, Mr. Bulldog?"

"John Austin!" Summer's face crimsoned. She was used to her brother's insatiable curiosity, but strangers were sometimes put off by him. But she needn't have worried about Bulldog. He was too interested in the fight to have noticed what the boy said.

John Austin looked up at his sister, inquiringly, to see what caused her rebuke.

"A bastard is the child of a woman who ain't married, Summer. I read it in the dictionary. I just wanted to know if Mr. Bulldog was a friend of Cal's mother."

Summer said nothing as she brushed the dark hair back from the boy's forehead and pressed his head against her. John Austin was exceptionally bright. By the age of three, he had known all his letters, was able to write his name and draw pictures. At five, he could read all the books the family possessed, and any other reading material made available by people passing on the road near their home, from the newspaper to wanted posters. Summer recognized his talent for drawing after his one glimpse of a train. He made a sketch of it, complete with locomotive, cars and caboose. She was amazed at her brother's ability to remember detail. However, in other, simpler things, childish things, he was completely inept.

Bulldog took off his hat and slapped it against his leg. "Yore right as rain, young feller. Ol' Cal got his ass whupped proper! He shore got his squawker plucked this time. He won't be a crowin' fer a while!"

John Austin's eyes glinted as he glanced at his sister. This was trashy talk, and people with breeding didn't talk this way, so Summer said. His sister was looking out the window, so he smiled indulgently at the grizzled cowboy. He liked him a lot.

"If we'd a made a bet, buster, you'd a won my drawers! I wouldn't a bet a pinch of snuff on that skinny feller." Bulldog's eyes shifted down and he backed away from the window. "Got to be a goin'. I'll tell Graves to send ya some grub up." He went to the door. "I'll be back in the morning ta fetch ya home."

"Fetch you home." The words flashed across Summer's mind, and a picture flicked behind her eyes. A cabin set beneath a spreading oak. A rope swing made from a sack of straw . . . her legs wrapped around the sack and someone pushing her back and forth. The breeze hit her face as she went higher and higher. She was commanded to hold tightly in the same voice that said, "Go get all growed up and I'll come and fetch you home." The picture faded and she turned to the man waiting beside the door.

"We'll be ready."

She scarcely heard the door close or the boot heels pounding down the plank stairs. She was searching out the window for something that had caught her attention before Bulldog spoke. There he was, leaning against the side of the building. He was tall and powerful, though not very heavy in build. It was something about the way he carried himself that drew her eyes to him. They had settled on him and couldn't seem to look away. She had noticed him skirting the crowd that surrounded the fight. He was the only person on the street who didn't stop to watch. He stood quietly and lit a smoke. His hat was pulled down low and the light from the flared match scarcely made a pinpoint of light in his cupped hands.

He moved away from the building and strode across the road. Summer watched. He walked as if he owned the earth! Bulldog emerged from under the hotel porch and hurried to meet him. He talked. The tall man tilted his head as if listening intently. Bulldog lifted his hand toward the upper window of the hotel. The man stood stonestill, never lifting his head to glance up. Finally, he started walking down the street. Bulldog's shorter legs worked to keep pace with him. The two passed out of Summer's sight and she felt odd and nervous, knowing something was going to happen—something apart from just the new life on their old homestead. Something, she felt, that for her was truly new and unimaginable.

Chapter Two

While her brother leaned on the window sill, oblivious to everything except the sights, sounds and smells of the street, Summer washed her face and hands. Every so often, she thought she could hear a sound coming from the other side of the thin wall and would turn her head a little, trying to catch the sound.

For a minute, she heard nothing. Then the sound came again and she knew what it was. A child was crying. She glanced at John Austin. It seemed so long ago that he was a child, with only crying to speak for what hurt him or what he needed. It was hard for her to believe this little brother of hers was merely eight years old. He had not even cried when their mother died. Instead, he had comforted her, telling her that Mama had gone to heaven to meet Papa. She would be able to walk there and would be happy.

A pounding on the door brought her up with a start, and she went to it. The hotel man stood there with a pan of stew, bowls, a flat tin of cornbread and a jug of milk, all balanced on a heavy tray. He set the tray on the bureau.

"Leave the pots outside the door when yore done, or else come down with 'em." His bold eyes appraised her.

"I'll leave them in the hall," she said stiffly, and moved to close the door the instant he passed through. Seconds later, she heard a loud thumping, and pulled the door ajar. The man was viciously kicking the door down the hall.

"Hush yore mouth! I ain't a havin' no goddam bawlin', hear? Yore botherin' payin' lodgers."

A louder wail came from the room, as if the child was suddenly terrified by the man's loud voice.

"Is that child alone?" Summer demanded, coming out into the dimly-lit hallway.

The man turned on her angrily. "She shore as hell better be! I ain't havin' no whorin' done in my hotel! I hadn't ort to a let her leave the snotty-nosed brat here. I never figured she'd bawl all night."

"Where is her mother?"

"At the dance hall or the saloon. A whore's what she is!"

Summer's lips tightened. "Well . . . that's not the child's fault. Open the door, and I'll talk to her."

"She locks the door afore she goes off nights."

"I can't believe a mother would do such a thing. What . . . what if this building caught fire?"

"I got me a notion," he growled, ignoring the question, "to haul that squallin' brat over to the dance hall. I ain't a havin' no more of it."

"That's no place for a child, and you know it. Open the door, and I'll take care of her until morning." Summer's anger was rising.

"I'd have to get the key," he protested.

"Then go get it!" She pulled herself up to her full height of five feet, four inches and glared at him.

He looked for a moment as if he was going to protest again, but seeing that she was not going to back down, he growled something under his breath and turned away. At the head of the stairs, he looked back at her standing firmly by the door, her arms folded, watching him.

"Damn lucky fer you I ain't a wantin' to tangle with that bastard Bulldog works fer." Still growling to himself, he stomped back down the stairs.

Summer kept her back straight and her chin lifted until the man was out of sight. It wouldn't do for him to know how tired and small she really felt. She placed her ear to the door. The child's sobs were ragged.

The room was dark as night when she opened the door. The faint glow from the lamp in the hall showed the outline of the bed and the small bundle huddled on it. Large, wet eyes looked up at Summer from a chubby face framed by long, curly hair. Small lips trembled as she peered past Summer toward the hotel man standing beside the door.

"Come stay with me until your mama comes back." Summer held out her arms and the little girl went into them eagerly and hid her face against her shoulder. Summer got to her feet holding the child.

"I'll take care of her," she said to the sullen man as she walked past.

In her own room, she kicked the door shut, and her eyes sought her brother. He was still looking out the window, and she doubted if he knew she had been gone.

The child's large, sad eyes tugged at her heart. She couldn't be more than three years old. And such a beautiful child, even in the huge shapeless nightdress. Her hair was copper-brown and curled in tight ringlets. A spattering of freckles crossed her short, pert little nose. She looked around the room with interest and her eyes caught John Austin by the window.

19

"What's your name?" Summer was pouring water into the wash bowl. She wet a cloth and wiped the child's face.

The little girl hiccoughed. "Mary Evelyn."

Summer barely heard the little girl's shy voice.

"My name is Summer and the boy is my brother. His name is John Austin."

Shaken from his reverie, John Austin turned to look with astonishment at the little girl sitting on the cot.

"Where'd she come from?"

"From the room next door. She's going to stay with us till her mama comes back."

The two children eyed each other.

A pleased smile came over John Austin's face. He went to the cot, sat down, and picked up the little girl's hand.

"She's so pretty, Summer. Look at that curly hair." He reached up and pushed the hair back from the child's face. "What's she been cryin' for?"

Summer had thought nothing her brother could do would surprise her anymore, but she wasn't prepared for his interest in and compassion for the little girl. Involuntary tears of love sprang into her eyes, and she swallowed the lump in her throat.

"I suspect she's hungry." She lifted the lid on the stew pot. "Wash your hands, dear, and I'll dish up the stew."

By the time the meal was over, the little girl's eyes were dry, and only wet, spikey lashes remained. She smiled often. Once she laughed out loud at John Austin's antics.

Seeing them together, Summer thought she could remember another time when a small child gazed with adoration at a boy; a tall, slim, dark-haired boy, who held her hand and walked with her on a log spanning a creek. He told her not to be afraid, and because he asked it, she wasn't. The child was herself, but the boy . . . ? Was he just a figment of her imagination?

These flashes were so brief—she couldn't be sure if it was a memory or a wishful dream.

She bedded John Austin down on the cot and lay, fully clothed, beside Mary on the bed. The child snuggled up to her and was soon asleep. Resentment toward the child's mother curled deep in Summer's stomach. She and John Austin would be gone tomorrow, and then what would become of the little girl?

Soon the nagging worry of how she and her brother were going to survive out on a homestead, without having to depend on Sam McLean for every bite of food that went into their mouths, crowded all other thoughts from her mind. It wasn't too late to put in a garden. She could certainly do that. But she needed money for other things; shoes, yard goods, a warm coat for John Austin. They shouldn't have come! The money spent on the stage fares would have kept them for a long time if they had stayed in the Piney Woods. One thing was sure, she couldn't ask Sam McLean for any more help. Although his letter had promised no more than that a homestead was waiting for them, she had expected more. Now she had only herself to blame.

Summer couldn't prevent her eyelids from drooping. She was tired and regretful, regardless of the promise she had made to her dying mother. They had traveled all day for many days, and her body ached from the bouncing stage. Soon sleep came, though she didn't know it.

A piercing scream and the slamming of a door woke her. She tried to gather her wits. She shook her head, stretched her stiff back, and came to her senses. It had to be the child's mother.

Summer hurried to the door and fumbled with the key. The instant she stepped into the hall, another door opened and a man sprang into the hallway. Summer almost laughed. He wore only his breeches and a hat and had two big six-shooters in his hands.

"What the hell?"

A large blonde woman, making no attempt to cover her voluptuous breasts, came out of the man's room.

"Come on back, honeybunch." She clutched his arm and rubbed her bare bosom against him.

With face aflame and eyes averted, Summer edged past them.

A woman's voice was coming from the stairway and had risen to an almost hysterical pitch.

"Graves! Graves, you bastard! Where's my baby? If you let anything happen to her, I'll . . . I'll crucify you! Mary Evelyn! Mar . . . ry!"

Summer hurried to overtake the woman before she bolted down the stairs.

"Your little girl is with me," she called, but the woman was already at the foot of the stairs and didn't hear.

The hotel man came up from a cot behind the counter.

"Shut yore goddam mouth! Yore waking up the whole place."

"You . . . you yellow-bellied . . . skunk! Mar . . . ry!" The woman was sobbing now.

"She's with me," Summer called again.

The woman turned. She was no more than a girl. Green eyes stared up at Summer out of pain-darkened sockets. Tight, matted curls framed a thin face with a short, upturned nose. A pink satin dress, much too large for the slight frame, hung to the floor on one side and came up to midcalf on the other. She raced back up the stairs.

"Where's she at?"

"You get that little bastard and get outta here!" The hotel man was standing at the foot of the stairs, his face twisted with rage. "Whore! Slut! Out . . . do you hear? Out!"

"You have Mary? Oh! Oh, thank God! I was so scared! I was scared that piss-ant had done something

22

to her. I'd a killed him! I swear, if he'd a hurt my baby, I'd a killed him."

"She's all right. She's sleeping in my room. Come, I'll show you."

The man with the gun went back into his room and slammed the door when Summer marched by him without as much as a glance. Inside her own room, she closed the door firmly and turned the key. The girl went to kneel beside the bed. The child was awake and reached out to wrap her small arms about her mother's neck.

"Mama . . . Mama . . ."

"Oh, baby! Oh, God, baby, I was so scared! I couldn't find you, lovey."

Summer stood at the end of the bed. The light from the flickering lamp played on the girl's pitifully thin shoulders and arms. When she looked up, her eyes were swimming with tears, her mouth looked puffed and bruised, and there were teeth marks on her neck.

"Thank you," she said simply.

"No thanks are necessary. I think my brother was smitten with her," she said, indicating the sleeping boy. "They took to each other right away."

The girl looked searchingly at Summer, then at the boy on the cot. She covered the little girl and got shakily to her feet.

"I'm at the end of my rope," she blurted out. "I just don't know what I'm goin' to do." Tears streamed down the tired white face, and her lips trembled. "I'm not a whore, ma'am. Not yet! But I'm just the same as . . . 'cause I don't know how much longer I can hold out without going to bed with 'em! I don't care about me, anymore, but I got to find a place for Mary Evelyn. You like her, don't you? She's sweet and real . . . good." She sank down on the bed and buried her face in her hands.

Summer put her arm across the shaking shoulders

and the girl's story poured out in sobbing, broken sentences.

Her name was Sadie Irene Bratcher; married at fourteen, mother at fifteen and widowed at seventeen. She'd married a young drifter and they had tried homesteading, but the lure of town was too much for her young husband. He died in a shootout over a card game, and Sadie and the little girl had been on their own for almost a year. She had come to Hamilton about a month ago. The only work she could find was in the dance hall, and it took most of her earnings to pay the hotel man.

"I'll go to whorin', if it's the only way I can feed my baby," she said firmly, then trembled violently. "Oh, God, ma'am, you can't know what it's like . . . pawin' . . . slobberin' . . . and they stink and dip snuff and spit! But I could do it if I had a decent place for Mary to stay." The girl rocked back and forth in her misery.

Summer went to the window and looked down. The street was empty, except for a horse tied to the rail in front of the saloon. The horse stood, head down, stamping or pawing occasionally, to relieve the boredom of waiting. Summer felt the shadowy presence of Sam McLean more distinctly than any time since her mother had died. He was in the back of her mind, a person to lean on. He stood solidly between her and her becoming like this poor, miserable girl. The girl was desperate, and Summer knew what she was leading up to; the request she was about to make. She couldn't take on the care of another child. She couldn't. But . . . Bulldog had said something . . . something about if she wanted a woman . . .

Not one to hesitate after making a decision, Summer went back to the bed and faced the girl.

"I've a solution, if you're willing to go out to a homestead with me and my brother." She sat down on the bed. "We have a homestead about thirty miles south of here. I don't know what kind of place it is, but

24

it's near a large ranch owned by . . . our guardian. We're going out there tomorrow. You and Mary are welcome to come with us. I don't really look forward to being the only white woman for miles and miles around. Another thing, Sadie, we don't have much money, but we'll have a place to live. We'll have to work hard, put in a garden first thing and . . ."

Sadie was speechless, stupefied with disbelief. Then the words burst from her.

"Oh, ma'am! You'd take me and the baby with you?"

"Why not? And my name is Summer."

One girl laughed, the other girl cried. Summer felt as if a load had been lifted from her shoulders. Here was someone she could talk things over with, someone who, hopefully, would work beside her. The girl's need was even greater than her own. They began to talk, to plan, and finally slept when dawn was just a few short hours away.

By sun-up, the town was astir.

Through a crack in the door, Summer watched the hotel man's retreating back. She closed the door softly and smiled reassuringly at Sadie. Green eyes stared unsmilingly back at her. The freckles stood out, each one like a grain of brown sugar on the fair skin. The girl who stood, clutching the hand of her small daughter, didn't remotely resemble the dance-hall girl of the night before. A well-worn cotton dress covered her from neck to instep, but the bodice was loose and the waistline clearly showed a recent loss of weight. The bravado of last night, when she found her daughter missing, was gone; fear of what the hotel man would do when he discovered she didn't have the money to pay for last night's lodging took its place.

When Summer opened the door for Bulldog, he stood and gaped at the two women and two children waiting for him.

"Mrs. Bratcher is going with us," Summer said, by

way of introduction. Her voice was confident this morning. She had set a course, and felt she had command of their future once again.

Bulldog shifted from one foot to the other. "Wal . . . now . . ." He clearly didn't know what to say.

Summer thought it best to tell him the complete story.

"And we're not paying him one cent!" she said firmly. "He's been charging her a dollar a day!"

The whiskered cowboy shook his head. "A dollar! Wal, now . . . Did he want to take his pay out in trade, Sadie?"

The girl nodded.

Summer looked from one to the other. Of course Bulldog would know who she was. There weren't that many women in town that Sadie would go unnoticed.

"I'll be back fer ya." Slamming his dusty hat down hard on his head, the cowboy gathered up two arm-loads of boxes.

The trip from the room to the wagon in front of the hotel went smoothly. The hotel man wasn't at the desk, and when Summer asked about him, Bulldog spit contemptuously into the dirt.

The sun was only half an hour above the horizon when their light wagon rolled to a halt in front of the store and the pile of supplies stacked on the loading dock. Hangers-on called out good naturedly to Bulldog as he lifted the heavy bags and boxes onto the wagon bed.

Since leaving the hotel, Sadie had relaxed, and her lips were tilted continuously in a smile. Summer was immensely glad for her presence. The two children stood behind them, watching all that was going on with large, excited eyes.

"I'm glad you're with me!" Summer clasped Sadie's hand.

"Yore glad! Oh, Jesus Christ . . . Oh, I mean . . . I

still can't believe we're out of that . . . place. I'll work hard, miss. I'll work my fingers to the bone!"

"You'll do nothing of the kind. We'll work together. And for Pete's sake, call me Summer."

"I ort to be a callin' you angel, that's what I ort to do!"

At the sound of Summer's laughter, the loafers in front of the store all turned their heads in unison to look at the lovely, raven-haired girl. She had piled her hair in a loose knot on top of her head because of the heat, and curly tendrils floated about her face and clung to the nape of her neck. The dark cotton dress she wore set off her violet eyes, and with the flush of excitement spreading over her fair skin, she was quite beautiful. But she was completely unaware of the picture she made, and the eyes that couldn't seem to look away from her, as she held out her sunbonnet to Sadie.

"I'll be right back, John Austin. Sadie, don't let him get out of the wagon. After you know him better, you'll understand why. I'm going to get us some garden seed."

Summer paused in the doorway of the store to allow her eyes to adjust from the bright sunlight to the darkened interior. It was filled to capacity with goods needed to sustain life on the vast cattle ranches that surrounded the town. Barrels of flour, sugar, salt pork and cornmeal crowded the aisles; jugs, tools, baskets, rope and harnesses hung from the rafters. Her eyes settled on a table of bright yard goods, and as she walked toward it she passed behind a man counting out a stack of silver dollars to the store clerk.

The man was very tall, whiplash thin, but with broad shoulders and long arms. His dark hat was pulled low, the broad brim shielding his face, and a long, thin cheroot in his mouth trailed a waft of not-unpleasant smoke. His clothes were dark and free of dust, and against his thigh rested a holstered gun. But Summer wasn't aware of these impressions until later. She was only dimly aware that the man stopped clinking the silver until she passed him.

After looking over the yard goods and thinking how nice it would be if she could afford to buy the blue for herself, the green for Sadie and the sunny yellow for Mary, she put the thought from her mind and moved to the now-vacated counter.

"Mornin', miss." A youngish clerk with a large Adam's apple, which rose and fell as he spoke, stood wiping his hands on a once-white apron.

"Morning. How much are the seeds?"

"The seeds? Oh . . . they're ten cents for this scoop."

"Ten cents?" Disappointment and uncertainty tinged her voice. "You'd pay two cents for that scoop back in the Piney Woods where I come from. Ten cents, you said? Well . . . give me a scoop full of bean, beet, turnips, corn and okra. I'll also need some potatoes to eye."

The clerk looked over her head. "If you're the lady Bulldog got the supplies for, ma'am, you ain't gonna need none. Bulldog said you ain't . . . he said that . . . well, he gave me a bill of what to lay out, and warn't no potatoes on the bill. He said you ain't goin' to need . . ."

"Is that stuff out there all for us?"

The clerk's face turned a beet red. "Well . . . I was told to lay out a stock; I was given a bill to fill."

"I can't pay for those things." Her voice was flat, angry. "I can't pay for them now, and maybe never!"

"They're paid fer, miss." The clerk smiled broadly, but Summer didn't.

"Bulldog paid for our supplies?"

"Mr. McLean paid, miss." For some reason the clerk's face burned a bright red again, and he kept his eyes on his hands.

Summer's lips tightened. "I'd like a copy of the bill, please." She stood proudly, looking steadily at the fidgeting clerk who stood as if cemented to the spot. "The bill." Summer held out her hand.

The clerk's eyes roamed the store, looking everywhere except at her.

"I'll make it out and give it to Bulldog—later." He began to scoop out seeds, wrapping each batch in a piece of brown paper.

Summer regretted her quick remarks. She had no doubt the story would be all over town by noon—if not spread by the clerk, then surely by the tall customer. Pretending to look closely at the bins of dried beans and rice behind her, she let her eyes wander until she located him. He stood with his back to her, and it was something in his stance, in the way he held his head, that drew her eyes to him again and again. He bent his head to light another cheroot, and she knew. He was the tall man from the street, the one Bulldog had talked with the night before. She turned to face the counter; her heart had started to beat at an alarming rate and her face felt suddenly flushed.

"Two sticks of peppermint candy, please." For some reason she lowered her voice to a mere whisper.

When Summer left the dimness of the store, she was aware that the crowd of loafers had increased. She was also aware that the sun was higher, and that it had grown warmer. All this she knew, but in a secondary way, for her attention was on the handsome buggy, escorted by half a dozen riders, pulling up in front of the store. The driver eased his long length out of the seat, and reached up a hand to help the woman who was sitting beside him. She was lovely, and her clothes were the finest Summer had ever seen. She was dressed all in gray, from the soft, high-button shoes to the wide-brimmed hat set atop high-piled blonde curls. She lifted gray-gloved hands, deftly folded back a gauze of gray veil up and over her hat brim, and laughed softly into the man waiting to help her. He reached up and encircled her narrow waist with both hands and lifted her gently to the ground. He handled her as if she were a piece of priceless porcelain, and Summer marveled because he was a large-framed man with a stern, unsmiling face.

Summer headed for the steps, hoping to slip past the party unnoticed. To her embarrassment, the woman stopped and smiled at her.

"Hello."

Her voice was musical and seemed just the right sound to come from such a beautiful creature. It was difficult to determine her age, for though her face was smooth, her eyes bright and her hair shiny, she had a very few wrinkles at the corner of her eyes and around her neck, where the lace collar of her dress was secured with a delicately-carved brooch.

"Ah . . . hello." Summer was ashamed of the stammer in her voice, and moved to pass on.

The woman reached out a gloved hand and placed it on her arm.

"Have you just arrived in town?" She smiled so sweetly and her voice was so friendly that Summer couldn't help being flattered by her inquiry.

"Since yesterday."

"I thought so." She smiled up at the stern-faced man. "I was right, Jesse. I thought I knew all the lovely young ladies for miles around." Summer felt a flash of pleasure on hearing the compliment. "I'm Ellen McLean, dear. And this is my son, Travis." Reaching around, she placed her hand on the arm of another man standing slightly behind her. He had blond hair and dancing blue eyes and winked openly at Summer when she glanced at him. She could feel the color come up her neck. She held out her hand to the woman.

"I'm Summer Kuykendall." She made the announcement and waited.

The name brought no hint of recognition from the woman, and it occurred to Summer that perhaps Sam

McLean hadn't told his family about her and John Austin.

"I'm happy to meet you, Summer." Mrs. McLean placed both hands around the forearm of the stern-faced man. "This is my good friend and manager of our ranch, Jesse Thurston."

Summer looked into the coldest eyes she had ever looked into. They were light gray, almost the color of the woman's dress, and absolutely expressionless. He raised his hand to the brim of his hat, his eyes holding her as if he could pin her to the wall. Summer inclined her head and her eyes shifted to Travis McLean, who was grinning at her in open admiration. He was somewhat younger than the other man, but still looked too old to be the son of the fairylike creature dressed in gray.

"Are you, by any chance, related to the Kuykendalls that homesteaded here some years back?" Mrs. McLean smiled up at the big man again. "I don't like to think of how many years back, Jesse, really I don't!" Her smiling eyes came back to Summer. "You can't be Nannie Kuykendall's daughter!"

"But I am. Did you know my mother?"

"Yes indeed, my dear. Your mother lived near Sam McLean's ranch. My late husband, Sam's brother, took up land a bit further west."

A flicker of regret crossed Summer's mind, and at the same time relief that this wasn't Sam McLean's family. She felt she was not yet equal to the task of meeting the McLeans.

"You'll be living out on the homestead? I haven't been there for years. May I call on you?" Not waiting for her question to be answered, she rushed on. "I didn't visit your mother as often as I liked, but I'll visit her daughter." Her eyes sought the stern face. "Won't it be nice for me to have a lovely young woman to visit, Jesse?" The man looked down into her wide-eyed face and his hand came up and patted the gloved hand on his arm.

During this pause, Summer had moved to the steps.

"I'll look forward to your visit, Mrs. McLean."

"I'll call on you soon. Goodbye, my dear."

Travis McLean swept his hat and clasped Summer's elbow to assist her down the steps.

"*I'll* bring my mother to call." His voice was low and he emphasized the first word. His hand gently squeezed her arm.

Trying not to notice the intimacy, and vastly relieved that this man was not Sam McLean's son, Summer walked quickly to the wagon. She took Bulldog's hand and climbed up over the wheel and sat beside Sadie. Then she noticed how quiet the street was. All activity, it seemed, had stopped while she conversed with Mrs. McLean. Even the store clerk stood in the doorway, his hands folded across his apron. Suddenly, Summer wanted to get away from this place, away from the watching eyes. Now Bulldog and Sadie seemed full of quiet, unspoken disapproval, and Summer felt uneasy.

Bulldog slapped the ends of the reins against the rumps of the horses, and the wagon rolled down the rutted street. Even John Austin hadn't anything to say. Summer turned to smile at him, but he was looking back, as was Mary, at the group watching them from the porch of the store.

Chapter Three

Summer was glad when they left the town behind. Bulldog clucked and snapped the reins sharply on the horses' backs as they ambled out of the rutted street and onto the prairie. A slight breeze kicked up little eddies of dust along the trail, but did little to dissipate the early morning heat. Summer put on her sunbonnet to take advantage of the shade it offered, and for a time rode silently, reflecting on Bulldog's mood and trying, fruitlessly, to comprehend his silent, scowling countenance. The area surrounding them was like a vast ocean, only solid and hot. Some half a mile ahead, a small grove broke the emptiness, and it was there that they headed. A group of horsemen waited beneath the cottonwoods.

"Mr. Bulldog?" Summer gestured toward the men when Bulldog turned to look at her.

"McLean men."

He reached into his pocket and drew out a flat tin,

dipped a small twig, the end of which was chewed into a brush, into the brown powder, and coated the inside of his lower lip. Summer had seen this done often. Even people in the Piney Woods dipped snuff.

"Mr. McLean's men?"

"Yup."

Sadie glanced nervously at Summer and pulled her sunbonnet from beneath the seat and tied it securely under her chin.

When Bulldog pulled the team to a halt under the shade trees, the men on horseback sat motionless and stared at the women. Summer looked at each face before confusion forced her to look away. Not one of the men fit her imaginary picture of Sam McLean, the one who would be the man in charge. The silence was broken by Bulldog's low laugh. It drew attention to him.

"Wal, now! You fellers just pull in yore eyeballs. This here's Summer Kuykendall, and the other'n is Mrs. Bratcher."

"Are you outlaws?" John Austin stood behind Summer, gazing with awe at the horsemen.

Summer looked around in horror. "John Austin!"

Grins appeared on the weathered, toughened faces, and one rider urged his horse forward.

"I'm not sure 'bout the rest of 'em, boy, but as fer me, I'm the ramrod of these galoots when the boss ain't around. Jack Bruza's the name."

"What do you ram, mister?"

Summer cringed. Her brother's questions were often unintentionally upsetting. He would invariably pick out the word that interested him the most and ask about it.

"Uh?" The expression on the man's face was typical of those who talked with John Austin for the first time.

The loud guffaws of laughter from the men didn't affect Jack at all. He grinned with them, took off his hat, scratched his head and allowed his restless horse to edge closer to the wagon.

"Wal . . . I'm a gonna have to study on that one, boy. How'd ya like to ride along with me while I tell ya 'bout it?"

John Austin didn't hesitate. He could never be accused of shyness.

"Can I, Summer? Can I?"

It was hard for Summer to suspend her habit of concern for her small brother. She looked first at the man and then at the prancing horse.

"I don't think. . . ."

"Jack ain't gonna let no hurt come to him," Bulldog growled. "Ya don't aim to make no sissy-britches out of him, do ya?"

She felt a flush of embarrassment at the rebuke. "Well . . . all right. But . . . be careful, John Austin."

Mary set up a howl as soon as the boy was lifted from the wagon.

"Me . . . me ride!"

An old man urged his horse up to the wagon. He looked inquiringly at Sadie.

"Ma'am?"

Sadie nodded, and with one arm he scooped the little girl up and placed her carefully in front of him.

"Jist come on up here with ol' Raccoon, lit'l purty gal, we'll jist have us a fine ride."

A youth, not more than fourteen, swept off his broad-brimmed hat, his young face creased with a teasing grin. He turned his horse in a circle, then caused the animal to rear up on its hind legs.

"One of you ladies is welcome to ride with me," he called.

"Ya just quit yore showin' off, Pud. Or I'm liable to take a board to yore back side." Bulldog snapped the reins sharply and the team began to move. "Now cut out the tomfoolery, and keep yore eyes peeled."

"The man's name is Raccoon? The boy's name is Pud?" Summer couldn't suppress a small laugh. She turned to help the children onto the wagon.

"Yeah." Bulldog cocked his head to one side, as if surprised by her interest. "We call the kid Pud, 'cause he is the puddin'-eatin'est little bastard ya ever did see. I don't recall jist what his name is. But ya just let a batch of bread puddin' get made up and that goddam kid'll eat till his eyes bulge." He flicked the backs of the straining team. "Raccoon's name is Fox, but when the boss was a tyke, he couldn't remember what kind of varmit he was, so he called him Raccoon, and it stuck."

"Do the boy's folks live at the ranch?"

"Naw. They was dirt farmers. The old man was a lazy mule and the old woman took off with a peddlin' man. Jack brought the kid out a few years back. Keeps an eye on him. He's a good kid, if'n he is mouthy. Stick his head in the fire if'n Jack tol' him to."

The day rocked on. It was pleasant sitting on the high seat. The country was lush and beautiful. They followed a creek south, the trail coming so close at times they could see the swiftly-running water. Bulldog explained the creek was running full now, due to the rains in the north, but would more than likely be a dry sand-bed before the summer was over.

The riders kept their distance from the wagon, riding mostly to the side and behind. Jack came to talk occasionally with Bulldog. They said as few words as possible, as was the way of men who spent much of their time alone.

"Seen any sign?"

"Nope."

"Nothing of Slater?"

"Nope."

"He ain't far off. Keep yore eyes peeled fer a signal."

"Ain't likely to do nothin' else."

"I got me a hunch."

"Yeah?"

"Could be we'll cross 'em at the gorge."

"Yeah?"

"Don't let Pud do nothin' hare-brained."

"He ain't gonna do nothin'. He's just full of mustard."

"We ort to be to the gorge in half an hour."

"Yeah."

Jack wheeled his horse and rode away. After that, the men were spaced further out from the wagon.

Happily sucking on the candy sticks, John Austin and Mary lay down in the wagon bed.

"When will we get home, Mr. Bulldog?"

Home. The word came so natural from her brother that it was seconds before it registered with Summer.

"Afore dark, most likely, if we keep on a clickin'." Bulldog's keen eyes were constantly shifting, and he had neglected to dip his snuff for a while. "You younguns lay down, and don't be makin' no racket."

It had all been so peaceful. Summer suddenly felt the sharp spur of anxiety.

"Are you expecting . . . trouble?"

"Ya'd be plumb bad off not to be 'specting trouble in this country. It's somethin' that comes sooner or later like a skeeter bite." Bulldog's tone was grim. "If'n it comes, 'n I ain't sayin' t'will. You hop over the seat and plop down on top them kids, 'n don't be pokin' yore head up fer nothin'."

Summer smoothed her dress down over her knees with a nervous motion. She started to say something, but would not trust her voice. She looked ahead at the hills. They seemed now to advance on them.

"We'll do as you say, Mr. Bulldog." Sadie's voice was quiet, confident. "Don't you worry none. Me 'n Summer'll take care of the kids."

"I wish you'd put a stop on callin' me 'Mr.'. Makes me itchy. Name's just plain ol' Bulldog. Ain't been called nothin' else fer so long, I'd not answer to nothin' else but."

They traveled on in uneasy silence, the rattle of the

harnesses and the clip-clop of the hoofs on the hard-packed prairie trail the only sounds to break the stillness.

Slater McLean sat motionless on his buckskin. He rolled the cigarette in his lips, liking the taste of the fresh tobacco, squinted his eyes against the sun's glare, and gazed down into the valley. He was a big, lean, wide-shouldered man. A quiet man with a weathered face, straight black hair, and eyes so deep a blue that they almost seemed black.

He sat easily in the saddle and studied the terrain with care, beginning with the far distance and working closer, letting no rock or clump of brush go unscrutinized. He had learned long ago that careful scrutiny and patience were essential in this country if you wanted to live. It was hot and he drew on his cigarette. A few clouds drifted across the sky, and their shadows traveled the length of the valley. Nothing else moved.

Finishing the cigarette, he let his eyes wander to his right, where a dip in the ridge would be the logical place to hide and wait for the wagon. It was too logical a place for an Apache, he would wait behind the broken boulders that lined the ridge—and if he took his time and made no sudden moves to attract the eye, he would be on the wagon before Bulldog could spit. Sweat trickled through the dust on Slater's face. His neck itched from the heat and dust. Nowhere in all that vast distance was there a movement. Yet, somewhere out there were Apaches. He was sure of it.

Yesterday, on his way to town, he'd crossed the trail of a band of Apaches. They had been riding without women and children, which meant they were young bucks out raiding, hot to lift hair and steal horses. No doubt they were a rag-tail outfit of half-starved renegades, and Slater hoped to hell he wouldn't have to kill them.

The Apaches were not the only problem Slater had

to worry about. There was another gang in the area, led by a man named Findlay. Bushy Red, he was called, and as far as Slater knew, he was the only white man in a gang of renegade Apache scouts, runaway slaves and Mexicans. Several times lately he had come across their sign, had found tracks of as many as a dozen or more. They were a mean outfit. The Texas Rangers had run them out of the Brazos River country, and they had drifted south, rustling and raiding.

Slater eased his weight in the saddle and checked the eagerness of his horse. They had been motionless for half an hour. Both had welcomed the rest after the grueling ride across country from Hamilton. But now he gave himself a mental shake. He couldn't keep his thoughts from the small dark-haired girl who got off the stage. Somehow, he hadn't expected to see such a proud little creature. She walked with her head up and her chin tilted as if she were six feet tall. He had often wondered what kind of woman the little girl had grown into; she was spunky from what he could tell. But still, he was puzzled by her bringing along the girl from the dance hall. He shrugged. As long as she didn't cause trouble among the men, he didn't care.

Slater's eyes were alert, but his thoughts traveled. The little brother was quite brainy, if Bulldog could be believed. At least the kid was well-behaved. Both of them will be better off at the ranch, he mused. Especially now that Travis had set eyes on the girl. The McLeans hadn't bothered him for a long time now, but he knew the meeting was no coincidence. And if Ellen had said anything about Sam, the girl wouldn't have left town with Bulldog.

And there was Jesse Thurston to deal with. His toughness was ingrained. He wasn't a cruel man, yet he was quick, hard and dangerous. Whatever wells of softness there were in him, were only apparent where Ellen McLean was concerned. That was a strange alliance. He was still lapping up every word or gesture from the woman, and she old enough to be his mother for all her beauty and careful grooming. He had seen Jesse almost beat a man to death for making a remark to Ellen, and she had stood by loving every minute of it. That was before . . . he raised a hand to his scarred cheek, rubbed the rough ridges. Every time he saw his reflection in a mirror, his eyes hardened and he felt almost choked with hate. Yes, he had been right to send Bulldog to meet the stage. His face might have been a shock to her now. He put his heels lightly to the horse's flanks. Even if she hadn't written, he had always had it in the back of his mind to fetch her home.

Slater pulled the buckskin up short of the ridge and moved against a dark clump of juniper where it was as invisible as possible to be on the hillside. A small cloud of dust rose above the brush on the opposite side of the slope. He studied it. It could have been a deer scrambling up from the creek, but it should stir up more dust. He waited. The dust appeared, then vanished, and that meant it was not a deer, but someone not wanting to be seen. He eased himself from the saddle, moving slowly, and lifted his rifle, being careful the streaks of sunlight shining through the branches didn't strike the metal. His eyes were glued to the spot where he had glimpsed the dust. He watched and waited, crouched down behind a clump of brush and weeds. He had stayed high up enough on the slope to be able to see the side of the draw, and yet see the wagon coming from the east. The sun was in the west, giving full light to the valley and shade to the sides of the slope.

Watchfulness was no new thing for Slater. Watchfulness and patience will keep you alive, he had been told more than once. The first to move is often the first to die.

In the hot stillness of the afternoon, Slater could hear the jingle of harness, the soft thud of hooves on the packed trail, Bulldog's muffled curse as the wagon jolted over a stone. He dared not to take his eyes from the willow clumps. The Apaches would wait until just the right moment. They knew the value of waiting. He had to have a sign soon, so he could fire . . . there it was. A movement of brown and his finger tightened, the rifle leaped in his hands. The sound of the shot echoed in the valley even as the Apache stood, then crashed over, his arms flung wide.

The sudden attack caught the Indians by surprise. They were shrewd and careful fighters, elusive, never trusting a wild charge if they could accomplish their purpose by concealment. Now mounted, whooping Indians came racing toward the wagon, firing and missing. It was diversionary action that Slater and his men were too experienced to fall for. The men crouched behind the wagon, the women and children lay flat in the wagon bed, the frightened team, their heads pulled up by the quick-thinking Bulldog, stamped their feet and moved restlessly. Slater put the butt of his Winchester against his shoulder and fired, his shots seeking out the hidden enemy, firing carefully, squeezing off every shot. Answering fire from the hillside suddenly ceased.

The silence seemed to charge over the hill. Rifles lowered, and in that instant the nearer Indians sprang from the cover of the willows. One big brave lunged his horse straight at Slater. Slater sidestepped and hit him in the small of the back with his rifle butt. The Indian hit the ground and rolled over, lance in hand. Slater hit him again to make sure he was unconscious. A horse was down, screaming. Colt in hand, Slater wheeled, and felt a sharp, stinging pain in his thigh that almost brought him to his knees. From behind the wagon came a crash of shots. Two more Indians fell, and a third fell headfirst off his racing pony and turned head over heels in the grass. The other two broke, seeking shelter. Firing coolly, the men of McLean's Keep poured lead into the brush. Then again, the sudden silence.

Slater waited. No sound followed except from the

wagon; a child was crying, the sound low and muffled. The attack was over. The Apache, like ghosts, vanished, melting into the landscape.

Summer had been trying to figure out the reason for Bulldog's anxiety when the first shot was fired, the sound bouncing off the hills. The reaction was instantaneous. Bulldog hauled up on the reins and the horses turned halfway across the trail in their effort to stop. Before she realized what had happened, she and Sadie were over the seat and she was flat on top of the squirming John Austin, who was trying to get out from under her so he could see what was going on.

"Stay down and be still, or I'll hit you!" Summer gasped out the words.

With pounding heart, arms and legs locked around the boy, Summer fought off panic. The noise from the guns beside the wagon was deafening. She heard something far away on the side of the slope that sounded like a shriek. The team stirred restlessly, and the wagon creaked as it followed the movement of the horses. During the lull in the shooting, she could hear hooting and yelping noises that made her blood run cold.

Time dragged. The shooting was unpredictable. Once, Summer heard a muffled curse; shortly after, the whine of a bullet hit the end of the wagon. There was silence, then someone began shooting up on the right of them. This was the hardest part, not knowing what was going on. She opened her eyes and stared into Sadie's green ones. They were large with fright and the freckles stood out on her white face.

"Shhh, baby. Shhh . . . Mama's here," Sadie crooned to the frightened child in her arms.

"You're heavy, Summer. Can't you get off now?" John Austin's voice was tired, bored. It made Summer angry.

"You hush up! We're not getting up till they tell us we can."

The wagon creaked as someone climbed up into the bed. Hands beneath her armpits lifted her to her feet.

"You done good. You done real good." Jack helped Sadie to sit up. She cuddled the frightened little girl to her.

"Was anyone hurt?" Summer held onto the wagon seat, her legs suddenly weak.

"Only a couple little nicks. Ain't nothin' that needs to be messed with. You all sit tight." He jumped down from the wagon. "Slater'll be glad when you get home tonight!" He turned to Summer gravely.

Slater. Later, Summer was to remember it was the second time she had heard that name. It had a familiar ring.

"We'll take the guns and that's all," Bulldog instructed the men. "They 'spect it. The rest of their plunder we leave. It's sacred to 'em. N'other thing. We don't go a killin' any wounded, if'n there is any. Killin' in a fights one thing, bashin' in heads of wounded is another. We ain't out to kill no 'Paches if'n they ain't out to kill us."

Now Bulldog rushed up the slope to where Slater sat on the ground. The wound in his thigh was throbbing painfully, and he took the handkerchief from around his neck and tied it tightly around his leg.

"Did they get ya, boy?" Bulldog knelt down, but Slater held out his hand to ward him off.

"Only a scratch. Anybody else?"

"Luther got a little nick and Jay got caught with a flying splinter."

"Why the hell didn't Jack have somebody out there riding point?" Slater got to his feet.

"Thought you was doin' that, sonny," Bulldog said impudently, but his eyes were full of concern.

Slater grinned. "Don't be givin' me any of that 'sonny' sass, old man. I can still whip your ass."

"Wal, now . . . I don't know nothin' of the kind. Ya ain't tried it fer a spell."

"Ain't had to, you old buzzard." Slater reloaded his weapons and Bulldog brought his horse over to him. "Better get back down there to the women. Tell Jack I'll ride point from here on." He looked at Bulldog, then away. "How did she do?"

"Cool as buttermilk. Threw herself down on top of the kid. Never heard a whimper. Sadie did good, too. Both of 'em got grit. Ain't ya comin' down? She's gonna be askin'. 'Sides, you ain't ort to be a ridin' with that gunshot."

"No, I ain't coming down. I'm going to ride. Tend to your own business."

"Ya are my business, ya . . . stubborn jackass." Grumbling, Bulldog went back to the wagon.

Chapter Four

Sundown came, and with it the happy anticipation of homecoming. Summer was tired, but strangely stimulated. Youth is wonderfully resilient. Not even Bulldog's irritability could dampen her spirits.

The wagon rolled up and over a rise. The house came into view. It was impossible for Summer to tell what her feelings were at that moment, or even if she had feelings at all. The house, set close to the ground, blended into its surroundings as if it had been born there. Built of heavy logs, it looked solid and permanent. A lean-to porch roof had been added recently, the heavy support posts showed the bark had just been peeled. Two doors led into the house from beneath the porch roof, and two stone chimneys rose from each side of the house; one emitting a thin plume of smoke. Summer's eyes took in everything, from the pole corrals behind the cabin to the plowed garden spot to the side, out from under the shade of the large oak trees that surrounded the house.

They were going alongside the stream. The water gurgled darkly over the stones and swirled around a branch as it bent its way through the long grasses. Summer was scarcely aware of it, her eyes reluctant to leave the house.

"Is this where we're gonna live, Summer?" John Austin held onto her shoulder to steady himself in the swaying wagon.

"Yes, John Austin. We're home."

The riders, except for Jack, abruptly turned, crossed the creek and disappeared down a well-worn trail.

"Did ya tell Raccoon to light a shuck up there and see to the stubborn mule?" Bulldog fired the question at Jack as soon as he rode up beside the wagon.

"Yes, I tol' him."

"'Times, he don't use no gumption a'tall."

"It's his pride what makes him what he is. That 'n not wantin' any coddlin'."

"Might be prouder than a game rooster, but he bleeds anyhow," Bulldog grumbled.

"Was someone . . . hurt back there?" Summer asked.

"Ya could say t'was back there or a long time ago." Bulldog spit into the grass and screwed his hat down tighter on his gray head.

Closer to the house now, Summer could see a large pile of freshcut stove wood and a horse tied to the pole railing. Her pulses quickened. Perhaps Sam McLean was waiting to welcome them, after all.

In the back of the wagon, Sadie was shaking Mary awake. Summer looked back and met the girl's dancing green eyes.

"This is the prettiest place I ever did see, Summer. This is the prettiest place in all of Texas. Look, there's a sack swing tied up to that tree."

Summer's eyes followed the pointing finger and her heart lurched again with a distant, familiar memory.

She heard that voice: "Hold tight, summertime girl."
Happiness, such as she hadn't known for a long time,
swept over her. This was home, the place of the fleeting
memories that had haunted her for years.

When she looked back toward the house, Pud was
coming out the door. He stood by his horse and waited
for the wagon to reach him.

"Put yore horse in the corral, Pud," Jack called.
"Yore gonna stay and make yoreself useful to the
women for the time bein'."

The boy threw his dusty hat in the air. "Yaaa . . .
hooo! Ain't I gonna be the spite of every galoot on this
here ranch?"

"Quit a shootin' off yore bazoo, boy, and start
unloadin' this wagon. The womenfolk are all tuckered
out."

Summer stood in the yard, forgetting for once about
her brother. Somehow, the fact that Sam McLean had
not been there to welcome them didn't matter at all.
The homestead was so much more than she had hoped
for. It was better, after all, to have a place of their own.
Now, in her heart, she gave thanks to Sam McLean for
bringing them here.

The house was divided into two rooms; one for
cooking and eating and the other for sleeping. At the
end of the room used for cooking, a ladder led to the
loft and a good-sized room tucked under the roof. John
Austin came in the door and went up the ladder, not
bothering to look at the rest of the house.

"I'll sleep here, Summer. There's two bunks with
ticks on them."

On a double bunk nailed to the wall in the kitchen,
Sadie placed her bundle of belongings.

"This here will do fine for me and Mary."

Summer looked into the other room with its large
rope bed and thick shuck mattress, clean bedclothes
and faded quilt folded neatly at the foot. This was the

bed where she was born! She felt a sharp pang of homesickness for her mother, who had suffered here so she might live.

"I don't need this whole room to myself."

"Well, you'll just have to get yoreself a husband then." Sadie laughed. "I don't 'spect you'd have no trouble."

To hide her blush, Summer went to help unload the wagon. She lifted a box, but had it taken out of her hands.

"Here, boy," Jack called to John Austin. "This here's man's work."

"I can take it," Summer said. "He gets to thinking about things and doesn't hear you call."

Jack frowned. "Boy!" His voice was sharp and loud. John Austin turned and stared at the man, who had removed his dusty hat and slapped it against his thigh when he called. "Over here, boy. Help yore sister. Men don't dawdle 'round while the women work."

John Austin didn't exactly hurry to pick up the case, but that he came at all surprised his sister.

"What's dawdle, Jack?"

"Dawdle's when a man stands 'round with his head up his arse and lets his womenfolk do the work." Jack heaved a large sack onto his shoulder and started toward the house.

John Austin flashed a glance at Summer's red face and giggled.

"Why is it," she mumbled as she retreated to the house, "that he always hears the things you don't want him to hear?"

Bulldog came hurrying through the door.

"Has someone been living here?" Summer asked.

"It's been used from time to time. Teresa cleaned it up a bit."

"Mr. McLean's wife?"

He swiveled around in surprise. "Ain't married.

Teresa's the Mex woman what cooks 'n cleans for . . . the boss."

Summer watched him hurry to the wagon for another load. He was anxious to be gone. She and Sadie were putting away supplies when Jack stuck his head in the door.

"Ma'am, I'm a goin' now. Bulldog already lit a shuck fer the Keep. Pud'll be stayin' here. He's a good lad for all his cuttin' up."

"Is the . . . Keep far from here?" For some reason, Summer's face burned when she asked.

"It's no more than a hoot and a holler. You go right on down there to the creek and look off yonder." He pointed toward a cluster of trees partially hidden by an incline. "And you can see the top of the house. There ain't no need for you all to be a worryin' none. Pud'll fire a signal shot if'n there's anythin' a'tall."

"We're grateful that Pud will be staying with us." Summer smiled at the boy and held out her hand to Jack. "Thank you for bringing us here."

Sadie clung to the door frame, shy, not yet sure how she was regarded. Jack smiled at her, the leathery skin around his eyes crinkled. On impulse, she held out her hand.

"Me, too."

Jack's smile deepened, and Summer thought the weathered face the kindest she had ever seen. Something like she had imagined Sam McLean would be.

Jack turned to the boy. "You behave yoreself with the women." He hit him a gentle blow on the stomach. Pud doubled up, as if in pain. "You'll have to feed him, ma'am. That's sure 'nuff a chore, 'cause them legs of his are holler."

They stood beneath the new porch roof and watched him splash across the creek and disappear up the slope.

"Ain't he nice, Summer? Ain't he about the nicest

man you ever did see?" Sadie sighed. "It's a pity all men ain't like him."

It was during the night that Summer decided she couldn't stay in this house another day without seeing Sam McLean and thanking him for his assistance. Midmorning, she left the security of the log house and walked down to the creek and the two huge tree trunks lashed together to make a footbridge. She had taken pains with her appearance—she was wearing a blue calico dress with a full skirt and scooped neckline. Her dark hair was coiled on top of her head to make her look older, more sophisticated.

At the footbridge she paused, and her eyes sought the roof of the house where she was headed. She knew she must have been there before, but she remembered it no more than the home she had lived in until she was almost four years old. She stepped up onto the big split logs. High water had washed the far bank, causing the logs to tilt downward and barely clear the rushing water. "Don't be afraid, I'll hold your hand," whispered the voice from the past. A feeling of homesickness for that distant time caused her to pause on the footbridge and look back at the house.

Sadie's laugh and Mary's squeals came drifting down to her. Up at dawn, Sadie moved about the kitchen as if she had found heaven. She was making bread and she sang happily to entertain her daughter. John Austin was drawing a picture in the dirt for Pud. The sight of her young brother brought Summer back to the present. And to her need to speak to Sam McLean.

The trail to the ranch house was sandy and up-hill. By the time Summer reached the top and the house came into view, she had a thin coat of perspiration on her brow. Cockleburrs caught at the hem of her dress and she stopped to pick them off, wipe her face, and push the damp curls from her cheeks. Pausing, she stood listening to a scolding bluejay and studied the ranch house. It was a square building made of heavy stone in the style of a Spanish hacienda. A wide veranda held in place by axe-hewn timber pillars was hung with baskets of flowers trailing their bright blossoms from the beams. Massive live oaks shaded the house from the strong sunlight, throwing black shadows on its stone walls. It was beautiful, peaceful.

She walked on slowly, feeling the sun hot on the back of her neck. Excitement stirred inside her. Be calm! she commanded herself. She *had* to appear calm.

The floor of the veranda was made of stone set deep in the earth. The shade of the veranda, the cold stone floor and wall, made coming in from the outside a cool retreat. A heavy wooden door with wrought-iron hinges stood open, and she could see a spacious room running the width of the house. Overhead, huge, ancient-looking timbers supported the ceiling connecting it to the stone walls, directing the eye to a massive fireplace. Bright Mexican rugs dotted the stone floor, and large, deep chairs, a couch, several tables and a glass-fronted secretary furnished the room.

She hesitated in the doorway. It was so quiet it was eerie. She took a deep breath.

"Mr. McLean." Her voice didn't come out very loud and she called again. "Mr. McLean."

There was nothing to break the silence but her voice. She moved into the room and toward the door beyond. She peered down a long hallway into the first open door. A large trestle table and handsome cabinets filled with dishes and silver assured her that Mr. McLean was not poor.

A large black cook-stove dominated the kitchen. Behind it, arranged neatly, hung an assortment of pots and pans. From the rafters hung bunches of dried spices, chili peppers and colorful gourds. A skillet was left burning on the fire, greasy smoke filling the air.

Instinctively, Summer went for the stove, her eyes searching for something with which to grasp the hot handle of the skillet. Seeing nothing, she bunched her skirt in her two hands and moved the pan to a cooler part of the stove. Standing back, she let her skirt fall back down around her ankles. In spite of the quiet, she had the feeling she was not alone. Swinging around, she jumped with surprise, her hand going to her mouth.

Someone was standing in the gloom at the far end of the room, standing quite still and watching her. While she stared, the figure moved and materialized slowly, became a tall man with a dark shirt and pants, straight black hair and a lean, swarthy face, whose right cheek was badly scarred. There was something about the outline of him, the way he held his head, that caused Summer's legs to tremble and her heart to pound in the most alarming way. It was him. The man from the street in Hamilton and the man from the store where they loaded the supplies.

"I'm looking for Mr. McLean." Her voice seemed dreadfully loud.

"You found him." He didn't look at her, but moved toward the stove.

"I mean . . . Sam McLean." Summer looked at his back. He had pulled the skillet back over the flame and dropped a piece of meat into the hot grease. The only noise that broke the silence was the sizzle of cooking meat. He didn't answer.

"I'm Summer Kuykendall, from over across the creek. I came over to thank Mr. McLean for . . . letting his men escort us from town. John Austin and I . . . John Austin is my brother. We came from the Piney Woods. You see, our mother died and she told me that. . . ." Suddenly, she couldn't stand the sound of her own voice. Her words seemed so trite, so unnecessary. The man was ignoring her, keeping his face turned away from her, and it made her angry. "Is there someplace where I can wait for Mr. McLean? It's . . . it's just not my nature to be beholden to someone and not be able to thank them."

"There's no need to feel beholden." The man's curt tone matched hers.

Summer was about to make a sharp retort when the man moved. His leg almost buckled under him. It was then that she noticed his feet were bare.

"Sit down. I'll fix your meal while I'm waiting."

She had expected him to protest, but he limped over to the table and eased himself into a chair, extending his leg out in front of him. Summer moved swiftly and efficiently between the work counter and the stove. Lifting the meat from the skillet, she broke two eggs into the fat; while they were cooking, she took biscuits from the warming oven.

Scarcely looking at the bent dark head, she placed the plate of food on the table and returned to the stove to pour two mugs of coffee. With both her hands curled about the warm cup, she sat quietly and watched him eat. The light from the window shafted across his right cheek, showing up an ugly white scar that curved from the middle of his ear up and over his cheekbone and down to the corner of his mouth. Thick black lashes hid deep blue eyes, when he looked up to see her looking at him. There was an awful, strained silence as they stared at each other.

"S. McLean?" Summer said carefully, as if the words were strange and she were terribly afraid of them.

"Slater McLean." His voice held a tinge of regret.

"You wrote the letter?" Summer's eyes held his.

"Yes." He looked down at his plate. "It's what Pa would've done if he was alive."

"Sam McLean is dead?"

"Five years now. But even then, he wanted you to come home."

"Why didn't you tell me? Or meet me in Hamilton?"

"Would you have come with me?"

She studied his face; one side so smooth and handsome, the other puckered, distorted. Most men, she thought, would have grown a beard to hide at least part of the disfigurement.

"I don't know what you mean," she said at last. "My mother told me to find Sam McLean and I. . . ."

"Say no more," he interrupted curtly. "I understand."

"What ever happened to your face?" The words were out before she could stop them.

There was an awful moment of silence while the enormity of her rude question shamed her. His thick dark lashes came together over the hard gleam in his eyes, and the left corner of his mouth slanted upward as he smiled.

"You're not supposed to mention it. You're supposed to look away and pretend it isn't there. It's ugly and offensive, but I'm grateful it's where it is and not two inches to the left—where it would have cut across my eye, nose and mouth. I can see, smell, eat, and I'm alive. And that is important to me."

His mockery affected her more than she was prepared for.

"I'm sorry. It was rude of me to ask, but I had no idea you were so sensitive about it. No amount of pretending is going to make it go away, you know."

"On second thought," he said icily, "I think I prefer your outspokenness to sly glances." He made to get up. "More coffee?"

When he was seated again, she asked, "Why didn't you ride with us? I saw you in the store."

"On my way to town, I found Indian signs. We haven't had Indian trouble for a year or two. Figured I'd better scout ahead."

"I was scared," she confessed.

"Only a fool wouldn't be scared of Apaches," he said drily.

"You were the one Bulldog was worried about." She made it a statement. "He called you a stubborn mule."

He almost smiled. "He's an old cluckin' hen."

"I don't mind his gruffness. I like him. Jack, too." She laughed, remembering how surprised Bulldog was when he met her at the hotel. "Didn't he know I was grown up? He thought he was meeting two children."

Slater's eyes never left her face. Her sparkle was infectious. He smiled, showing even white teeth, and she was surprised at the change it made in his grim face.

"Time doesn't mean much to Bulldog." He continued to watch her.

"I invited Sadie and her little girl to come out and live with us after Bulldog said we were going out to a homestead. I had the idea John Austin and I would be living out on the prairie, miles from anyone else."

She stopped talking. With a sense of shock, she realized he was waiting for her to say something more. She straightened her back and said nothing, but her eyes were drawn to his, and he held them, probing them, before moving from her eyes to her hair and down the full length of her body. Her cheeks flamed.

When she did speak, her voice was calm, firm; it surprised her.

"We're going to plant a garden right away. And there's another thing. . . ." Her voice trailed away only because she didn't know how to put into words that their cash money was gone and she needed a way to earn more.

"And . . . what?" he prompted.

She folded her hands in her lap and bent her head, her lids drooping over suddenly moist eyes, her courage leaving her.

"I want to discuss the bill at the store." She hoped, desperately, that he didn't know how nervous she had become. Looking straight into his eyes, she added, "You needn't feel you must be responsible for us."

"You're not a charity case, if that's what you're

thinking. The land was your mother's. We only used it all these years. Sam's instructions were clear. He wanted you to come home and have what was yours. He was . . . fond of your mother.''

Her spirits rose a little. But she wished he had said it was what he wanted, and not what Sam wanted.

"Sam left you a small amount of cash money. I'll keep it, if you like, until you need it. In the meanwhile, if there's anything you need, let me know. Your place is part of the Keep, and we take care of our own."

Their eyes met in silent assessment of each other. He knew every question and answer that flitted through her mind; she could see it in his eyes. Summer's chin began to tilt and she tossed her head back as if to shake the hair from her face. She knew this was her outward sign that inside she was nervous, afraid, uncertain. She wanted to remember another time, but his eyes drew all coherent thinking from her mind, and she asked rather absently:

"Why did he name the ranch McLean's Keep?"

The rare smile surfaced again. "To Scots, the word 'keep' means fortress, castle, lands, possessions. Sam McLean loved everything Scottish. He built this Spanish-style house because it suited the land and the materials were available, but everything else on the Keep is Scottish. He worked hard and was frugal as only a Scot can be. This place proves what one determined man can build in a lifetime. I intend to hold it in trust for the next generation of McLeans."

Summer carried the cups and plate to the counter to hide her unexpectedly flushed face. He was standing when she turned, and she saw him wince as he put his weight on the injured leg.

"Shouldn't you stay off that leg?" She tilted her face up to look at him, and almost automatically he turned the smooth cheek toward her.

"Yes," he assented begrudgingly. His eyes glinted

briefly when he looked into her wide violet ones. "Don't tell Bulldog I admitted it."

Her eyes searched his face, her hand on the back of the chair steadied her.

"I came to thank Sam McLean," she said quietly.

He grinned down at her. "Consider it done."

She smiled back, somehow not wanting to leave, but since he didn't say anything, she moved to the door. He followed, and they walked through the dining room and into the large room fronting the house. His pace was slow and he held his leg stiffly.

"It's a beautiful house," Summer said admiringly.

"You don't remember it at all?"

She looked about the room and shook her head.

"You don't remember hiding behind the couch and jumping out at me when I came through the door?"

That made her look up at him, her eyes wide. She studied his face. It told her nothing except that he was fascinated by her expression.

"And the swing I made for you?" The smile left his face. "And how afraid you were to cross the footbridge?" It seemed to Summer he watched her with his whole body, not just his eyes, and that all his muscles were coiled, taut, in anticipation of her answer.

She moistened her dry lips. She felt as if she were in a vacuum, being drawn toward him.

"You . . . You promised to come . . . and fetch me home." Her eyes were filling with tears and her lips trembled.

"That I did, summertime girl." The words were so softly spoken they barely reached her ears.

Summer opened her mouth, but no sound came out. She stared at him as if stunned, her mind stumbling and forming no logical thoughts. The desire to cling to him burned so strongly in her that she had no will to resist his arms as they closed about her and he hugged her tight. Strange sensations went zig-zag along her nerves, and her fingers fanned out across his back as she hugged him in return. Finally, she tilted her head and looked up into his face.

"You're the boy? The one that called me summertime girl—I tried and tried to remember." Her voice was tremulous with elation.

He loosened his arms and she stepped back, her face radiant.

"Yes," he said slowly. "I was about your brother's age when you were born in that cabin. You belonged here."

"Thank you for bringing me back."

"Thank you for coming back, summertime girl."

Their glances met and measured each other again. Her head whirled and she gave him what she hoped was a smile.

"I must go," she said breathlessly. "I better see about John Austin. He's . . . kind of a handful sometimes."

"So Bulldog said." He was reluctant for her to leave. "Turn him over to Jack. He's the best I ever saw with kids. Likes them, too. He'll have your brother eating out of his hand in no time."

Summer sobered. "John Austin is one of the reasons I came out here. After you get to know him, you'll understand. He's terribly bright, but what worried Mama and worries me is that he doesn't have what you call . . . horse-sense." Their eyes clung for a breathless moment, then she dropped her lids and continued. "Mama said Sam McLean would know how to handle him."

"And he would have." His voice was husky. "Now I'll see to it."

Summer's heart gave a frantic leap and lodged in her throat. She was agonizingly aware that he wanted her to stay, but her thoughts were not functioning the way they should, they seemed to stumble about in awed bewilderment. She turned her back, then halted a pace away. Bootheels rang on the stone floor of the veranda, and Bulldog appeared in the doorway. He looked from one to the other, then tugged his hat from his head.

"Got company down to the other place." In spite of his calm manner, indignation showed in his tight lips.

"Company?" Slater moved out from where he was leaning against the door frame. "Who?"

"Miz Ellen, that's who! Miz Ellen 'n her whole tribe!" Bulldog now bristled like an enraged porcupine. "Come a ridin' in jist as pretty as ya please, that big galoot by 'er side along with that sorry cur she calls 'son.' Same bunch what was in town. Now you just tell me what they's come fer, after all this time of not settin' a foot on the place?"

Slater's eyes had narrowed. "Anyone down there?"

"Jack." Bulldog flung a hand out irritably. "We saw the dust and went to look. Then we high-tailed it over to the 'little place' to be a waitin' fer 'em."

Summer's interest grew with every passing second.

"She didn't lose any time." Slater leveled his sharp gaze on Summer and she met his eyes. Sensing that somehow this crisis had to do with her, she felt compelled to ask:

"Are the visitors at my mother's place?"

Slater lowered himself into a chair and sat rigidly erect. He studied her for a moment before he spoke.

"Ellen McLean and her son have come to call on you." He bit the words out icily. "Enjoy your guests. They're not welcome here." Abruptly, he hoisted himself up from the chair and limped out of the room.

Summer stood as if he had struck her. She turned wondering eyes to Bulldog, but he slammed his hat down on his head and walked away from her. She went to the door Slater had just passed through.

"Slater." He was going down the hall and stopped when she called to him, but didn't turn around. "Why are you angry? Is it because of Ellen McLean? Why has she come all this way to call on me?"

He turned around, showing her only the scarred side of his face.

"She wants you for a daughter-in-law." He ground out the words in a low, husky voice. "And Ellen usually gets what she wants."

Summer turned her head away before he saw the distress in her eyes, and when she looked back he was gone.

Chapter Five

When Summer reached the footbridge, she was still trying to find an explanation for Slater's sudden change of mood and boorish behavior. She pushed it back into a corner of her mind and fastened her attention on the figures waiting for her in the shade of the veranda.

Ellen McLean rose from a chair where she sat fanning her face. She snapped the fan shut and allowed it to dangle from her wrist as she came forward. The men, lounging casually against the rough logs of the house, watched her. One swept off his hat and ran his fingers through thick blond hair as he stepped out into the bright sunlight. The other scarcely moved. There was no sign of Sadie or the children.

"I hope you won't think it presumptuous of me to call on you so soon." Ellen came toward her with hands extended. "You have no idea how excited I've been, just knowing you were so near. It's been ages since I've been able to talk woman-talk." She took Summer's hands and clasped them warmly; her smooth, lovely face wreathed in smiles. Summer's reaction to the older woman was spontaneous.

"I don't think it presumptuous at all, Mrs. McLean. I'm happy to see you again."

"Oh, my dear! You've no idea how relieved I am to hear you say that." Her lilting voice deepened with sincerity, then lightened as she glanced at the men behind her. "It was no mean task to persuade those two to bring me," she said confidentially. "Jesse is champing at the bit to get back to the ranch. He's my foreman, you know, and I must say there was never a better one, but this scamp is like his mother." She placed her slim hand on her son's arm. "If there's a pretty girl around, he wants to know her."

Summer looked up to meet bold blue eyes. She was startled to find them locked on her with a smiling intensity. It was like being caught naked in a public place, the way he looked at her. Her face must have reflected her feeling, for he lowered his lids and his face took on a friendly, boyish expression.

"My mother will give you the wrong impression, Miss Kuykendall, but I'll admit it didn't take much persuading on my part." A smile flashed rakishly across his handsome face. "It was well worth a half-day's extra ride."

Innocently confused, Summer turned back to Ellen. "Is your ranch far from here?"

"It's really close by, as far as distances go in this vast country." Ellen took her arm and they walked together toward the house. "It must be about fifteen miles as the crow flies, but slightly more than that by the time we wind around and get across those troublesome streams that are either dry or overflowing."

Summer found Travis once more scrutinizing her with a thoroughness that made her again feel undressed. His gaze moved unabashedly over her softly-rounded breasts and trim waist, then moved leisurely along the full length of her. She struggled to keep the tide of color from her cheeks, and in looking away met Jesse's steely eyes. He held her gaze for an instant, then raked his thumbnail over the head of a sulphur match and held the flame to the cigarette dangling from his lips.

Summer's mind groped like some small, drowning creature. She was at odds as to how best to proceed with her guests.

"Mrs. McLean . . . ?" she began, in a questioning tone.

"Ellen. I couldn't possibly allow Nannie Kuykendall's daughter to call me anything but Ellen." The soft friendly voice continued, "If you don't mind, Summer, I'll sit here and catch what cool breeze there is and Jesse will fetch me a cool drink."

Travis squatted down on his heels and leaned his back against the heavy post supporting the veranda roof. Jesse moved away from the wall and toward the door.

"Bucket in here?" he asked, the soft timbre of his voice seeming to go with the rest of him.

"I'll get it for you." Summer escaped inside the house and Jesse followed.

When they entered, Sadie backed from the stove, her large green eyes going from Summer to Jesse. She continued to back away, until her legs struck the edge of the bunk where her daughter was sitting. Her fright calmed Summer's nerves.

"This is Mr. Thurston, Sadie." She placed her arm across Sadie's shoulders. "My friend, Mrs. Bratcher." She laughed down at the small face peeking from behind Sadie's skirt. "And her daughter, Mary."

Jesse nodded. He had noticed the girl's fright the moment he stepped into the room, and now that he had a closer look at her, he understood why. She was the dance-hall girl he had rescued from Travis several weeks ago. He allowed no recognition to show in his face as he mumbled a polite greeting and looked down at the impish little face peeking up at him. His stern face relaxed, and memories of his own childhood came flooding back; every kind word, every pat on the head was to be remembered and cherished. He fished into his pocket, came out with a peppermint stick, and held it out to the child. She hid her face in Sadie's skirt and refused to look at him. He chuckled, and handed the candy to Sadie.

"She scares easy," Sadie murmured as she accepted the offering.

"It's natural." The piercing eyes rested once again on Sadie's face, and remained so long that it seemed he was counting every freckle on her slightly upturned nose, before going to the shelf for the water bucket.

Sadie's eyes followed him out the door. "I'll get the meal ready, Summer, so don't you be frettin' how you're gonna feed 'em."

"That's a relief. I never dreamed we'd have visitors so soon. Where's John Austin?"

"He's all right. Jack said to tell you not to worry, he'd keep a tight rein on him."

"I hope to heaven he does." Summer's voice took on the serious, worried tone it always did when she spoke of her brother.

"You go on out," Sadie urged. "I'll call when the meal's ready."

It was later in the afternoon, as she and Ellen were sitting in the shade of the oak tree, that Summer thought about the tall ranch foreman and Travis. They were not openly hostile toward each other, but they were certainly not friendly either. She had not been able to observe them more closely because Ellen kept her occupied with woman-talk. Up to now, the talk had been about dress patterns, new novels and hairstyles.

"How is Slater?" Ellen asked suddenly.

"I only met him this morning."

The friendly blue eyes searched hers, then saddened as she shook her head.

"It's a shame the way that man has withdrawn since Sam was killed." She paused, and her face turned toward the footbridge and the ranch house beyond. "He blames us, you know. I could never understand how he could think that Travis or I had anything to do with such a thing." The sad eyes came back to Summer. "I loved Sam McLean like a brother. After all, he was my husband's only living kin." Tears welled in the corners of her eyes.

Summer reached across and clasped her hand. "I'm sorry, Ellen. I didn't know Sam McLean was dead until this morning."

Ellen wiped her eyes. "That's just like Slater, to bring you here without telling you." Summer didn't speak, so she continued. "It's been about five years now. Or maybe four, time goes by so fast. Sam and Slater were camped in the hills, and men rode into the camp shooting. I suppose they thought Sam had money on him. They killed him. Slater was badly injured. One of them rode his horse over him time and again . . . so he said. It's a wonder he lived. Some of Sam's men were bringing in fresh horses and heard the shots. They rode in and killed the men on the spot. They said one man got away by riding through a nearby pass, but they found no trace of him. The dead men worked for us at one time, so Slater believes the orders came from us. It's beyond me how he can think such a thing." Ellen turned her face away to dab her eyes.

Summer didn't know what to say. The woman's sincere distress made her half-angry at Slater. It was logical for him to be hurt and angry, but why carry on that hate, without proof, for five years?

"Slater was a strange little boy," Ellen said fondly. "He was so lonely. His mother was . . . well, there's no other way to put it, not quite right. It happens sometimes to women out here in this desolate country.

They can't cope with the day-after-day loneliness of never seeing another woman." She shook her head sadly and patted Summer's hand. "Men!" she exclaimed. "Men have their work, but women need more than that. We need to talk, need to be loved and told that we are loved. Poor Libby, so fat and unlovable. Who could blame Sam for spending most of his time as far away from her as possible? He adored Slater and Slater adored him, tagged after him everywhere. When you came along, he adopted you as his little sister." She breathed deeply and let out a trembly sigh. "Sometimes, I think Slater may have inherited some of what affected his mother."

"Did she die before the accident?"

"Yes. She died a couple years after you and your mother went back to the Piney Woods. It was a blessing, in a way, for toward the end she had to be locked in her room. But let's talk of more pleasant things. You have a beautiful place here. I've always loved this place. Your land borders on ours. Did you know that?" She laughed at Summer's expression. "No. Your land doesn't reach out fifteen miles, but ours reaches almost that far. You have a strip in here that borders the creek—I'd say it's two or three miles wide. You've a valuable piece of land as far as Slater is concerned. The south of your land is another part of McLean's Keep. That wily Sam!" She laughed again and shook her head. "He laid out this homestead. I don't think he thought J.R. would come back for Nannie. Maybe he thought he would marry her himself." Her eyes danced with mischief. "That Sam was a true Scotsman!"

The hint that Sam would have married her mother for her land didn't go down well with Summer, but she kept her eyes on the distant hills and never allowed her feelings to show.

"And you, Ellen," she asked, "have you been widowed long?"

Her eyes took on a sad, faraway look again. "Travis was just a little boy when Scott died. We stayed at the ranch for a few years, then went to Nacogdoches, where my people lived. We came back about twelve years ago and brought Jesse with us. It was about time, too. The man I trusted to manage the ranch had about stolen us blind. I do declare, you never know whom to trust. Jesse took things in hand. You know, I have the finest house in west Texas if I do say so myself. Do come and stay as long as you like, Summer. What good is having a fine house if you can't show it off?" She laughed and held her hands over her ears in mock dismay. "What must you think of me?" she wailed.

"I think you're a very nice lady, who is proud of her home."

"Oh, Summer. I want us to be friends."

"There's no reason why we shouldn't be." Summer's eyes found her young brother and she called to him. "I want you to meet my brother, Ellen."

Summer saw no more of Travis until the evening meal. He came in with Jesse. The two men stood side by side waiting for the meal to be placed on the table. How alike they were, and yet so different. Both were tall, lean and brown. One smiled easily, the other seldom, if at all. Travis was politeness itself. Gone was the lecherous image he projected earlier, and in its place a boyish friendliness. Summer privately conceded that her opinion of him could have been colored by Slater's bitter warning.

Sadie appeared when the meal was over, and Summer assisted with the clean-up. Sadie was unusually cross with Mary, and the little girl finally went to the bunk in the back of the kitchen and lay, sucking her thumb, watching with large, round eyes. Ellen was distantly polite to Sadie, and ignored the little girl completely. It was with relief that Summer invited Ellen to the veranda when the work was finished.

As soon as the two women left the room, Sadie went

to the washstand and bathed her flushed face. It was a struggle to crush the feeling of apprehension that stirred restlessly when in the presence of Ellen McLean and her son. Son-of-a-bitch! A mule's ass of the first string; a spoiled, conceited bastard, whose sexual urges ran to cruelties and perversions. The women in Hamilton had told her plenty about him. Even the whores refused his money unless they were desperate for cash. Her heart had come up in her throat when she first saw him, and the nightmare of his near-rape came bounding back to set her atremble. Only her screams had brought help. Just before his fist had smashed into her face, she had seen the tall dark foreman, his face frozen with anger, trying to jerk him off her. Today, the man acted as if he didn't remember her, but Travis had recognized her instantly. He had appeared once this afternoon and leaned briefly in the doorway of the kitchen eyeing her insolently, as if daring her to betray him.

Angry with herself for being so cross with Mary, she went to her and gathered her up in her arms.

"Mama's sorry, sweet baby," she crooned. "Mama's sorry she was cross. I tell you what we'll do. We'll go down to the swing. Would you like that?"

The little face broke into smiles. "Swing, swing!"

It was twilight when they walked hand in hand out the back door. Down by the creek, Sadie could see the fire from the temporary camp set up by Mrs. McLean's drovers. Several riders from the other ranch splashed across the creek to join them, and from the shouted greetings it was obvious the groups were friendly. Sadie and Mary turned toward the swing.

Mary ran ahead, grabbed the straw-filled sack suspended by the rope and wrapped her small legs about it. Sadie gave her a gentle push and she laughed merrily. The sound of her child's laughter was so dear to her that Sadie forgot everything except this small pleasure she was sharing with her daughter.

"High, high, Mama!"

"Hold tight," Sadie cautioned. "Hold tight, and we'll go higher."

After a while, Mary became weary of holding on, and her small feet dragged the ground until the swing stopped. She was content for a time just to push the swing, then turned her small face up to her mother.

"Mama swing!"

"All right." Her laughter equalling that of her daughter's, she jumped up and wrapped her legs around the sack. "Give me a push, Mary."

The small hands on her back barely moved her.

"Come on, Mary. Give me a push."

Large, hard hands touched her back, and she was given a hefty shove. She was so frightened that her hands froze onto the rope and she flung herself around to see Mary standing beside the tall foreman, clapping her hands and squealing with glee. The man's hat was pulled low over his eyes, and she could see only his mouth. It was slightly tilted.

"Mary," she gasped, and darted to take the child's hand. Mary jerked away from her and ran to the swing.

"Me swing!"

Sadie's heart was galloping wildly in her breast. She went to snatch Mary from the swing, but the man was there ahead of her and gave the child a gentle push.

"We was just goin'."

"No, you wasn't."

She wasn't sure she heard correctly and looked wildly about like a frightened child.

"I'm not the one you have to look out for. You know that." He spoke softly, gently, and kept a steady hand on the child's back as he swung her back and forth.

"Yes," she whispered, but the sound reached him.

"How come you was workin' in the dance hall?" Sadie was taken aback by his words and didn't know how to answer, so she remained silent. "Where's your man?" His direct questions sparked resentment.

"He got hisself killed, and I was working in the dance

hall 'cause I couldn't get no other work." She watched him, frowning, but her resentment died fast when his eyes met hers. To soften her blunt words, she added, "Thank you for what you done that night. I didn't have no idea he'd do what he did. He'd been so nice."

"He can be when he wants to. Don't let him catch you by yourself."

There was silence while they both watched Mary on the swing. Again, Sadie was taken aback by his words, and she searched frantically for something to say.

"How long you been working for Mrs. McLean?"

"Twelve years."

She wished he would say something more, but he stood silently, watching her, swinging Mary.

"Do you come over this way often?" She wished she hadn't asked the question.

"I will now."

Sadie was so nervous and strung up she could hardly think. What did he mean? For a second, she felt the prick of a thrill, but it faded quickly in the face of logic. He would be bringing Mrs. McLean to visit Summer. She allowed herself the luxury of staring at him.

His sun-bronzed face was framed by neatly-trimmed dark brown sideburns, accentuating high cheekbones and a thin, well-formed nose above a generous but unsmiling mouth. It was the sternest, most forbidding face she had ever seen. He turned to look down at her, and suddenly his gray eyes gave her the feeling he could see straight through her.

"This is a good place for you. Will you stay here?"

"I want to." The words came easier. "I want to help enough to pay for our keep."

"This is a good place for you," he said again.

Sadie watched him, noting the way Mary trusted him and how gently he pushed her on the swing. She looked into his face and wondered what was behind it. What was he thinking? And would he really protect her from his employer's son? She wondered how he had come

among the McLeans. What had his home been like?
What kind of woman could take him from Mrs.
McLean? A queer little shock went through her when
she realized her thoughts. How could it possibly matter
to her what kind of man he was? Come morning, she
would probably never see him again. Nevertheless, the
thought disturbed her, and she looked at him keenly.
There was no smell of evil about him like there was
about Travis McLean, but there was no real softness,
either, except what he showed with Mary. Yes, to be
with such a man would be . . . would be. . . .

"Have you made up your mind about me?" He
stopped the swing and lifted Mary down.

"What do you mean?"

"You were trying to decide what kind of man I am,
and if I'm to be trusted."

Mary reached up and took his hand and tugged. He
looked down at the impish little face and squatted down
on his heels. He patted his shirt pocket. Timidly, at
first, Mary searched until she discovered the slender
cylinder of candy. Her sparkling eyes found his. Jesse
got to his feet and patted her head.

"Somethin' we both got a fondness for, eh, little
girl?"

He took the makings for a cigarette from his pocket
and, scarcely looking at what he was doing, constructed
the smoke. He flicked the head of the match with his
nail and held up the flame. He watched Mary, sticky
spit from the candy running down her chin, then turned
his gaze on the mother. She was a woman all right—
scarcely more than a girl in years—but a spunky
woman. Pretty, too. He took the cigarette from his lips.
She was fidgeting and burning because he was looking
at her. She had looked at him, now it was his turn. She
must have really been brought low to take the job in the
dance hall. He knew when he pulled Travis off her that
she wasn't right for that sort of place.

It was growing late. Sadie took Mary's hand. The

man didn't turn or speak as she walked behind him, but her footsteps hesitated a little, as if she wanted to speak. He turned and she stopped.

"Mister?"

"Yes'm?"

"Thank you. And thank you for givin' Mary the treat." Her voice trembled, in spite of her determination to keep it even.

"Go on back," he said. Sadie was sure his voice gentled. "Go on back and I'll watch."

It was wonderful not to be afraid. She could feel his eyes on her until she let herself into the back door. Quickly, she washed the sticky sweet from the child's tired face and hands, undressed her, and put her in the bunk. Blowing out the lamp, she undressed and got in beside her. She could hear the murmur of Ellen McLean's voice coming from Summer's room, and the voices of John Austin and Pud in the loft. She thought of the coming morning with mixed feelings. Although she longed to see the last of Mrs. McLean and her son, she dreaded to think she'd not be seeing Jesse Thurston again.

It was near midnight when Jack tied his horse to the rail and crossed the stone veranda. He let himself into the house, and guided by the smell of freshly-brewed coffee, went directly to the kitchen. Slater looked up and motioned toward the stove. Jack hung his hat on the rack and took a mug from the shelf.

"How's the leg?"

"Better. Teresa made up a poultice that took off some of the soreness."

"How'd she get it past Bulldog?"

Slater grinned at that. "He was busy keeping his eagle eye on Ellen."

They sat in silence for a while before Jack spoke again.

"Ain't that kid a ring-tailed tooter?"

Slater refilled his cup and thought about the pleasant hour he had spent with John Austin.

"It's no lie about him being brainy."

Jack chuckled. "He got ol' Pud treed. Drawed him a picture of the world and showed him how the sun and the moon went around it. Ol' Pud jist sit thar with his mouth open. Kid tol' him he'd show him how to read and write his name. I thought ol' Pud would bust a gut when the kid said thar warn't no excuse for him to be ignorant now that he was here. Kid's smart. Ya gotta give him that. But the fool kid don't know nothin' else. Walked right up close to a rattler . . . wanted to look at it. I tol' Pud not to take his eyes off him, leastways till we get some sense in him."

"His sister said he lacked horse-sense, but she brought it about herself by protecting him too much, doing too much for him. It's made him selfish and forgetful of his manners. He needs a man's hand."

The older man looked down at the table, twisted his cup round and round in his large calloused hands.

"Travis has come a courtin', Slater. He's behavin' real good. If'n him and his ma get their way, we ain't gonna have nothin' to say 'bout the girl or the kid."

Although Slater was of the same opinion, the spoken words angered him.

"Who the hell says they're going to get their way? That girl is no fool. I'm counting on her seeing right through Ellen and that murdering son-of-a-bitch." Resting his elbows on the table and rubbing a fist against his forehead, he heaved a laborious sigh and continued, "Goddammit, Jack. I ought to kill the bastard and be done with it."

"There's times when I agree with ya, and then there's times when I don't. I ain't sayin' you're wrong in thinkin' he was in on the killin' of yore pa, but if ya just gun him down, not knowin' for sure, it could be a hard thing to live with. 'Sides, you might have Jesse to worry with."

73

"How about Jesse, Jack? He still lickin' Ellen's boots?"

"I'll tell you somethin'. I'd bet my bottom dollar Jesse is onto Travis. He'll do all he can to keep it from Ellen, but he's onto him. He dogged him all day, and once, when he was talkin' to Armando, you know that hand we hired a while back? Well, he kind of sidled up to them, easy-like, and Travis moved off. I ain't a likin' that coot a cozyin' up to Travis like he done."

"Maybe you ought to tell him to skeedaddle."

"Thought it might not hurt to keep him and see what he's up to."

"He's spying for Travis."

"Maybe."

Slater fingered the scar on his face as he sometimes did when he had something on his mind. Irritably, he jammed a cheroot in his mouth and, striking a match on the sole of his boot, puffed it until it glowed. A wraith of smoke curled into the air.

"Jesse see any Indian sign?"

"None. Said the bunch what hit us was likely an offshoot of Mountain Apaches in the hills south and west. Jesse's got good Indian sense, fought 'em a heap from the way he talks. Course the booger don't give away nothin' 'bout hisself."

"Jesse knows what he's about."

"Except for one thing."

A scowl came to Slater's face. "Every man has a weakness. Jesse's is Ellen McLean."

Chapter Six

Just after daybreak, Jesse brought the buggy to the front of the house.

"Must we go so soon?" Ellen, in her gray traveling suit, placed a hand on his arm.

He patted her hand and spoke to her as if she were a child. "You know we must. Say your goodbyes, so we can get goin'."

"I didn't see enough of Summer," she pouted.

"We'll come again," he promised.

Watching from the doorway, Sadie chastised herself for even daring to dream a man like that would be interested in her when he had that beautiful, dainty creature, even though she was years older than him. She folded her hands across the clean apron she had put on in hopes she would see him again, and scolded herself for the extra time she had spent on arranging her hair. He had not even looked her way.

Summer was not sorry the visit had come to an end. She liked Ellen, and her opinion of Travis had undergone a drastic change since the afternoon before, but it was a strain having guests when she had been in her new home for such a short time. Travis was friendly without being overly so, and he seemed to have faultless manners. He came up to her now, and extended his hand.

"It's been a pleasure, Miss Kuykendall. Thank you for your hospitality." He grinned boyishly and tilted his head toward his mother. "She'll be easier to live with for a while."

Ellen's sparkling laugh filled the morning stillness. "Don't mind what he says, Summer. He and Jesse would have you believe I'm a regular nag." She went to Summer and kissed her lightly on the cheek. "I would have loved having a daughter like you, dear. But," she raised her eyes upward in mock despair, "I was given this unbearable son!"

John Austin came out of the house, rubbing sleep from his eyes, followed by Mary holding up her nightdress so she could walk. The little girl made straight for Jesse, much to Sadie's distress and reached up and tugged on his hand.

Jesse's stern face softened, and his hand came out to fondle the dark red curls before he squatted down on his haunches so she could reach into his breast pocket for the candy stick she knew would be there.

The smile that came to Summer's face when she saw the amazement on Sadie's faded when she looked at Ellen. The older woman's brows were drawn together and she seemed to be repulsed by what she saw. She wrinkled her nose in disgust and moved a step closer to Jesse and placed a hand on his shoulder.

"Well . . . Mama!" Travis laughed teasingly. "You're gonna have to keep a tighter rein on your man. I do believe he's been out prowlin'."

"Shut up, Travis." Jesse barked the words as he lifted Mary up in his arms. Turning to Ellen, he said, "Get in

76

the buggy." He handed the child over to Sadie and raised his hand to the brim of his hat. "Ma'am."

They had moved only a few paces off when Travis spat: "Now ain't he being all godawful polite to a whore!"

"Travis, be nice," Ellen admonished.

Travis doffed his hat in mock salute. He swaggered to his horse and mounted, pulling the reins up tight so the animal danced nervously among the drovers that waited to escort the buggy.

"That red-headed mare's been rode so much she's got saddle sore, Jesse. Can't you do no better than that?" He said something out of the side of his mouth to the drovers, and one of them laughed nervously. "Hey, Jesse . . ." Travis had the attention he wanted and was making the most of it. "That filly of hers won't be ready for bustin' for a few years. You stakin' your claim now?"

Ellen took hold of Jesse's arm. "Jesse, no! He's just funnin'."

Jesse shook her arm loose and in a few quick strides reached Travis, who was crowded in tight among the drovers. Before the younger man could draw a breath, he snatched him from the saddle.

Travis hit the ground and bounced to his feet, his face twisted in anger.

"Goddam you," he snarled. "I ought to have killed you when you first came smellin' around my mama!"

"How about now?"

The words were calmly spoken and barely out of his mouth when Travis charged him. Jesse's fist flashed out and slammed him in the face. Travis's head snapped back and he stretched out full length on his back. He came up clawing for his gun. The drover, who had dismounted to hold the nervous horse, stepped on his arm and jerked the gun from its holster.

Travis got slowly to his feet, his face a mask of

hatred, blood from his busted lips running down his chin.

"You bastard! You son-of-a-whore!" He stood swaying, his hands hanging at his sides, his eyes darting from Jesse to his mother who stood with gloved hands pressed to her mouth.

"Jesse! Please!" Ellen pleaded.

The big man moved deliberately, and with his open hand slapped Travis across the face on one side and with the back of his hand on the other.

"Get on that horse, and count yourself lucky I don't stomp you to death."

Travis staggered back against the horse. His hand reached for the pommel and his foot for the stirrup.

"Jesse, how could you?" Ellen twisted her hands anxiously. "How could you hurt him over a . . ."

Jesse's look silenced her. Gently, he took her elbow and guided her to the buggy. Summer came to stand beside the step.

Smiling bravely, Ellen held out her hand. "I'm truly sorry our visit had to end so crudely. Please forgive them. You'll find men of the west are quick-tempered and brutal at times. Travis is a tease and Jesse takes everything to heart. In a few days, this will all be forgotten." She laughed nervously. "You'll come for a visit?" Summer nodded. "I'll be back to see you. I'll be back real soon."

Jesse climbed into the buggy and took up the reins. Ellen waved her handkerchief. Travis spurred his horse and disappeared in a cloud of dust. The drovers fell in behind the buggy.

Summer and Sadie silently watched Ellen's departure. They were stunned by the scene they had just witnessed. The insulting remarks hurled by Travis and the cold violence displayed by Jesse were so shocking to Summer that they seemed something from a bad dream.

John Austin broke the silence.

"What did he mean, Summer? Why did he call Mr. Thurston a son-of-a-whore? Why was Mr. Thurston so mad?"

Summer whirled on him. "Don't you ever say that word again, John Austin Kuykendall! Do you hear me? Don't you dare say that word again!"

"I just wanted to know."

"If you want to know something," his sister retorted angrily, "the woodbox is empty."

"Why are you so mad?" The boy looked puzzled. "You don't hardly ever get mad."

Suddenly, Summer was ashamed. She was also confused. Her emotions had run the gamut in the last twenty-four hours. She had been suspicious of the visitors because of Slater's attitude, been reassured because of Ellen's, and was now disillusioned because of Jesse and Travis.

"I'm sorry, John Austin." She hugged him to her. "I'm sorry."

The boy grinned up at her. "It's all right, Summer. I think I know what it means, anyway."

Summer looked horrified. "Get in there and eat your breakfast." She followed him into the house and sat down at the oil-cloth covered table and rested her chin in her hands.

"You won't be lonely out here, will you, Sadie?" Summer was suddenly depressed.

"Lonely? Me? It's grand here!" The smile left her face. "Why did you ask? Don't you like it here?" Her voice held a worried edge.

"Of course I like it. It's my home." Summer considered the worried look on Sadie's face. "And you and Mary are welcome to stay for as long as you like."

Big tears came to the green eyes and Sadie swallowed with difficulty. "I'll be a help to you. I promise."

"You already have been, Sadie. You're a much better cook than I am." Summer pushed back from the table and got to her feet.

Sadie was pleased and showed it. She smoothed her apron with nervous hands. "I like doin' homey things."

She went to the window. Keeping an eye on John Austin was an ingrown habit with Summer. He was squatting in the dirt with a sharp stick in his hand. He looked so lonely sitting there. She frowned and turned to Sadie.

"Mrs. McLean didn't take much notice of John Austin," she said, as if to herself. "Did you think she was pretty?"

Sadie turned her head away when she answered. "Yes, she's pretty all right."

"Mary took a shine to Mr. Thurston." Summer gave the other girl a teasing scrutiny.

Sadie tossed her head. "Nobody's likely to get him away from *her.*" She emphasized the last word.

Summer smiled at her defiance. Sadie was pretty, with her bronze curls and green eyes, but it was her quick wit and spirit that Summer liked.

"Did you like Mr. Thurston?"

"Heap more'n I liked Travis McLean." Sadie's face was turned away, but Summer knew from the sound of her voice her mouth was taut with anger at Travis. This puzzled Summer. Before she could say anything, Sadie was speaking again. "It ain't for me to be sayin' nothin' 'bout the McLeans. That Mrs. McLean can't see me for dirt."

"You didn't get to know her, Sadie. Every time we came near you, you scampered away. She was nice, real nice."

Mary squirmed out of Sadie's arms and made for the door.

"Not without your dress, you!" She dived for the child and carried her back to the bunk. "I'll swear to goodness, I don't know what I'm goin' to do with you. Ain't you got no shame?" To Summer, she said, "I'm thinkin' we should get started on that garden, Summer. It's the right time of the moon. My mama always planted ground roots; taters, turnips and the like, when the moon was gettin' bigger.'' Sadie didn't want to think about the McLeans or their tall, flint-eyed foreman. She had had foolish dreams, in the dark of the night, but this was morning and he was gone. The planting would crowd him out of her mind.

Ellen made her displeasure known to Jesse by her silence. She had the feeling she had been firmly put down in front of Summer, and she didn't like it at all. The humiliation, she reasoned, was hers for letting the scene between her son and Jesse erupt. She had always been a little thrilled by the wild, violent streak in Jesse, especially when it surfaced on her behalf. The cold, ruthless, calculating way he went about disposing of an adversary had, up to now, made her proud of his devotion to her; but when he turned that quick, hard, dangerous strength against Travis, it was another thing.

Silence was Ellen's only safety while she plotted what tactics she would use to deal with Jesse. Up until that last disgusting scene, Summer had been impressed with Travis. He could charm the skin off a snake when he set his mind to it. His desire to taunt Jesse about the dance-hall girl had just carried him away, that's all. And Jesse, damn him, had just about ruined everything!

The northwest road meandered along the dry creek bed before turning toward the foothills. The countryside around them lay utterly still. Beneath the June sun the buggy was like an oven, causing Ellen almost as much distress as her impatience with Jesse. She sat tense and silent in her corner, all too aware of her companion's scowling brow silhouetted in bold profile against the horizon. He had not moved, except to flick the reins, since he took his place beside her and propped one booted foot upon the guard rail.

"I don't understand you, Jesse. Really, I don't. That was a terrible thing you did to Travis. You've humiliated him so he'll never want to see Summer again. And all because of that girl."

He turned to look at her. "You heard what he said. He's lucky I didn't break his neck." The calm voice seemed somehow not to go with the tight lips.

Ellen wondered, at that moment, if she had ever really known this big, silent, relentless man.

"He just got carried away, Jesse. He was funnin', like he does sometimes." She looked up at him and allowed a teasing grin to tilt her lips. "You know, Jesse, you're making me think that maybe you have been slipping off to town, that Travis is right." Her soft laugh was to accent the absurdity of her words. Jesse continued to look at her and she sobered. "I didn't mean that, dear. I know you would never take up with a woman like that."

"A woman like what?" he asked quietly.

"You know what I mean," she said patiently. "That girl is a saloon woman. She is common and coarse. I can't imagine why Summer allows her to stay there. I fully intend to have a talk with her about it. I could hardly believe it when Travis told me who she was. Travis said that. . . ."

"Travis says too much, Ellen."

"You just don't like him, do you, Jesse? You're jealous of him." Ellen's temper was rising. "You never tried to be a friend to him, to show him how to keep the respect of the men. You belittle him, and make all his boyish pranks seem much worse than they are. I sometimes wonder about you, Jesse. How many other beatings have you given him that I don't know about?"

"Several." Jesse stared straight over the horse's back and Ellen gasped at his calm answer.

"He's just a boy! He's no match for you in a fight."

The cool look he gave her caused Ellen to draw another quick breath.

"He's no boy, Ellen. He's a twenty-five-year-old

man, who acts like a spoiled kid a grabbin' any and everything he wants. Keep him away from McLean's Keep, or Slater will kill him. He still thinks he had something to do with Sam's death, and he wouldn't think twice about killin' him if he gets to messin' around the women."

Ellen's face burned with anger. "That's ridiculous, and you know it. Travis may be a little wild, but that's all. Scott was wild as a deer when I married him, and Travis takes after him. Sam was always the steady one, the dull one, just like Slater." Contempt crept into her voice. "Travis will settle down when he has a wife."

"And you have someone in mind."

"Of course. Summer. It was a godsend for her to come back. She comes from good stock, and will make a perfect wife for Travis. And she'll not come into the family empty-handed, either. That strip of land of hers will make the Rocking S one of the largest holdings in Texas."

Jesse's voice was quiet, deep and abrupt. "You can't be foolish enough to think Slater improved on that claim and brought that girl out here to stand aside and let her marry Travis."

"I don't know what he can do about it."

"He can marry her himself, Ellen. So you better not get your heart set on the match."

"That's the one thing I am sure of, Jesse. Slater will never marry Summer." Ellen glanced at him, a strange, mysterious smile tilting her lips.

"You can't be sure of that."

"I'm sure," she said confidently. "Slater may take up with the dance-hall trollop. Women are scarce, and she may appeal to his rude nature." She let her hand slide down the inside of Jesse's arm. "I know you were merely being chivalrous this morning, dear, but it wasn't necessary. A woman like that is used to that sort of thing." She smiled with disarming gentleness. "I'm sorry for my jealous little comments. It's . . . it's just that I depend on you so. I don't know what I'd do without you, Jesse."

Ellen could not remember a time when Jesse had not responded to her coaxing. He sat as if made of stone. There was not even a flicker of an eyelid to betray what he was feeling at the moment. It was impossible to tell if he had even heard her words, or if he was feeling anger, surprise or resignation.

It wasn't any of these things Jesse was feeling. It was something else altogether. Something he hadn't felt for a long time. An emptiness flowed through him. Memory stirred, painfully, uncertainly, as the buggy traversed the lower slopes of the hill country. His childhood hovered, half-imagined, half-remembered. It was way back there, that childhood, but still familiar enough to imbue his stern face with a terrible loneliness. The inevitable waiting! The waiting was what he remembered the most. Waiting in that unloving, uncaring place.

It had taken a long time. And then Ellen had come, so pretty, so gentle and caring. His features relaxed for a moment, then tightened. The interval between the home and coming out here with Ellen had not been easy. The hardest, dirtiest jobs for scraps of food were freshest in his mind. "Kid do this . . . hurry up, kid . . . you goddam kid . . ." One day, he was no longer a kid, and the orders stopped.

He looked down at Ellen, and his steely-gray eyes lost the haunted look and stared with affection into hers. She began to smile, her flushed face and quivering mouth betraying only too well that she was aware she had been excluded from his thoughts, but that now his attention was back with her once again.

"I don't know what I'd do without you, Jesse," she said again, and tears misted her eyes.

He covered her hand and squeezed it.

Far ahead of the buggy, two horsemen rode out of

the gully. Travis was in the lead, Tom Treloar close behind. Tom was a thick-set man, with a thick bush of gray hair on his face as well as his head. It was he who had stepped on Travis's arm and saved his life. He had no doubt at all that Jesse would have killed him had he drawn his gun. Jesse's reaction would have been as natural as breathing. To Tom's way of thinking, it was going to come sooner or later, anyway, as Jesse had about got his craw full of this brainless excuse for a man.

They were only a few miles from the Rocking S. The shadows stretched from the hills. Travis reined up and stared down at the buggy coming along the track, and mopped sweat from his face. His shirt was sticky and uncomfortable, and the throbbing of his split lips was a constant reminder of the humiliation he had suffered that morning. He edged his mount closer to Tom's and spoke for the first time.

"Don't interfere in my fight again, Tom, if you want to live."

The drover's face showed no emotion as Travis voiced his threat.

"He'd a killed ya slicker than snot, Travis. Ya was in no position to fight."

Irritation mounted in Travis, stifling his own doubt. "He's not so all-fired fast!"

"Fast enough," Tom said quietly, "with you on the ground."

Travis was shrewd enough to know Tom was right. He had hated Jesse since the day his mother had brought him to the ranch, an eighteen-year-old who was almost as much of a man then as he was now. At first, he hadn't understood the relationship between his mother and the man who gradually took over the running of the ranch, but he was almost certain now. Well, if Mama needed a stud, it made no difference to him. Mama could open her legs for anyone she wanted to. It was other things that bothered him. Such as

Mama having joint control of the ranch until he turned twenty-six. His face darkened with anger, his lips twisted in a sneer of contempt. It wouldn't be long now, and he would settle with Jesse. He stewed in self-satisfaction. They would all find out, soon enough, who was the best man. Irritation mounted within him. The frustrating truth rang in his head and pounded in the sour pit of his stomach, feeding his hatred.

"No!" he muttered fiercely.

The sun was still above the hilltops when the buggy turned up the lane toward the house. Rising out of the prairie, the two-story, white-frame house was a splendid example of eighteenth-century architecture. Built square and high off the ground to catch the breeze, it had wide, railed verandas, with roofs supported by graceful columns decorated with elaborately-carved cornices. Long windows opened up onto the verandas on both the lower and upper floors. Stained-glass panes adorned the upper part of the windows as well as the doors. A drive curved through carefully-tended grounds to reach the broad steps leading to the veranda. The elegant house looked as if it belonged on a shaded street in exclusive New Orleans rather than on the Texas prairie.

Realizing he was home, the horse pulling the buggy stepped briskly up the circled drive and stopped beside the gate. Jesse handed Ellen down from the buggy as a black man in a white shirt and loose black trousers came out onto the porch and down the steps to take Ellen's boxes from the boot.

"Hello, Jacob."

"It's good you is back, Miz Ellen." The dark face beamed as he leaped to hold open the door. "Y'all got the army men a camped back yonder. Ah 'spects da cap'n done come ter see Mastah Jesse."

"Company? You said company, Jacob?"

"Yes'm. Cap'n Slane."

"Go down and invite the captain to dinner, Jacob." Her face wreathed in smiles, Ellen started up the stairs, then stopped. "Jacob. . . ."

"Pears ta me ah can smell me a big ol' turkey a roastin', 'n if'n ah smell real good, dem pecan pies is coolin' by da door." Jacob rolled his eyes and chuckled.

Ellen laughed with velvety softness and watched him bask beneath her fond gaze.

"I should have known. You're just a wonder, Jacob, that's what you are, a wonder!" Halfway up the stairs she turned again, "Jacob. . . ."

"De hot watta is on de way, Miz Ellen."

It was good to be home. Jesse had come to like the quiet elegance of the house, the carefully-prepared meals served on the white cloth, but he knew it was temporary. He had no doubt his future here was over the moment Travis took over. In that one thing, he had been a failure. It was Ellen's greatest wish that he make a man of Travis, and he had failed. Nothing he could do was going to change Travis in the least. He was hell-bent for destruction and he, Jesse, was determined not to go along with him.

Ellen was beautiful that evening in her plum-colored muslin gown with a high neckband and long, fitted sleeves. The narrow bodice was pert and pleasing on her slender figure. Jesse watched her charm the captain. The gentle, smooth tone of her voice and the radiance of her smile affected the captain so much that he was scarcely aware of what he was being served.

Captain Kenneth Slane was ten years out of West Point. He was one of the officers sent by the army in 1848 to establish a cordon of eight frontier forts about sixty miles apart, across Texas from the Rio Grande northwest to the upper Trinity River, to protect the settlements to the east from Indian raids from the west. The town of Hamilton spread around Fort Croghan, one of the forts in this cordon. The fort guarded the northwestern approach to Austin, the state capital. Captain Slane was in charge of Company A, Second Dragoons, stationed at the fort.

Light conversation halted as the last course was served. The dessert was pecan pie topped with a generous helping of cream flavored with sherry sauce. Ellen beamed approvingly at Jacob, who hovered in the doorway until his mistress signaled. When the talk resumed after coffee, she could no longer resist broaching the subject that challenged her curiosity.

"What brings you out from the fort, captain? Whatever it is, we are indeed grateful for your company."

"Thank you, ma'am. My reason for being with the troops is such an unpleasant thing to discuss in a lady's presence, but the truth is, I am making a tour. The policing of the territory has been shifted to the army now that the Texas Rangers have been moved out. In the last few months, almost one hundred settlers have been killed and scalped between here and Fredericksburg. My outriders and scouts are watching various scattered bands of Apaches in the hills. I mean to come to grips with them and determine their strength."

"Slater McLean had a run-in with mountain Apaches a few days ago." Jesse's eyes searched those of the captain. He was curious, and suddenly aware there was more to the expedition than the captain's answer implied. "They were a rag-tailed outfit, and Slater had to kill half a dozen of them. He said they were a wild bunch, without leadership."

"Oh, my!" Ellen looked from Travis to Jesse, her eyes large and questioning. "Why didn't you tell me? I never gave a thought to Indians today."

"You wasn't supposed to," Jesse said softly. "Tom and Travis were scouting ahead, and we had the drovers."

"Did you see any sign of Indians, Travis?" Ellen was attempting to draw her silent, sullen son into the conversation.

"Wasn't looking for any." There was an edge of sarcasm in his tone. "I doubt it would take a company of cavalry to flush out a few half-starved Indians."

Captain Slane flushed a little. "My platoon could hardly be considered a company." His voice was dry, but when he turned to his hostess his face was clear of anything but polite admiration.

Nothing like a bright smile to cover an awkward moment—Ellen turned the full force of her attention on the captain. She glided to her feet.

"Perhaps you gentlemen would rather retire to the parlor for cigars and brandy," she suggested cordially.

She allowed the captain to escort her across the hall. They paused briefly to watch Travis stride purposefully out the front door, without a word or backward glance.

"You must excuse my son, captain. He's not in the best of moods these days." There was a whiteness around her tense lips that did not go unnoticed by the captain.

On previous visits, Kenneth Slane had been able to converse with Travis, still, he didn't consider him to be much but lazy and irresponsible. This beautiful, gracious woman had been short-changed where her son was concerned, though blessed in having a man like Jesse for a foreman. He wondered if the rumor that they were lovers was true. Jesse was fond of her, it was certain, and he couldn't blame him. No, sir, Ellen McLean was a beautiful woman, and if he was any judge, a passionate one.

It was much later when the captain got a chance to speak with Jesse alone. They walked down the trail to where the platoon was bivouacked.

"A week ago, an army caravan was ambushed, twelve men were killed. It just so happened it wasn't the pay wagon or one carrying weapons. The wagons were ransacked and clothing and food taken."

Instinctively, Jesse knew this wasn't all the captain had to say, so he waited.

"It was meant to look like an Indian raid. One dead Apache was left behind and several dead horses. I've never known of Apaches leaving their dead, and I know for certain they don't kill horses unless there's no other way. The four horses were deliberately shot in the head."

"Don't appear to me it *was* Apaches."

"My scouts swear it wasn't, but I'm keeping it under my hat for the time being."

"According to Slater, the bunch he ran into couldn't have whipped their way out of a tow-sack. He picked off most of them himself. Said they were disorganized and hopped up on loco-weed or whiskey. He wouldn't a killed a one of them if he could have helped it." Jesse stopped and lit a smoke. "Good man, Slater, he'll meet you half way to be decent. But he don't take no shit."

"I've heard that about him. I'll be going his way in a few weeks. I'd appreciate your company; that is, if Mrs. McLean can spare you."

"I'd like that. Thanks for asking me. There's more here than meets the eye."

They stopped on the trail, the familiar sounds of the encampment reaching them: clinking of pans, low masculine voices, blowing and stamping of tethered horses.

"I hear a mighty good-looking woman came in on the stage and went out to McLean's Keep. Slater import himself a bride?"

"Well," Jesse answered carefully, "I don't know if it'll come to that. The girl and her brother own the claim across the creek from Slater. It seems her mother filed on it, and Sam and Slater improved on it for her. It's the strip that runs between McLean's Keep and the Rockin' S."

"Interesting," Captain Slane said slowly. "I'm anxious to meet the lady." He started to say more, but stopped. His sharp eyes were peering into the darkness behind Jesse. "We'll be pulling out early. I'll say goodbye, Jesse. It was an enjoyable evening."

"Goodnight, captain. Send word when you're ready to patrol south."

Jesse turned up the trail. The shine from a silver belt-buckle caught his eye. Travis, obviously listening. Jesse pinched out his cigarette and, flipping it toward the glint in the darkness, went back toward the house.

Nothing can hang on for long when its time is past, Jesse mused, as he lifted the whiskey bottle and poured himself a drink. His time here was coming to a close. It was time for him to consider what was best for him. And for Ellen. This was her home. She would never leave it. The thought of parting with Ellen was not as disturbing as it would have been a few years—or even a few months—ago. There had been a time when he would have killed Travis; waylaid him and killed him in cold blood, if necessary, in order to stay with Ellen. Now, the simple truth was he had become dissatisfied with his life.

Mentally, he saw the girl again: big green eyes, unruly bronze curls, her lips, face and neck marked by Travis's attack. Then, the frightened eyes that turned on him when he stepped from the shadows to give her a push in the swing, the color draining from her cheeks on hearing Travis's insults. All day, he had been seeing that face.

He finished his drink and started up the stairs, his mind lingering on the woman and her child out at McLean's Keep. She would be safe there. As safe from Travis as she would be anywhere.

He was still thinking about her when he opened the door to his room. He stood still for a moment, trying to bring his thoughts back to the present. In the faint glow of the oil-lamp burning on his bureau, he saw Ellen, lying relaxed and smiling, on his bed. He quietly closed the door.

When he turned, she was beside him, dressed in a simple, flowing pink robe, her blonde hair parted in the center, falling freely to her waist, her half-shut eyes containing the unmistakable look of longing.

Jesse looked down at her critically, as if assessing her for the first time. For a moment, he felt awkward. He couldn't greet her as he had in the past when she had surprised him in his room. The image of the girl at McLean's Keep created a formidable barrier between them.

"Jesse, darling," she said in a deeper, softer voice than the one she usually used, "I've missed you."

"You knew where to find me," were the only words he could find.

"It wasn't convenient, darling. I'll deny myself before I'll be indiscreet."

She kissed him lightly with her hot, moist, eager mouth, and pressed her softness against him, pressing the area of his sex firmly with a circular motion of her hips. Then her eyes narrowed.

"I love how you touch me, Jesse. . . ." Her voice was a whispering monotone. "You make me come alive, Jesse . . . be good to me, darling. Love me . . . a little."

For an instant, Jesse hesitated. She kissed him again. The scent of her filled his nostrils. In seconds, the warmth of her body fused into his and he felt a surging excitement, a tingling warmth. He lifted her hair and buried his face in her neck. He could feel her heat, the warmth of her breath on his ears and neck. His mouth covered hers and he kissed her like a hungry child. His hands moved hesitatingly; then as he could feel her assent, he gripped her hard.

When she struggled a little, he loosened his arms and stood away from her obediently. He made no move to resist her when she began to remove his coat, then his shirt and trousers. It was a ritual between them. When he stood nude before her, she slid her hands down over his chest, feeling the smoothness of his ribs, the powerful muscles in his shoulders and back. Her experienced hands moved quickly, unnerving his body with their probing and caressing, seeking the response she desired. She loved the powerful feeling of knowing that her touch brought vulnerable animal sounds from him, and he stood quivering when she stroked certain sensitive areas. It was only when his powerful body had taken as much as it would endure and his clenched fists and twisted face told her his control was about to break that she allowed him to touch her.

He jerked the robe from her body and snatched her up in his arms. In two quick strides, he reached the bed and literally threw her onto it. His mind was a complete blank. Only his own release and the pleasing of Ellen was important to him now.

Chapter Seven

Summer was toting a bucket of water up from the creek to water the garden when she heard the sound of a horse splashing. Looking over her shoulder she saw Slater, seated on a big black horse, leading a small sorrel. Almost a week had passed since she had gone to the ranch house and he had turned his back on her.

Instantly, she was aware of the sweat-soaked dress clinging to her bosom and the flying hair escaping down her neck. She cursed the color that came up to flood her face.

The horse came up alongside of her. The saddle creaked as Slater reached down and took the bucket from her hand.

"John." His voice was not loud, but it had authority. John Austin, lying on his stomach in the dirt, jumped to his feet.

"Hello, Slater."

"Any man worth his salt don't laze around while his women work." He handed him the bucket.

"Jack said it was dawdling."

"Whatever it is, we don't do it."

Summer wanted to say something in the boy's defense. She wanted Slater to know that John Austin was the way he was because she had not had time to stop and teach him practical things. All the time she could spare had been used to satisfy the boy's craving for schooling. Slater's eyes shifted to her and she was certain, from the way he looked at her, that he knew what she was thinking, feeling.

"He helps when I ask him." Her chin went up. "Sometimes, his mind is on other things."

"You do too much for him," Slater said quietly. "He's lazy."

"He is not!" she protested. "He just thinks about . . . things."

He ignored her and turned to the boy. "Have you ever had a horse?" John Austin shook his head. "You've got one now." He handed the boy the reins of the small sorrel. "He's yours for as long as you take care of him. You are to take care of him, understand? I don't mean your sister or Pud. *You.*"

Summer's heart lurched. "Oh, I don't think . . . I mean, he doesn't know about . . . he's never. . . ."

Slater was faintly amused. "It's time he was put in the traces."

"You misunderstand me. I don't want him to get hurt."

"He'll survive a few knocks. Get on the horse, son."

When Summer made a move to assist her brother, Slater edged his horse in between her and the sorrel. She looked up to protest. The horse had turned and the scarred side of Slater's face was turned to her. She caught her breath sharply, involuntarily wincing at the pain he must have suffered. He misunderstood her reaction and his mouth tightened and his nostrils flared. A strange gleam came into his eyes.

"Ugly, isn't it?" Her innocent amazement seemed to

anger him, and the livid expression in his eyes made her take a step backwards. "Not handsome like Travis McLean." His drawl was taunting. "Never judge a man by his looks. Judge him by his actions."

"What makes you think I'm judging you?"

"The way you're looking at me. Like you've suddenly seen the devil himself."

"I was only thinking of how you must have suffered."

He shook his head slowly from side to side, as if he didn't believe her. His hard stare never eased from her face.

"It was nothing compared to seeing my pa shot down by cowards with covered faces, and knowing who was responsible and not being able to do anything about it!"

From under straight dark brows she studied him curiously. His scarred cheek, his hard dark eyes, the derisive slant of his well-shaped, firm mouth, the pugnacious jut of his jaw. All gave the impression of toughness. He looked as if he lived and worked for only one thing—revenge. Slowly, her glance drifted down to the gunbelt strapped firmly about his hips and the revolver resting against his thigh. She guessed the gun had been a part of him for so long he would feel naked without it.

He continued to watch her, his thick lashes almost hiding the blue-black eyes. She had the impression that all his muscles were coiled and ready to spring into action, as if she were an Indian. A tingling went down her spine, and was followed suddenly by overwhelming weariness. Almost without realizing it, she rubbed a hand across her brow in a gesture of near-exhaustion.

When he spoke, his voice was soft as velvet. "I'll snake water up in a ditch if you insist on having the garden. You don't need it, you know. There's plenty at the Keep for all of us."

"No. You've done enough. We don't expect you to feed us, too."

From under the brim of his tilted, broad-brimmed

hat, his eyes glared at her, wicked, livid light flickering in them.

"You heard me," he retorted curtly. "There's no need for you to exhaust yourself carrying water to this garden. Sam McLean planned for this ranch to be part of the Keep. We plant corn, wheat, and grow vegetables. We raise chickens, keep bees, and run cattle. We also have an orchard. This place is part of us." Bitterness edged his voice. "Or have you already decided to join your land to Travis McLean's?"

"No!" Her cry of protest came straight from her heart. She was on the verge of tears, suddenly, because she couldn't bear the thought of him being so angry and suspicious of her. She realized how distant she had grown from the boy she had once adored. "I don't know you," she managed to say, "and I don't know them. I only wanted a place to bring John Austin." Her mouth trembled and she blinked rapidly to keep the tears from disgracing her. "I won't be in the middle of your feud with Travis and Ellen. And . . . another thing . . . I don't want this land. My brother and I are not entitled to it. You and your father made the improvements on it. All I ask of you is a place for John Austin until he is old enough to make his own way."

She stood in troubled silence while Slater looked at her. He couldn't help but wonder at the grit of this woman. He hadn't counted on her disrupting his whole life, as she had done since the first day he saw her getting off the stage at Hamilton. She stood stiff and proud and he saw her fine-boned profile set with the effort not to betray her tears.

"No, you don't know me at all, Summer. But you're going to." He touched the brim of his hat obligingly. "I'll be back." He looked over his shoulder and gave a short whistle. The sorrel pricked up its ears and moved slowly in behind the big black. Slater turned his horse toward the creek and the sorrel followed. John Austin, feet flapping against the mare's sides and holding tightly to the pommel, gave Summer a huge smile as he passed her.

She stood wiping the tears from her cheeks with her fingers, wondering vaguely why she wept, why he affected her emotions in a way that she couldn't control. She was losing her hold on the person she had always tried to be: composed, competent, well-mannered.

Sadie walked over to her quietly. "Let's rest a while."

"Suits me."

The strong sunlight had caused the freckles to pop out in surprising numbers on Sadie's pert nose, and her bronze hair, damp with sweat, was kinking into tight curls. She looked searchingly at Summer, trying to decide if the dampness on her cheeks was caused by tears or sweat.

"Who was that man?" she asked, after they had refreshed themselves with a cool drink.

"Slater McLean."

"I remember seeing him in town. He came to the dance hall and watched. You'd not forget a face like that. Not 'cause it's cut up some, but 'cause he didn't smile a'tall. I never saw him till the last couple nights I was there." Sadie's green eyes watched Summer through red-gold lashes. In all her young life, Sadie had known little love, and much loneliness, longing and hardship. There had been years of impossible struggle. And from that struggle, she had learned to judge men. "I'd say he's a man who wastes no time once he gets his mind set. I've seen his kind afore. He don't go swaggerin' around huntin' trouble, 'cause he's had it a plenty. He's been up the creek and over the mountain, as my pa used to say, and takes to fightin' and standin' up for hisself like you and me take to makin' a batch of cornbread. It's everyday work to him. Now, he's the kind of man I'd tie to . . . if'n I ever got the chance!"

Summer avoided her eyes. "I knew him when I was a

little girl," she said. After that, it was easy to talk to Sadie, to tell her about her mother, Sam McLean and Slater. She didn't say anything about Ellen or Travis or Slater's hatred. "My mother was so sure Sam McLean would take care of us that she made me promise to come here. Slater is just carrying out his father's wishes and I'm grateful, but . . . I don't like feeling so . . . obligated!"

"Don't ya like him?" Sadie asked shyly. Then, before Summer could answer, she blurted out, "He's ten times the man that varmit of a Travis is, I tell you! I ain't never even talked to the man, but I can tell that by lookin'."

Summer had to laugh at Sadie's vehemence. Then she said seriously, "We must do everything we can for ourselves before we ask for help, Sadie. And if there is anything that we can do for them. . . ." She left the words hanging and drew her brows together in thought.

Sadie's green eyes twinkled. "I know what we can do! Cowhands like nothin' better than doughnuts. Well, I'm here to tell ya that I'm the best doughnut-maker in all of Texas! We'll make up a dishpan full, that's what we'll do. Those cowhands will wonder how they ever lived without us!" She got up. "I'll do it right now, Summer. That is, after I see what that Mary is up to. She's mad 'cause she didn't get to go with John Austin—had herself a regular spell—thinks he's the grandest thing ever hatched."

"I must have felt that way about Slater when I was young." The words were an echo of what was in her mind. Wanting to change the subject, she asked, "Why do you dislike Travis, Sadie? Was he unkind to you at the dance hall?"

"Unkind!" The word exploded from Sadie. "That polecat passed right over 'unkind' and went over to downright horrible. Take my word for it, Summer, that man ain't worth doodle-de-squat!" She disappeared around the corner of the house. "Mary!" Summer heard her. "Don't eat that worm! You ain't no bird!"

In the quiet of her departure, Summer sat thoughtfully. A big June bug buzzed against the glass window pane. Behind the house, she could hear Sadie scolding. Down by the creek, a mockingbird sang. Then she heard the sound of a male voice and Slater and John Austin rode into the yard. Summer watched the man on the big horse and the boy on the sorrel. Her little brother was slipping away from her.

Slater dismounted and glanced at the boy. The kid had grit and staying power; he had taken him over a rough trail and the tyke had hung on like he was glued.

"Get off the horse, John, and come 'round and talk to her. She'll learn you're not afraid. That's the first thing she needs to know about you. After that, she'll know who's boss and will be your best friend, could save your life someday. You take care of her and she'll take care of you." He talked evenly and confidently, showed the boy how to strip off the saddle and bridle, stood aside while John Austin struggled, and then helped him turn the mare into the corral.

"You're not going, are you, Slater? Can I come with you? Can I look at your books?"

"I'll bring some over for you after you finish your chores." They walked to the woodpile. "Stack this wood in a neat pile, John. And gather the chips in that tow-sack and leave them outside the back door for the women to use to start the fire." Slater picked up the axe that was lying on the ground and sunk the blade in a log. "Never leave the axe on the ground when you're through with it. Always sink the blade into the stump and it will stay free of rust. Another day, I'll teach you to use it. Now I'll show you how to stack the wood so if we get a downpour it won't all get water-soaked."

As long as Slater worked, John Austin worked. When Slater stopped to roll a smoke, John Austin stopped until Slater motioned him to continue.

An hour later, the two of them walked into the kitchen. Slater hung his hat on a peg and stepped outside to the wash-bench. John Austin, his face covered with sweat, bark and wood-dust, headed for the table and snatched a cake from the pile of freshly sugar-dusted doughnuts.

Slater appeared in the doorway. "Wash first, John."

To Summer's annoyance, her brother sat down at the table and stuffed his mouth with the warm cake. Before she could say anything, Slater spoke again.

"Up, John!" It was as unexpected as the crack of a whip.

The boy looked at his sister and wiped his hands on his shirt. Summer's face flooded with embarrassment.

"John Austin!" she hissed. At that moment, she could have slapped him.

"Did you hear me, John?" Slater was behind him. He glanced at Summer. Her face was flushed, but her chin was up and her eyes wide.

"He don't usually. . . ." she began.

John Austin glanced unconcernedly at Slater. Summer would take care of it. She always did. He reached for another cake. A hard brown hand engulfed his, and he was lifted from the chair.

"It's time you had a lesson in obedience and manners, boy." He headed for the door. Summer's heart leaped into her throat when her brother looked back at her with pleading eyes. "Get out to the woodpile and finish stacking the wood. Then, wash your hands and apologize to your sister and Mrs. Bratcher. Do you understand?"

There was a long silence when Slater turned from the door. Summer stood, dusting the hot doughnuts with sugar, not trusting herself to words because they would have been indignant ones. They would have been in defense of herself, and only partly because of John Austin.

"Well?" A flicker of anger was in his eyes. "You allow him to get away with such behavior? Run rough-shod over you? Haven't you taught him any manners?"

Manners? Obedience? How could this man know what it was like to raise a fatherless boy? A daydreamer of a little boy, who had been hers to care for and to worry about while caring for a sick mother. Summer's face, in the soft light of the kitchen, was stolid, her eyes like empty stars. She stood beside the table and smoothed out the cloth with a few quick, graceful, and totally unnecessary movements. There was not a single word to be said, because he would never understand. He would have had to have gone through the ordeal himself to have understood.

It was Sadie who broke the silence, rescuing Summer and not Slater. She poured a mug of coffee and sat it on the table.

"I'm the one who is forgetful of my manners," Summer said tightly. "This is my friend, Mrs. Bratcher."

The rapid thrust of his gaze moved over Sadie, interest in his eyes.

"Slater McLean, Mrs. Bratcher."

"Do you take sweetnin', Mr. McLean?" She pushed the cup toward him.

"No, but I have a fondness for doughnuts." He smiled his one-sided smile.

Sadie seemed to be perfectly at ease. Her face lit up and she grinned at him.

"I ain't never seen a cowhand that wouldn't trade his pocket knife for a pan of doughnuts. 'Pears you ain't no different than the rest, Mr. McLean."

"I get a craving sometimes for something other than refried beans and tortillas."

Sadie giggled and Slater laughed back at her. Summer swallowed with difficulty. It seemed to her she was the only person in the whole world whose stomach was tied up in knots. Sadie's catlike green eyes absorbed the lines of distress on Summer's face.

"Take yore coffee to the veranda, Mr. McLean. It's powerful hot in here. Here's a cup for Summer, too. I'll bring you all a hot cake from the next batch." She tossed her head and grinned at him. "I'm gonna need this here table for my doughnut-makin'."

Slater's glance at Sadie held a quality of conspiracy that caused Summer's heart to beat painfully.

"I can see that we would be in your way." He picked up the two mugs. Summer followed him on wooden legs.

She sank down on the bench and accepted the mug Slater held out to her. She felt tired and strangely bewildered. Her face was quite still, depleted of all her strength. Under Slater's sharp gaze, she was still, small, young, alone.

"You don't like the way I handle your brother?" There was a tiny hint of a taunt in his voice. He sounded as if he wanted to hurt her, and not because of the way she had failed with John Austin. She was convinced it was something personal about her that angered him.

She bit her lower lip, looked at the expanse of blue sky and didn't answer him.

"Well?" The expression of anger was still on his face; the muscles clamped above the jawline.

She had to meet his eyes, because to have avoided them would have been the last indignity.

"It isn't that." She closed her eyes to escape the mesmerism in his. "You can't know how it was."

"I think I know." His voice was softer. "We'll share it now."

Her eyes flew open.

He turned away, reaching into his pocket for his tobacco. In that silence, the match flared; he lit his smoke and blew out the flame. Then, he picked up her hand, turned it palm upward and looked at it. It was a small hand, still very young, but it had the callouses of hard work on it. Her eyes came up to his. They were sad, sober eyes, but deep down in them Slater could see a yearning beginning to dawn.

"This is what you brought your brother here for, isn't it, Summer? You wanted my pa to help you guide him, discipline him. He's a very clever and unusual child . . . and strong-willed. You do too much for him, protect him to the point of making him weak. I'll not allow you to do it any longer." He sat looking at her. They were so near they touched.

"But he's so young. . . ."

"Not so young that he doesn't know how to manage you. He has that age-old wisdom and knowledge of how to work a woman, far beyond his years. He's not an ordinary boy, and he'll need a heavy hand for a while."

"You think I tied him to my apron strings." Summer looked at the smooth side of his face, the scarred side turned away from her. He opened and shut the fingers of the hand she allowed to lie in his.

"It was necessary. Without those apron strings, you couldn't have gotten him here. But there comes a time to cut him loose."

"Now is the time. Is that what you're saying?"

"Now is the time." He gripped her hand tightly. "It's time someone took care of you, too. I'm going to take care of you both. You belong to me now."

Slater's eyes were suddenly like dark glowing coals. They met Summer's. Hers were startled. He had said, "belong to me." And she could see he meant it. Suddenly, something had changed, forever. They both knew it.

Summer sat frozen, yet waiting. Very slowly, he raised the cigarette to his mouth. Smoke floated away like a dream, lost and gone. He stared down at her.

"What we have, we share." His eyes were inscrutable.

This wasn't a game, or a fantasy. He meant what he said. Her heart pounded and she drew the tip of her tongue across dry lips. Under his slanting black brows, his eyes were clear and searching.

The silence was long, breathless and deafening.

Slater flicked the cigarette into the yard and took the mug from her hand. Then his arm went around her and she was so firmly against him that she could feel the hard bones and muscles of his body thrusting through her thin cotton dress. The intimacy of that contact sent waves of surprise and pleasure through her. Strange, tempestuous feelings threatened to swamp her, and she struggled desperately to keep her head.

The smooth side of his face pressed tightly against her cheek, and the feel of his mouth against her ear made her panic. Writhing in the trap he made of his arms, she uttered a faint cry of protest.

"Sh, sh . . . hh. Sh, sh. . . ." His voice was soothing. His lips touched the side of her neck and his hand moved up and down her back. She was panting a little, the wild beat of her heart against his. "Do I frighten you?" His lips were against her cheek.

"No." It was scarcely more than a whisper. Her brain commanded her to fight free of him, but her senses ignored the order. Her eyes closed and all conscious thought was wiped away by new and pleasant sensations.

Long ripples of tranquility flowed through her as she lost the desire to struggle. Her body became pliable and molded itself tenderly against his as a new need grew within her, a sort of ache for something—she wasn't quite sure what—something like a joy beyond anything she had ever known, and which she might be able to reach if she stayed close to him.

Still holding her with one arm, he raised her face to him. She opened her eyes.

"Is there anything you want to say?" His voice was thick, but she didn't notice. She was too aware of the hard warmth of his body and the faint smell of tobacco on his breath to take notice of anything else.

"I . . . don't know. I . . . have to think."

"I'm staking my claim," he said tensely.

The bold possessiveness of his words, the sheer arrogance of them, sent a thrill of excitement through her even while her intelligence rejected it. Once again, she made an effort to assert absolute control over her mind, only to find that her senses were being led into open rebellion by the touch of his fingers as they wandered down her chin and over the hollow of her throat. Gently, the tips stroked the soft skin.

"I won't rush you," he murmured. "We'll take time to get to know each other." He looked searchingly into her eyes, then his arms fell away abruptly and he stood up. "From here on, I'll handle your brother. He's not going to grow up to be a spoiled bastard like Travis!" He walked away with sure, quick steps. At the end of the veranda, he paused and threw her a wary glance over his shoulder before disappearing around the corner of the house.

Summer sat for a moment, then went to the end of the porch to peek out. Slater was talking earnestly to John Austin. Perhaps he intended to take care of them like a younger brother and sister. He hadn't mentioned marriage. Her confused mind groped for an answer. Confusion darkened her eyes, and her heart began to pound again. It hadn't been a sisterly embrace when he held her. *You belong to me now* . . . the words refused to leave her mind. She went back to the bench and sat down, her pulses beating feverishly, wondering what would happen the next time she saw him.

Chapter Eight

In the days that followed, Summer learned much about Slater and McLean's Keep. What impressed her the most was the fact he was a person who didn't give away his feelings easily. He was the undisputed boss of the significant number of people that lived and worked on the ranch; his was a position of great responsibility. He had to know how to do everything he expected his men to do, and do it better. They respected him and depended on his judgment. Summer had never met a man of his type before. She hadn't, for that matter, met many men of any type—a lack she was terribly aware of, in a frightened way.

John Austin recognized Slater's authority and bowed to it. When he was harsh with the boy it shook Summer, for she had brought her brother up with dedicated tenderness and care for his young feelings. However, Slater was just, and while he reprimanded John Austin, he also made every effort to give the boy his heart's desire—books from the ranch house.

One evening, more than a week after he had taken John Austin in hand, he returned at dusk; bathed, shaved, his dark hair wet and slicked back from the small white strip near his hairline where the suntan stopped, his strong brown throat protruding from a freshly-washed, open-necked shirt. He had come to "walk out" with Summer. He made his intentions clear the first evening.

"Evening, Summer, Sadie." He lowered himself down onto the bench and leaned back against the rough logs of the house.

While Summer was struggling to bring some semblance of order to her thoughts, Mary slipped off Sadie's lap and went straight to Slater. She stood between his knees and looked curiously into his face. Summer held her breath for fear the child would mention the scar on his face.

In the gathering darkness it was hard to see Slater's expression, but his voice was gentle, and opened up whole avenues of conjecture as to his real nature.

"Isn't it about your bedtime?" He lifted the child and set her on his lap, one large hand cupping her bare feet. "You could get into a cockleburr out here in the dark."

On hearing Slater's voice, John Austin came out the door.

"Slater!"

"Hello, John." Slater turned his attention back to the little girl. She cuddled up against him and he chuckled softly, a sound that caused an inexplicable emotion to rise in Summer. "You're a little scalliwag, that's what you are!" He hugged her tighter in his arms.

While Summer and Sadie watched, fascinated, Mary's small hand came out and reached for his face. Summer sucked in a long breath as Mary's little fingers moved up and down over his scarred cheek. Slater stayed very still, his eyes looking down on the child's face. It seemed like an hour before she rested her curly head against him, wrapped her arm about his neck, and closed her eyes.

"Slater. . . ." John Austin said impatiently.

"In a minute, John."

In the silence that followed, Summer wondered exactly what his visit meant. She thought of his telling her he was staking his claim, and it brought an unexpected flush to her cheeks. If only she didn't feel this terrible constriction in her heart when he was near!

Slater got to his feet and held the child out to Sadie. "She's sound asleep."

"Slater. . . ." John Austin hovered beside the door.

Slater waited until Sadie went inside the house before he spoke. "What is it, John?"

"You promised to teach me to play chess."

"And I will, but not tonight. It's time you were in bed."

"But—"

"It's time you were in bed," he said again. "The evening hour is for me and your sister. It's going to be our private time together. You may join us when you're invited, and only when you're invited."

Summer stirred and Slater put out his hand and caught her elbow, commanding silence.

"Say goodnight to your sister, John," he continued. "Be careful not to disturb Sadie and Mary. Goodnight."

"Dear. . . ." Summer started forward.

Slater, holding her elbow, held her back.

"But Summer always comes with me and. . . ."

"No. You put yourself to bed, tonight and from now on."

"Please, John Austin. Do as he says."

"Goodnight, John," Slater said again. There was no mistaking the foreboding in his voice. John Austin retreated a few steps.

"Goodnight," he said with a catch in his voice; then, anxiously, "you'll be back tomorrow?"

"Right after sun-up." Slater's voice was softer, friendlier.

With his hand on her elbow, he turned Summer and guided her firmly away from the house, down the path toward the creek.

"How could you?" she said in a hoarse whisper.

"I could and I did. It was very easy. I intend to manage him my way, Summer. Its best I begin in the way I intend to go on."

"But . . . you're so abrupt . . . unfeeling." She had a sob in her voice. "He's not used to that."

"He'll get used to it."

She walked beside him in silence. There seemed to be nothing more she could say. They crossed the yard and stopped under the cottonwood where the sack swing hung. Absently, she gave it a push.

"It can't be the same swing," she said, half to herself.

Slater moved away from her and leaned against the tree.

The cottonwood leaves were whispering and the stream seemed unusually loud in the quiet night. With no other noise, the smallest sounds were obvious. Summer tried to see Slater's face in the deepening shadows, but the outlines were gone, and she could only see that he was standing there.

Abruptly, he struck a match and held the flame unusually long to the end of the cigarette he held between his lips. The light flickered on his scarred cheek and outlined it briefly before he blew out the flame.

"This is a hard, lonely land, Summer. I'm a hard, lonely, impatient man, made more so by the murder of my pa and my own . . . injuries. I'm asking you, now, before this thing between us goes any farther, if this thing on my face repulses you, if I repulse you."

She had expected him to say almost anything but this. Shocked, she stared at his shadow, at the small glow of his cigarette. Finally, she found her voice.

"I've said that I didn't know you, Slater. Well, you don't know me, either, or you wouldn't ask me such a question."

"It's an important question and I demand that you answer."

"All right, but I'm disappointed that you think I have no more depth to me than to be put off by a scar." She stopped and caught a long, ragged breath. "I have a few questions of my own, Slater. Where do we stand with you? It appears to me that you're taking over our lives. I have the right to know what to expect." She finished breathlessly, her heart thumping like a mad thing in her breast.

He drew on the cigarette, then dropped it to the ground and stepped on it.

"I've told you what to expect. You've had several days to think on it. Why are you angry?"

From anxiety and anger, her mood changed when he spoke.

"I'm not angry. Confused, but not angry."

"Then answer my question. I need to know if the woman I plan to spend the rest of my life with finds me unbearable to look at."

Summer stood motionless, staring at his shadow, transfixed, literally shaking inside. She swallowed hard, fighting back the tears. There was a poignant longing in his voice, and for a moment all the years rolled away and she remembered him as he had been . . . the tall, slim boy: *You go on and get all growed up, summertime girl, and I'll come and fetch you home.*

"How can you ask?" The warm night air almost suffocated her as she waited for him to reply. He said nothing, and finally she cried out helplessly, "No! No! You make it seem so important and it's not! It's not!"

"Then come to me," he whispered huskily.

It didn't occur to her not to obey. She stopped in front of him and his arms reached out and drew her close. Her palms pressed against his chest. She looked

up at him, into his eyes. He studied her face, the
sparkle of tears on her lashes, her trembling mouth. He
grabbed her hand and held the palm hard against his
cheek.

"You're sure?" he asked, and she nodded. "You are
absolutely sure?"

"Yes, I'm sure." She was crying to herself inside that
it was so hard for him to believe her.

Slowly, he released her hand, but she held it there
against his face and let her fingertips trace the rough
ridges and plains of his cheek. She looked up at him
searchingly. The pale light slanted onto his scarred
cheek and his thick lashes made fans of darkness in the
hollows beneath his eyes. The moment quivered with
electric tension. As her hand caressed his cheek, her
soft, slim body changed and grew taut with a strange
longing. And out of the longing grew a new feeling, a
wish to take away his hurt, to absorb his pain.

"I don't want you to be hurt . . . ever again," she
said in a low, stricken voice. Her breath was coming
quickly, and she felt his body shivering against hers.

"My summertime girl," he whispered, and leaned his
head forward, kissing her reverently on the forehead.
His voice was merely a breath in the night. The
softly-uttered words and the caress of his hands on her
back sent tingles of excitement racing through her. "I
had to hear you say it," he said against her hair.

Her hands moved up to encircle his neck and she
lifted her face. A sound, half-groan and half-sigh,
exploded from him, and he strained her closer.

He tilted her head so he could look directly into her
eyes. His eyes devoured her. "You want me, too!"
Relief and surprise made his voice husky and transformed his anxious face.

They stared at each other for a moment that was so
still that it seemed time had stopped moving. Then,
slowly, haltingly, he lowered his mouth to hers.

Summer's breath left her in a sudden gasp. The

shock was abrupt. The first, gentle touch of his lips awakened fires, the bittersweet ache of passion. A strange feeling, until this moment unknown to her, fluttered within her breast. Although his lips were soft and gentle, they entrapped hers with a fiery heat that flamed her cheeks and spread down her throat. The tobacco taste of his mouth, the woodsy, musky smell of his face as her nose pressed his cheek, and the hard strength of his embrace made her head swim—she was only vaguely aware that his hand had traveled down her back to her hips and pulled her to him.

Her arms tightened about his neck and she clung to him, unaware of his restraint, unaware of the tremor in his arms. She came to him with eagerness. Their lips blended with an impatient urgency, and locked in each other's embrace, glowing waves of pleasure spread like quickfire through her body. Somewhere, she had lost the fumbling uncertainty of her feelings for him, and untamed intensity swept her on. They were two beings blended together in a whirling tide that set them apart, for the moment, from the world.

He drew his head back and looked into her flushed face. He knew that he was the first man she'd ever loved. His hoarse, ragged breathing accompanied the pounding thunder of his heartbeat as he realized that she was not frightened of his passion, that she had responded. It was more than he had dared to hope for so soon.

"It's a gr-rand thing that's happened to us!" he said against her mouth. He stuttered with the power of emotion, and his voice sounded vaguely Scottish, like his father's.

"Yes!" She could feel life pounding in her throat, her temples.

"Sweet, sweet, wonderful Summer!" His whisper was warm against her lips. He was trembling violently, and as he looked into her shining eyes, half-closed in ecstasy, his mouth went dry. He seemed to be drowning in her violet eyes. Mesmerized, he watched as the tip of her tongue came out and moistened her lower lip.

"Slater, I. . . ."

"Shhhh . . . don't say anything," he cautioned. "We've said enough for tonight."

He drew her arm around behind him and held her hand tightly between his arm and his body. With his arm around her, they walked slowly back to the cabin. At the door, his lips fleetingly touched her forehead.

"Goodnight." His hand gently squeezed her shoulder, and he was gone.

Summer moved into the darkened room. Nothing in her young life up to now had prepared her for the emotions that churned inside her. It was as if she was outside of herself. Her heart still hammered furiously and her lips felt warm and throbbing. A fluttering in the pit of her stomach refused to go away, even as she pressed her hands tightly to it. Automatically, she undressed and slipped into her nightgown, took the pins from her hair and combed through it with her fingers before plaiting it into one long braid.

For some reason, she thought of her mother as she climbed into bed, and the words she had murmured as she lay dying . . . "Such a wonderful summer . . . so wonderful."

When morning came, Summer had no time to prepare herself for Slater's arrival. He came in through the back door while they were having breakfast.

"Mornin'."

Summer's tongue froze to the roof of her mouth and a rosy flush came up from her neck to flood her face. Sadie's quick glance took in her confusion and she jumped to her feet.

"Mornin', Slater. Had yore breakfast yet? You did? You got room for coffee and a cake, I reckon." She took her cup from the table. "Sit right here, where I was a sittin', cause I'm done, anyhow. That John

Austin has been a rarin' at the bit a waitin' for you to get here. I'll swear to goodness, I don't know what we'll do with that youngun. He's a corker, he is.'' Sadie knew she was talking too much, but she was desperately trying to make time for Summer to gather her wits about her. She sat looking down at her plate. "Did those big galoots up there at the bunkhouse eat up all those doughnuts? In all my life, I never did see men what could get rid of so many doughnuts. Filling them up is like pouring sand down a prairie-dog hole."

Slater's sharp eyes had caught the blush on Summer's cheeks, and he understood her friend's unnecessary chatter. He smiled at the pert red-headed girl.

"You're right about that, Sadie. They think it's Christmas and the Fourth of July all rolled into one."

"Well, I guess I'll just have to stir up another batch. If'n there isn't anything else I ort to be doin'."

Summer looked up. Slater's eyes on her face brought her color up again. She looked away from him and despised the blush that flooded her cheeks.

"I don't know of anything we have to do that can't wait, Sadie. It's a hot day, though, for you to be standing over a stove."

"Summer is right, Sadie. If you're going to be the doughnut-maker for McLean's Keep, the least we can do is build you a fireplace in the yard."

Sadie looked disbelievingly from Summer to Slater, then her green eyes sparkled.

"An outside fireplace. Why, that'd just be heaven!" She grinned impishly at him, and Summer envied her her easy manner. "You make me a cook-place, Slater, and I'll make doughnuts . . . till the cows come home!"

Slater laughed and Summer couldn't help noticing that when he did, it spread a warm light into his eyes. She found herself beaming with pleasure.

"I'll get Jack on it. He's real handy with that sort of thing." He looked directly at Summer and met her smiling eyes. "Where's John?"

Summer's eyes were fastened on his dark blue ones, and her pulses leaped in stupid excitement. Her slightly-flushed cheeks made her violet eyes seem all the brighter, clearer. Her mind groped like some wild creature caught in a bed of quicksand.

The voice from the doorway saved her from answering.

"Here I am, Slater. I already got the saddle on Georgianna. Pud didn't help me, I did it all by myself, and I left her in the corral like you told me."

"Georgianna?"

"She's a girl, ain't she? You told me I could put my own name on her, and I like Georgianna."

Summer got to her feet, filled with remorse for being so wrapped up in her own affairs that she had failed to know what her brother was about. He could have been stepped on . . . trampled.

Slater intercepted the worried look and got his hat from the peg. "Well, we'd better go take a look and see what kind of a job you've done on . . . Georgianna." He followed the boy out the door.

"He's gonna do just fine, Summer." Sadie came to stand beside her. "Don't worry, Slater'll make a man out of him."

Summer turned and caught the look of yearning on Sadie's face, which quickly changed to a saucy grin.

"Why, if'n I ever do find me a man like that, and if'n he would take to my baby, I'd just about lick his boots every day of the week." The green eyes sobered. "I'm a tryin' not to envy . . . I swear to God, Summer, I'm tryin'."

"He wants to marry me." The words burst out.

"Course he does, any fool'd see that. Can't hardly take his eyes off you."

Summer threw her arms about her friend. "It was meant to be that I'd meet you, Sadie. I'm so glad I did."

"Well, I been thinkin' on that too, Summer. I must a

done somethin' right back there a ways for the good Lord to let you come to that hotel. Now, if'n the good Lord would just let some big, old, handsome cowhand come and sweep me right off my feet, like he done you, well, then I think I could give out 'n die!"

Summer laughed. "Well, until he comes, Sadie, you'll stay right here and become the doughnut queen of Texas. But I just know before the summer is over, you're going to meet that big, handsome cowboy."

"Well, let's see. There's Bulldog, old Raccoon, there's Pud and Jack. Oh, Jack's nice. Real nice, Summer, but he don't make my heart flutter. Just once, I want a man what would put a shine to my eyes like Slater puts to yours."

"Does it show that much?" Summer put her hands to her cheeks.

"Don't be shamed by it!" Sadie pulled her hands away. "It shows to me 'cause I been lookin' for it. And it shows to him. He was early this mornin', just like he couldn't hold hisself away."

"Oh, I'm not shamed. It's just so new, is all." Summer's violet eyes danced and she couldn't keep the smile from tilting her lips.

"He's a man what would make any woman proud," Sadie said softly. "I ain't seen but one other what would make a woman feel so safe, so taken care of."

Summer gave her friend a sharp look, but Sadie had turned away and was plucking her newly-awakened daughter from the tangled bedclothes.

Summer could hardly contain her bubbling spirit as the morning progressed. Sure that her hair was smooth and her dress was clean, she paused frequently to look out the door toward the corral. She was agonizingly aware when Slater and John Austin rode into the yard, and fervently wished she could conceal herself beside the door and watch, but she went to her room and busied herself with the quilts in the big, wooden box at the end of the bed.

She had spread the patchwork quilt out to refold it when she heard Slater's voice in the other room. Her heart was pounding, her knees were weak, when he appeared in the doorway. His searching eyes found her, then swept the room before coming back to hers.

"I always liked this room."

Summer clutched the quilt to her, her eyes devouring his face, her heart galloping wildly.

"My mother loved it," she managed to say. "She said the most wonderful time of her life was spent here. When Papa came back from the fighting, he wanted to go back to the Piney Woods, but I think Mama wanted to stay here."

"Yes, I think she did," Slater said slowly. He walked over to the high chest and ran his hand over the small, carved box that had belonged to Nannie Kuykendall. It was in this box that Summer had found the letter from Sam McLean. "I remember this box. Your mother kept her treasures in it. There was a small gold ring she wore when she was a baby. You wore it, too."

Summer moved over to stand beside him. She lifted the lid of the box and took out the circle of gold. It was small and thin and she slipped it over the tip of her little finger for him to see. He was standing close to her. She could feel his breath stir the loose tendrils of her hair. She stepped away so she could look up at him. Their eyes caught, held, and Summer thought she would suffocate.

Quickly, she returned the ring to the box and drew out a flat package and unwrapped it.

"For as long as I can remember, Mama had this hair necklace. I never saw her wear it, but sometimes she took it out and looked at it. I think it's beautiful and must have taken hours and hours to make." She held it up between them. The hair was glossy black, and fine as silk. It was crocheted into a beautiful rope design to form the necklace. "I don't know whose hair it was."

She smiled at him. "But it could have been yours, Slater. It's the same color."

"Or yours." His eyes teased her and he reached out to touch the coils atop her head.

"I think if it was mine, she would have told me. I know it isn't Papa's. His hair was reddish-brown." She folded the necklace in the paper and returned it to the box. Slater didn't move. She could feel his eyes and looked up. He smiled at her with amused tenderness in his eyes. His voice had reached into her heart with a thrill of joyful recognition so strong that it caused her to catch her breath. She knew him! She knew him with her heart, her soul, as if he was the other half of herself and they would never be content until united.

It was a highly emotional moment, everything else in suspension, till Slater reached out a hand and stroked her forearm.

"Get something for your head. I want you to come with me to the Keep." It was a softly-spoken request.

While Summer tied on her sunbonnet, Slater spoke to Sadie.

"Decide where you want your outdoor cook-spot, Sadie. I'll send Jack down with a load of rock and an iron grill. Jack's good at rock work. He'll fix it up high, so you won't have to be bending all the time."

Sadie flushed with pleasure. "That'll make things real handy."

John Austin looked from his sister to Slater. He was clearly puzzled as to why Slater preferred her company to his. When Slater spoke again, it was to him.

"I'm taking your sister over to the Keep, John. You keep a sharp eye out here and look after Sadie and Mary. If you think there's a need, you climb up on a chair and get this handgun off the shelf. It's loaded, so be careful. Point it up and pull the trigger. It kicks like a mule and will probably knock you down, but by the time you get up someone would be on the way over.

121

Remember that? Don't get it down unless you mean to fire it."

"I won't, Slater. And I'll take care of things while you're gone."

To Summer's startled eyes, her brother seemed to grow inches.

"I know you would, John, or I wouldn't leave you in charge."

Out in the yard, Summer started walking toward the creek and the footbridge. Slater took her elbow and turned her toward the corral.

"We'll ride over."

"Oh, but. . . ."

He laughed. "Oh, but . . . what?"

"I can't ride in this dress."

His mouth twitched and humor came into his eyes. "We'll have to get you one of those fancy riding skirts that's split somehow. I never did like a side-saddle. They just don't do for this country."

Summer looked up at the tall black gelding, her voilet eyes full of apprehension. As if guessing the sensation, Slater stepped close to the horse's head and the animal nuzzled his hand.

"Estrella's gentle, but won't tolerate a heavy hand or a sawing bit."

"Estrella? What does it mean?"

"Means Star. When I got him, his name was Esteril, which means sterilized, but I thought it rather cruel to keep reminding him of what had been done to him." He turned her face toward him with a gentle finger under her chin. His dark eyes, as they watched the crimson flood her face, glinted devilishly. Weakened by the pulsing flame traveling from his hands through her, Summer tried to turn her face away, but he held her with tender strength. "The only thing that's keeping me from kissing you is John. He's watching from the door."

"You wouldn't?"

"No, but I want to."

Before she could retreat, he swept her up and placed her in the saddle sideways, thrust a foot in the stirrup and swung himself up behind her, his arms encircling her as he held the reins. Summer gripped the saddle-horn. The horse's movement brought her in rhythmic contact with him—there was no way she could escape his closeness, not that she wanted to. She longed to melt back against him, to feel his broad chest against her back, but she held herself erect.

"I wish I hadn't told you to wear that damn bonnet." His voice was close to her ear. The horse stopped in the middle of the creek. "Take it off."

Her hands were gripping the saddlehorn so tightly, she doubted if she would be able to loosen them. He laughed softly and she thought it the nicest sound she had ever heard.

"Don't be afraid. I won't let you fall." He untied the strings beneath her chin and lifted the bonnet from her head. "I want to see you, touch you. I've thought of nothing else." His arms drew her back and cradled her against him. Her head fit into the curve of his neck.

All thought left her. She closed her eyes and gave herself up to the joy of being held by him. The smooth side of his face was pressed to hers, and she lifted her hand to caress the scarred cheek. It was warm and rough and his whiskers scraped gently against her palm. This was the part of him she loved the most, this part that had given him so much pain.

He moved his head and his lips searched for hers. There was no haste in his kiss. Slow, sensuous, languid, he took his time quite deliberately, and every move of his lips increased the deep buried heat in her body. She kissed him back, hungrily, her hand moving back to pull at the crisp hair at the back of his neck. She relaxed in his arms and offered herself to his possessive lips.

His brown fingers moved to her chin and his thumb gently stroked her lower lip. Their breath mingled for an instant before he covered her mouth once again with his. She was filled with a driving physical need, which drummed through her veins like thunder, turning her body into helpless fluidity. She was conscious only of a need to please him, to satisfy him.

His hand curved around the back of her head in a sudden movement of possession, pushing her face to the curve of his neck. Against her hot face, the coolness of his skin was thrilling. Breathing fiercely, she kissed him, her mouth tasting the rough saltiness of his skin for the first time. She felt as well as heard the hoarse sound he made in his throat. Reluctantly, he held her away from him, looking at her with eyes that moved over her hungrily, lovingly.

"We'll marry soon," he said thickly. "I've been waiting for you . . . forever."

The horse moved restlessly, but it was of no concern to either of them. Summer tilted her head and pulled away so she could see his face.

"I'm all growed up and . . . I've come home to you."

"Sweetheart. . . ." His voice broke off, shaking. "Sweetheart. . . ." His hand caressed her arm, shoulder, and moved to her breast with trembling gentleness. He looked at her with a consuming tenderness in his dark eyes.

She gazed back at him, the ache of love in her tremulous mouth.

"Oh, God, I've wanted to hold you, kiss you, for days," he said thickly. His mouth parted her lips, desperate in search of fulfillment, and she clung to him, bonelessly melting into his hard body. The kiss lasted endlessly, as if they each found it impossible to end it. "Summer," he groaned against her neck. "Summer."

"Slater. . . ." she said, half-laughing. "Someone might come by."

He kissed her quick and hard. "Very well, what's a few more hours? But when night comes . . . my girl. . . ." he threatened teasingly.

She ran a finger over his hard mouth. "Are you threatening me, Mr. McLean?" Her eyes sparkled at him through the thick lashes.

"Warning you, Miss Kuykendall." His hat was pushed to the back of his head, and his dark eyes were alive with the smile-lines that fanned out from the corners. This relaxed, smiling man in no way resembled the stern-faced man she had met in the kitchen a few short weeks ago.

Her own shyness gone, she giggled softly and tried to tuck the stray tendrils back into her braid.

"Put your bonnet on, summertime girl. I don't want you to get a blister on your nose."

The horse, grateful to be leaving the water, scrambled up the bank. Slater, holding Summer between his two arms, grabbed the saddlehorn to keep from sliding off the horse's rump. Their laughter mingled. They were like excited children; everything was new and wonderful.

At the ranch house, Summer looked around with interest. The ride and the pause in the creek had brought color to her cheeks. Slater watched her with appreciation. There was a depth to her and a quickness of mind that he liked, and yet she was a woman, with all a woman's instincts. He felt an indefinable surge of pride.

"You belong here." He said it suddenly as he lifted her from the saddle. "This is your home."

She studied his confident expression, then looked around her at the sunlit, hard-packed earth, the soft shadows along the walls, the coolness of the place after the heat of the ride from the "little place". The house was stately with its verandas, shaded by the oaks that spread their branches some fifty feet in each direction.

Summer nodded her head, too happy to speak.

His hand came out to enclose hers, a smile of pleasure on his face.

"Come. You got to see it all."

The house stood at one corner of a rectangle of ranch buildings. South and west, no more than forty yards from the house, was the chuckhouse. Built adobe-style, the walls were thick, the windows and doors wide to allow the air to circulate. Beyond it was the long, low, stone bunkhouse, and beyond that an equally long building divided into rooms. These were respectively the saddle and harness rooms, tool house, storerooms and blacksmith shop. Behind this building was a barn filled with hay and three corrals.

In the space between the long building and the next group of buildings was the most beautiful garden Summer had ever seen. There were two acres or more of carefully-tended plants of every kind. Several rows of fruit trees bordered the back and one side. A small stream of water flowed in deep irrigation furrows beside the rows.

Watching the expressions flit across her face, Slater couldn't help laughing.

"We have a heap of people to feed here. Now you can see why I told you not to bother with a garden."

"But. . . ." Her violet eyes narrowed as she frowned, wrinkling her nose. "Why was the plot plowed and ready for planting?"

"Ol' Raccoon is the gardener. He's the man in charge and no one puts a foot in his garden till he says they can. He wanted to try a crop of peanuts and that's good sandy soil over there." He laughed at the troubled look that came over her face, and put an arm across her shoulders as they walked on. "It's all right, sweetheart. He's so glad you're here, he just chuckled when I told him he had lost his peanut land."

At the far end and to one side of the garden was a brush arbor, and beneath it roughly-made tables on which to spread and sort the foodstuff and prepare it for storage. Near this was a root cellar, the plank door folded back.

"Does Raccoon do all this work by himself?"

"No. We have four Mexican families living here. Some of the men are drovers, but some are too old or too young and they and the women help Raccoon. They share the work and share the bounty. But Raccoon is the boss, make no mistake about that." He laughed, then turned serious. "Some people can't seem to forget the Alamo, but there's a heap of good Mexican people in Texas. They love their children, keep their places neat and clean, are loyal to you if you treat them decent. Look at the flowers around the adobes."

Summer looked toward the group of houses. Flowers grew in profusion along a rail fence, and clay pots filled with an assortment of bright blooms lined the small verandas. Children were running and playing in the yards and clean clothes lay drying on the bushes. McLean's Keep was like a small town. As if reading her mind, Slater explained:

"Pa came here when there was nothing but hills and plains, outlaws and Indians, and he planned very carefully. To this new country, he brought some of the best of the world he left behind. His life went into making the Keep a self-supporting ranch. We must keep it that way, do all we can to preserve it for the next generation of McLeans."

They walked slowly back up the dusty track toward the house. Summer's hand was engulfed possessively in Slater's. The drovers tipped their hats and spoke politely, then grinned and winked at each other when they had passed. Bulldog sat on the veranda in a chair made from a large tree stump and worn smooth by years of use. He was whittling on a stick with a long, slim blade. He eyed them as they approached, his mouth puckered and twisted to the side.

"Wal," he said, rubbing his foot over the shavings on the stone floor. "It don't seem like any work's gonna get done a'tall, what with you out a strollin' and Jack a bustin' his tail to put up outdoor cookin'-spots. This whole place could just dry up and go ta seed, 'n I'd be the only one ta know it." He got up and walked to the end of the veranda and spit a stream of brown juice onto the dirt, then returned to his chair.

Summer squirmed uneasily and glanced up at Slater, expecting to see a scowl on his face. His eyes had narrowed to mere slits, but his lips were twitching at the corners in an effort to keep from smiling.

"And what are you doin', old man, but sittin' on your butt in the shade and cuttin' up a mess for Teresa to clean up? How come you're not rousting steers out of the brush?"

"Why, I can't do that, boy! Some folks got to stay on this here place ta see that things don't get out of pocket. Others I know of has got so bedazzled, a late, they don't know what end's up."

"You just got to hang around and see what's going on." Slater drew Summer's hand up into the crook of his arm and covered it with his. "Just to satisfy your curiosity, old man, and to get you off your hind and back in the saddle where you belong, there's going to be some changes around here. When my wife comes over to take charge, she might just take the broom to you when you get to flapping your mouth."

"Humph!" Bulldog didn't look up from where the blade was slashing long, thin strips from the wood. "I 'spect I can whup her hindside same as I whupped yores."

Slater looked down at Summer, his eyes twinkling, a mock-frown on his face. He put his arm across her shoulders and urged her forward.

"Come on, sweetheart. Pay no mind to that old goat. He's ornery as a brindle steer turned tail-over-teakettle. Don't plan on winning an argument with him. He just talks to hear his head rattle."

Bulldog's grizzled face broke into a grin when they

passed, and he rubbed his chin with the blunt edge of his knife. He cocked his head to listen to the voices coming from the kitchen. The girl and Slater were with Teresa. Whistling a tune through his snuff-stained teeth, he kicked the shavings off the porch with his foot and sauntered off toward the bunkhouse.

Chapter Nine

The days slipped past. After two months in the hill country, memories of the Piney Woods crossed Summer's mind only rarely. This was a busy time on the Keep, but Slater came to "walk out" with her almost every evening. Sometimes he was late, as they were driving steers out of the hills and into the river bottoms where the grass was thick and green. Later, after rain, they would be allowed to drift onto the higher plains. They were all hoping for rain, as the work was hot and dusty; they came in off the range with dry throats and dust-caked faces. In this country, rain meant not only water in the water-holes and basins, but also grass on the range.

Slater toyed with the idea of sending someone to town to bring out a preacher so he and Summer could marry, but the chance one would be found were slim, and the chance he would make the long ride out into the hills slimmer. He decided to wait until the work was finished and they would ride to Hamilton together—if necessary, on to Georgetown.

It was midmorning and John Austin was reading to Mary. She didn't understand any of what he was reading, but she liked sitting close to him and watching the pages turn.

Summer and Sadie were washing clothes and hanging them on the ropeline that stretched from the corner of the house to the big oak tree. They saw a lone rider coming up the creek road. They didn't pay much attention, at first, thinking it was a McLean rider bringing a message from Slater. Few travelers came this far alone, but when one did happen by, it was the unwritten rule that he immediately became your guest and was entitled to hospitality.

Sadie recognized the rider before Summer did.

"It's Travis McLean! It's Travis McLean sure as I'm a standing here!" Her voice was almost a wail, and Summer looked at her with surprise, then laughed. Sadie didn't like being caught looking so untidy. "He's up to no good. He's up to no good a riding in here by hisself." Her voice was softer, almost resigned.

"You don't know that, Sadie. Maybe he's bringing a message from Ellen."

"He's bringin' trouble, if'n he's bringin' anything." Sadie grumbled and picked up the empty wash tub and dropped it with a bang beside the black iron pot. With a long stick, she punched the clothes down into the boiling water again and again.

Travis rode into the yard and sat his horse. He removed his hat and wiped his forehead with his shirt sleeve. His light hair glistened in the sun, and Summer noticed he had grown a mustache since she'd seen him last. He was a handsome man, and now he smiled, showing rows of even white teeth. It was a friendly, boyish smile, and Summer couldn't help but respond to it.

"You're just as pretty as I remembered, Miss Summer. It was worth every mile of that hot, dusty ride to see that sweet smile."

Summer smiled again at his brashness. There was no doubt in her mind that he was putting his best foot forward.

"Get down and have a cool drink, Mr. McLean."

"Thank you, ma'am." He urged his horse over to the rail.

Summer walked with him to the washstand beside the back door. His gaze made her uncomfortable. She wished Slater would come riding in.

"What's keeping you from calling me Travis . . . Summer?"

It was so unexpected that she couldn't think of anything to say.

"Nothing. Nothing . . . at all . . . Travis."

"That's better. Much better." He looked amused.

"The water should be cool. It's a fresh bucket."

He smiled and offered her the dipper. She shook her head.

"My mother asked me to stop by and give you her regards. We're having a party at the end of the month, and she would be proud if you came. And she's not the only one that wishes you would honor us with a visit." The last words were lowered in an intimate whisper.

"I'll think about it, but I'm almost sure I won't be able to come. But tell your mother I'd be pleased to have her visit me again."

Summer was at a loss now what to say or do. She knew if she asked him in Slater would be furious, yet good manners demanded she invite him to eat.

"I trust your mother is well," she said, stalling for time.

"Yes, she's fine. Planning this blow-out is keeping her busy." He stood looking at her, smiling, waiting to see what she was going to do.

Finally, she decided she was making a dilemma where there was none.

"We'll have a meal ready shortly, Travis. You're welcome to stay and eat."

"I'd like nothing better, if you're sure its no bother. Excuse me, and I'll water my horse."

Summer nodded and slipped into the house.

Sadie watched her leave with dread, realizing she was alone in the yard with Travis and would have to pass him to get to the house. Fighting her terror, she punched and probed at the boiling clothes with the stick, desperately wanting to break and run as she watched him approach. He wouldn't do anything here in plain sight of the house, she reasoned, but even those thoughts didn't stop the lump of fear that came up in her throat. He stopped scarcely two feet from her. With his hat under his arm, he bowed his head as if in respectful greeting.

"Hello, split-tail." He smiled with his lips, but his eyes remained steely cold. "You didn't think I'd forget what happened that morning and whose fault it was, did you?"

Sadie moved around to the other side of the boiling pot, her eyes never leaving his face. He stood with his back to the house.

"Stay away from me." Her brain hummed. She would wrap the boiling shirt around the stick and hit him with it if he came any closer.

"What makes you think I want to touch you?" His tone was conversational, but behind each nostril showed white, and his eyes shone a brilliant blue. "Touch you? I could have you begging for it in no time a'tall; that is, if I'd put myself out to please a whore."

She managed a breathless laugh. "I'd die first."

"I can arrange that, too. Better yet, I can arrange it for that little bastard of yours." He smiled pleasantly.

"You touch a hair on her head and I'll spill your rotten guts all over creation," she hissed. Fresh alarm shot through her. She had been too frightened for herself to give a thought that he might harm Mary. Horrified and trembling like a leaf, Sadie grabbed the stick with both hands. "You're crazy!" she gasped.

"Might be, but I sure do have me a time." He laughed and ran his hand through his hair, and to Summer, looking out the doorway, the two by the boiling pot were having a pleasant conversation.

"One of my reasons for making this long, hot, dusty ride was to see you. I've been a thinking about you since that morning. You thought you had a little something going with Jesse." He laughed, this time nastily. "You'll not get him away from my mama. He might crawl on you if it comes handy, but I'm thinkin' he's already got a place to go." His voice lowered menacingly. "I don't want you here with Summer! If you as much as breathe a word to her about me, you'll not leave this place alive."

A tight hand seemed to be squeezing the breath out of her body. Through a daze, she heard him talking again, his voice taut with restrained anger.

"It won't be like the last time. There won't be no Jesse a chargin' to the rescue."

"I ain't said nothin' to Summer about you or what you . . . did!"

"Goddammit! Do you think I'd believe a slut? Go! I don't aim to be looking at you every time I come here to see Summer." His face had grown dark with anger, and she thought his eyes almost shot sparks of blue flame. Suddenly, he laughed in a boastful way that made her despise him all the more. "From that hill yonder, a man with a good rifle could pick off a chicken in this yard." He cocked his head to one side. "That kid of yours is quite a bit bigger than a chicken."

"I'll tell Mr. McLean. . . ." she blurted out in desperation.

He lifted his shoulders in resignation, glancing over his shoulder toward the house; then his eyes played over her, bringing a helpless, humiliating flush upward to the roots of her hair.

"I'd get you. If I didn't get your kid first, so you'd know what to expect. I got friends up in the hills and they owe me plenty." His lips curled in a sneer. "You didn't think I was dumb enough to ride in here alone?"

"Sadie!" The call came from Summer. "Can that batch of wash wait till after the nooning?"

Sadie tore her eyes away from the man's leering face and thought with lucid remoteness that she could call out to Summer, tell her to get the gun from the top shelf and kill this rattlesnake. Her eyes flicked back to him. His face was tense, waiting. She made a helpless gesture and his face relaxed.

"Wait right here." His voice was no more than a purring whisper. "I'll water my horse and we'll go in together." He led his horse past her to the watering trough.

"I'll be there in no time a'tall, Summer." Sadie called on all her inner resources to keep the fear that was eating her alive out of her voice. She had no chance against a man like Travis McLean. He was handsome, rich, spoke too fast. Summer would never believe the conversation that had just taken place. Never believe it fast enough to act.

Sadie walked into the kitchen as if in a nightmare, numbly thinking that this couldn't be real. This place had been a safe haven for her and Mary. She had been happier than she could ever remember. Now this piss-ant coming through the door behind her was making it a hell. The thoughts of what he threatened to do to Mary were too awful to think about. Jesse Thurston flashed through her mind. Oh, but he was a world away, and she and Mary were here with Travis McLean.

Mary was sitting on the bunk playing with some paper dolls that John Austin had cut out for her. Sadie, weeping inside, picked her up, holding her tightly. Summer turned from the stove with a pan of cornbread.

"I put her box on the chair, Sadie. She can sit here beside John Austin."

"Your daughter is almost as pretty as you are, Mrs. Bratcher." Travis stood observing the two of them, a pleasant smile on his face. "Same green eyes, same beautiful red hair. It's been a long while since I held such a pretty girl on my lap. Come to me, young miss. Let's see how big you are."

"No!" The word burst from Sadie's lips. "No. She's . . . scared of strangers."

Summer's head came up and a puzzled look crossed her face. Even John Austin got to his feet. With his back to the others, Travis looked at Sadie with narrowed eyes.

"You're not afraid of me, are you, young miss?" His voice was pleasant, wheedling. "Come to Uncle Travis. I'll find a big, shiny penny for this pretty girl." He reached for the child and she went willingly.

Sadie's heart almost burst with fright. She went to the shelf, fighting back waves of nausea, grabbed up the crock of butter, anything to give herself time to compose her face before going to the table.

"This is her place, Travis," Summer was saying. "You can sit next to her, if you like, and John Austin on the other side of you."

"I'd like that." He lowered Mary to the box. "How are you, John Austin? What's that you got there? A picture book?"

"No, sir. It's about the Revolutionary War. Slater lets me read his books. He's got a lot of them. This one is about Nathan Hale, who was executed as a spy by the British. Next I'm going to read about the Marquis de Lafayette. He was a Frenchman and he. . . ."

Summer interrupted. "Will you say grace, John Austin?"

"Sure, Summer, then can I tell . . .?"

"Mind your sister," Travis broke in smoothly. "After we eat, we'll have a good, long talk."

The meal progressed smoothly. Travis buttered cornbread for Mary, put vinegar on John Austin's greens, chatted lightly with Summer. Sadie was quiet, but Summer put that down to shyness. Travis was fascinating company. The children listened raptly to his every word. Summer was sure he was making up stories to amuse them, especially the one about the pony that would rather eat apple pie than sweet clover, but John Austin loved it.

"Slater gave me a horse, Travis. Her name is Georgianna. I think I'll see if she likes pie. Maybe she'll like doughnuts, 'cause if she does, she could have lots. Sadie makes good doughnuts."

"Georgianna? Did you say your horse's name is Georgianna? Well, . . . what do you know about that?"

By the time the meal was over, the children were completely won over, and Summer had almost forgotten the unpleasant scene with Jesse. Ellen McLean's son had a nice way about him, she had to admit.

Travis sat on the veranda and talked with John Austin while Summer and Sadie cleared the table. Mary wanted to join them, but Sadie insisted she sit on the bed with her toys.

"We have all afternoon to finish the wash, Sadie. You've been whirling around like the house was on fire." Summer was teasing, but her face sobered when she saw the stricken look on her friend's face. "Don't you feel well?" She laid her hand against Sadie's white cheek. "You're so white. You've been out in that sun and standing over that boiling pot too long."

"I did get a mite hot. I'll sit down and rest once we get caught up here."

The food Sadie had forced down at the dinner table

was churning in her stomach, and she kept swallowing the wetness in her mouth to keep from throwing up. What could she do? Suggestion after suggestion raced through her thoughts, only to be discarded. She could get the gun from the shelf, walk up behind the bastard, and blow out his brains! Then it would be sure death for her and Mary. His friends would seek revenge. She would never know when she and Mary went out the door if they were out there waiting for them. Oh, dear God! The thought made her knees almost collapse under her. Which was safer . . . to stay here or go away? If she went away, she would have no protection at all!

Travis came into the house followed by John Austin, still talking.

"I'm glad you came, Travis. Next time you come, I'll tell you about the Battle of San Jacinto. My papa fought in that battle."

"I'd sure like to hear about it." Travis took his hat from the peg. "I hate to eat and go, Miss Summer. But my men will be wondering where I got off to. We're doing a little hunting in the hills. Slack time on the ranch, right now."

"We're glad you came by. Thank your mother for her invitation."

"I'll do that, Miss Summer." He swung around to Sadie, who was standing beside Mary, her face white, her eyes huge. "There you are, Mrs. Bratcher." He took several steps toward her and put his hand on Mary's head. "You take care of this pretty little girl. She's just too pretty for words." His eyes bored into hers and she felt a numbness in her breast. "If I get over this way, you can bet Uncle Travis will be back to see you, honey." A scream was building up in Sadie's throat, but she choked it off. Fear, like a thousand needles, rode down her spine, and her legs almost refused to support her. As if realizing he had pushed her almost to the breaking point, Travis turned and went to the door. "Goodbye for now, John Austin. Thanks again for the meal, Miss Summer."

"Goodbye, Travis."

Summer stood in the doorway and watched him leave. He swung lightly into the saddle and lifted his hat toward her. She smiled and waved. Watching him ride away, she had mixed emotions. She was glad he had come, but glad he was going before Slater came over. Of course she would tell him that Travis had been here. But she knew he would be angry, and knew it would be a frightening thing. She felt a flutter of apprehension and wished Travis hadn't come, after all.

Sadie lay down on the bed and gathered the drowsy little girl in her arms. She desperately wanted to cry, but there were no tears anywhere inside her. Only hate, fear and devastation.

"I'm afraid you're coming down with something, Sadie." Summer looked down at her with worried eyes. "You stay here in bed. I'll finish the wash."

"I'll rest a minute and be out to help you." Sadie managed a saucy grin. "You know I ain't used to layin' on my backside."

Grateful when Summer went out and left her alone, Sadie allowed her face to crumble, buried it in her daughter's hair and let her misery flow over her.

Summer's pulses quickened as darkness fell. Sadie, who usually sat with her for a while after the children went to bed, had retired early. Summer had washed, put on a clean dress, brushed her hair and gathered it at the nape of her neck with a ribbon. Lastly, she took out the small pouch of dried rose leaves and rubbed it against her neck, face and arms.

Sometimes, she felt unreal waiting for Slater. It was so wonderful to be in love. He filled every corner of her heart without her being able to stop it. Her realization that she loved him had given the world a new brightness, freeing her from many of her old, almost cherished inhibitions. She felt laughter bubbling inside her at the most unexpected times. Happiness seemed to flow in her blood, and little smiles of pure delight curved her mouth. The nagging worry about Sadie, the fear of Slater's reaction to Travis's visit were pushed to the back of her mind. There was no room for anything inside her now but her love for Slater.

Summer's ears were attuned to the night sounds, and she heard him coming seconds before she saw him. She left the bench by the wall and went to the edge of the veranda, waiting, her heart beating a happy tattoo. She heard the creak of saddle leather, then he was coming toward her. His light-colored shirt was a soft glow in the moonlight. He was hatless and his black hair framed his dark face. She ran out from the porch. He stopped and held his arms wide. She ran into them and he lifted her off her feet, swinging her around.

"My sweet! My sweet summertime girl! I'll never get used to you waiting for me, running to me." His voice was husky, teasing, tender, and his lips nuzzled her ear. "You smell like roses. Is your beau coming to call?"

"He's here!" Her arms tightened about his neck. "He's right here!"

The feel of her body warm against his and the scent of her filled his head. He swallowed hard because he wanted her so much. His hand moved up and down her back and over her rounded hips, pulling her closer.

"This day has been a year long," he whispered passionately against her lips, and kissed her long and hard.

She returned his kiss, her mouth answering his hungrily, feeling the familiar longing in her loins, pressing against him, her breasts tingling as they waited for his caress. He began to stroke her, his hands gentle.

"Sweetheart." His breath was warm on her face. "I've waited all day for this. It's getting harder and harder . . . to not do more than kiss you."

The knowledge that she could excite him so much, could cause his big, work-hard body to tremble and his breath to catch in his throat, made her brave. Her hands moved down and slipped inside his shirt. His chest was furry in the center and warm and smooth as her hand slid along muscles that quivered at her touch. Her exploration stopped abruptly. She turned her lips from his so she could speak.

"You . . . you've been hurt here!"

"It doesn't matter. Nothing matters now but you." He began kissing her again, his hand coming up under the hair at the nape of her neck to hold her head. She could feel the stirring in him and in her, and she wanted to melt into him, become one with him, so she could feel the pain he'd felt when these scars were made.

Gently, still kissing her, he eased her arms from around him and, holding her by the shoulders, he peered down into her face.

"Let me move you and John Austin to the house, sweetheart." There was urgency in his voice. "I want you to be there. I'll move to the bunkhouse until we are wed." He pulled her back into his arms.

Her heart hammered. The sincerity in his face, his voice, made her weak. Somewhere, she found the strength to whisper:

"It won't be long now." She placed slow, nibbling kisses along his jawline. "Until we're married, I'll be waiting right here, anytime you can come to me." She pulled away, laughing lightly. "Why are we standing here? Shall we sit on the veranda?"

"Let's take a walk down by the swing." He untied a bundle from behind the saddle, and arm in arm they moved away from the house.

Now is the time, she thought, to tell him about Travis's visit. While she was trying to form the right words in her mind, they reached the cottonwood tree, and he flipped out the blanket and lowered himself down. The moment was lost.

He leaned on his elbow and watched her. He was quite sure there was not another woman like her and never would be. How easily she had woven her web around him, yet she was like a fragile butterfly. The moon was up and skimmed the treetops. In its silvery light she was a vision of all that was wonderful. He had to have her close, and he reached up and tugged on her skirt. She knelt down beside him.

"Are you real, Summer, or am I having a dream? A wonderful dream." His fingers closed lightly around her wrist and brought it to his lips, kissing the soft skin, running his tongue along her inner arm.

She bent low to press her trembling mouth to his. "Oh, love," she breathed against his lips. "Even dreams are not this wonderful!"

With an arm across her shoulders, he rolled down onto his back and pulled her down beside him. A great peaceful sigh came from him.

"You're tired," she said, with concern. Her eyes searched his face in the meager glow, and her fingertips stroked his scarred cheek.

In the warm, wavering glow of the moon, her skin shone warm and pale, shadowed and highlighted, even more beautiful than he had seen before. There was a radiance about her that was different, but he couldn't name it.

"My beautiful Summer," he breathed, almost in reverence. "I could not have believed it, but you have grown even more beautiful. Are you a fairy princess, my love?"

"Yes." She smiled down into his eyes. "And I may turn into a green toad if you don't kiss me."

"Not that!" The words were a husky growl in his throat. He turned and bore her down to the blanket, leaning over her and gathering her close. His kisses came upon her mouth, warm, devouring, fierce with love and passion. Summer closed her eyes as the bliss of his greedy mouth swept her every nerve with intense excitement. She heard his harsh breathing in her ear, the hoarsely whispered words of love. His hand moved between them to the buttons on her dress, exposed her naked breast to his touch. He cupped, caressed, stroked, then pressed her nipples to his own bare chest, where his heart beat wildly.

Blindly, not daring to open her eyes, Summer moved her lips to his scarred cheek and kissed the puckers and ridges with her open mouth. His hands moved over her breast and down the length of her body, exploring its curves and hollows through the cotton dress. When his fingers unfastened more buttons, more hooks, she began to shiver, but she could no more have moved to resist him than he, at this moment, could have stopped himself.

His lips moved slowly and lingeringly from her mouth to her earlobe to her eyes and back to bury her mouth with his. He was trembling violently. She felt his mouth on her breast, lips and tongue caressing, nibbling at her nipples. Holding his head to her breast, she groaned, a muted, strangled, incoherent sound. She wanted this! She wanted to lie under his searching hands. None of her imaginings had ever been like this. This was more wonderful, more frightening.

"I love you and want you, but I don't want to do this to you. Tell me to stop, sweetheart!" Muttered words tumbled from his lips as he pressed fevered kisses along the soft skin of her throat and the beginning swell of her breast, arching her backward over his arm, while his other hand stroked her buttocks and thighs. There was an eagerness in him to know and touch every part of her, to go inside her, to fuse with her. "Is it what you want? Please . . . please, say it's what you want!"

Summer's eyes were soft with love as she gazed at him. Placing her palms on either side of his face she said soothingly, as if to a child:

"Yes, my love. It's what I want. A few words said by

a preacher won't make me any more yours than I am at this moment."

His mouth lowered to savor the sweet, heady nectar of her lips, and his tongue searched for entry. His fully-clad body lay half-covering her, his leg thrown over her, his arms clutching her to him. She lay soft and pliant, meeting his kisses with gentle ardor. "I must tell you, sweetheart," his words came against her cheek, "it . . . it may not be what you expect. It may. . . ."

". . . hurt. I know. I know." Her hands moved impatiently, pulling his shirt away and running her fingertips through the crisp hair on his chest and around to his lean, muscular ribs. His sharp intake of breath thrilled her. She felt briefly abandoned when he left her arms to help her slip out of her dress, but almost before she could voice a complaint he was back, bare and warm and covering her.

Her arms went up to hold him closer, her body straining against his. He covered her face with kisses, releasing his pent-up desire with each touch of his lips. He bent his head and kissed the soft firmness of her breast and his hand moved between her thighs, stroking the soft inner skin, moving upward. She gave a muffled, instinctive cry as his fingers found her wetness and probed gently inside.

He spoke to her softly and coaxingly, and after a while she forgot who she was, where she was, and opened her legs, letting his fingers have their way. Her excitement mounted, her body writhed and strained upward against his hand, aching for something she couldn't yet understand. "This is the first of a thousand times for us," he breathed. "I want you to know the pleasure that I will know. I want you to cherish the memory of our first time."

"Yes, yes! Please. . . ." she whispered, and he moved over her, his knees between her thighs, holding them apart. For an instant, she was afraid. Her hands slipped down his back and felt the clenching and unclenching of his muscles. He lifted himself above her and she felt him large, hot and rock-hard, pushing to enter her. He went inside her a little way and stopped. With ragged breath, he waited a full minute; calming her, reassuring her. Suddenly, he thrust, and her body arched in shock. His mouth stopped her startled cry.

"My precious love," he soothed her. He stayed inside her without moving, embedded in her, their bodies joined, his hard belly caressing the softness of hers.

The realization of it washed over her and she wrapped her arms about him, her hands pressing his back, his lean hips, truly wanting to become one with him. Lying there beneath him, with his arms around her, a part of his body inside her, she thought: Nothing can ever be the same again, nothing! From this moment, my life is changed.

Gently, he moved, slowly, his body rigid, trembling. He raised his head so he could see her face; it was glowing and full of love. His movements quickened. There was no more pain, he could read it in her eyes. With a stifled groan, he covered her mouth with his, and their bodies arched together, her movements meeting his. Tingling waves traveled like quicksilver through her veins. "I love you," she screamed inside, as her body twisted and he seemed to take her to the edge of the world and they flew out into space locked together.

Wave after wave of pure physical pleasure washed over them. They were two beings wrapped in the perfect bliss of their union, giving all to each other and in return receiving everything and more. Summer only suspected that theirs was a special love; Slater knew it. He had been a man burning for peace, for contentment. It was here, beneath him, in the body of this small woman. He poured himself into her, groaning,

shuddering, reaching for her very soul with his possession and binding his heaving body to hers in total
consummation.

Afterwards, still joined to him, she hardly had
strength left to return his kisses. She was weak and
lifeless in body, but her spirit soared, and she wanted to
tell him how it was with her.

"It was wonderful! You are . . . wonderful!"

Relief flowed through him. Tenderly, he pushed the
damp hair from her face and his heart swelled. He had
never dared to hope, to dream, of finding a woman like
this. He bent his head and reverently kissed her
forehead, her lips, her breast. He was filled with
indescribable joy and contentment. Lifting himself up
and out of her, he lay beside her and reached for his
shirt. Gently, he wiped the perspiration from her face,
drew the soft cloth across and around her breast, down
over her flat belly, and between her thighs, cleansing
her. It was an act of loving devotion, and Summer
recognized it as such.

He drew back and they stared at each other. She was
acutely aware of his naked chest and lean, muscular
body, and he was totally conscious of her slender
nakedness, but there was no shyness, no embarrassment.

"I love you," she sighed in a soft, trembling voice.

"And I love you," he said huskily. "Thank you for
loving me too."

Later, he slipped into his clothing, then helped her
dress.

"If you were in my house, I could love you all night
long." He said it softly, teasingly. And then, seriously,
"But I understand your reasons for not wanting to
come now."

Too tired, almost, to move, she sat still while he felt
about on the blanket for her hair ribbon, found it, and
slipped it about her neck, leaving her hair hanging free.

They looked at each other with new eyes. What they'd had before tonight was wonderful . . . now it was glorious. They had merged, blended, come together as man and woman, her softness yielding to his hardness, their wonder turning to rapture. It was enough to sit close to each other, quietly, letting the soft blackness of night curtain them from the world.

"I feel strange, new," Summer whispered. "I feel like music."

"Kiss me again."

Their lips met in the darkness, clung, and she pulled away from him. The moon was lost behind a wandering cloud. Somewhere, a coyote sent his lonely cry to the wide sky, an owl hooted, a squirrel chattered inquiringly, and then there was silence.

A faint, far-off sound caught Slater's attention. He listened. There was nothing more. He reached into the side of his moccasins and palmed a small handgun. With an arm about her, he listened a minute longer. In one fluid motion, he got to his feet and pulled her up beside him.

"What is it?" she whispered.

"A deer splashing in the creek," he said softly. Arm in arm, they left the shadow of the tree and crossed the yard.

"Travis McLean was here today." She said it abruptly, hurriedly.

They reached the veranda and Slater dropped the blanket on the bench. She was confused. She was sure he had heard what she said, but he said nothing.

"Slater." She looked up into his face. "Did you hear me say Travis was here today?"

"I heard you." His voice was bitter and cut into her like a knife. "Why didn't you tell me before now? What was he doing here?" he demanded. His anger seemed to reach out of the dark and envelop her. Involuntarily, she shrank back. His grip on her arm tightened.

"He said he was hunting in the hills and his mother asked him, if he was over this way, to invite me to a party." She looked at him fearfully.

"Hunting?" She could almost feel the burning, spitting rage that consumed him. "Hunting what? Some poor Indian to take for a slave? To torment?"

Shook out of her fear by his snarling, accusing words, anger overpowered her.

"He didn't say what he was hunting. I only know that he conducted himself like a gentleman, and I offered him a meal. What else could I do?"

"You don't know Travis McLean, or sweet, simpering Ellen!"

Her pride was nipped by the brusque manner in which he dismissed her opinion.

"I have no reason," she said calmly, "to believe they are my enemies. Ellen was good enough to call on me. She was my mother's friend and she wants to be my friend. You're wrong in thinking they had anything to do with killing your father. Ellen had nothing but good things to say about you and Sam."

"So!" He flung the word into her face like a slap. "You think she was Nannie's friend? She despised Nannie, despised my mother, despised me, despised anything or anyone that stood between her and my pa. When she finally realized she couldn't have him, she wanted him dead! With me dead, she would have at least a part of him—his ranch!"

"You don't know that, Slater." Angry frustration ran rampant through her and her argument burst forth in a torrent. "You're allowing your suspicion to cloud your judgment. If you had proof against them, why didn't you take it to the law?"

"The law? You little fool, there's no law here! The army does what it can, but that amounts to about as much as a pimple on a jaybird's ass. Do you think it's luck this ranch isn't overrun with outlaws, renegades,

Indians? It's safe for you because my men keep it that way. I lose one or two good men every year keeping 'law' on my land.''

Sheer desperation made Summer find words, any words, just so she could defend her stand.

"You still have no proof Ellen wanted you killed so she could have the ranch. She couldn't know she would get it if you were dead.''

"Yes, she did. McLean land always goes to blood McLeans, and sorry as he is, Travis is a McLean. Uncle Scott claimed him, though God only knows how he could have sired such a pervert.'' He cupped her face between his palms as if he thought to mold and memorize its contours as he studied it through narrowed eyes.

Summer's anger was over. Now she wanted to cry, but pride forbade the use of tears to soften him.

"Slater, please, try to understand.''

"Understand? You either believe what I tell you or what Ellen tells you. It's that simple. I love you more than life, Summer, and I was hoping, was beginning to believe, that you loved me in return. The foundation of love is trust, loyalty.''

"How can you doubt that I love you? Do you think I would have . . . could have? . . .'' A note of weariness crept into her voice, tears filled her eyes, and her soft mouth trembled. A brief pause ensued, while they searched each other's faces. Shyly, hesitantly, she slipped her arms about his neck and, standing on her tiptoes, she pressed a kiss on his stern, unyielding mouth. His breath left him in a sudden gasp, and his arms closed about her in a crushing grip. Slowly, her sobbing lips parted and yielded to his passionate kiss.

If she expected to see a softening in his face when he released her, she was disappointed. There was an uneasy silence, while he scrutinized her openly. Tears blurred her vision and she drew a ragged breath. She tried to pull out of his encircling arms and hide her face before she humiliated herself further, but he only held her more tightly.

"There's no reason for you to cry. You must listen to me," he said, in a strange, expressionless voice. "Don't be misled by Travis's glib tongue and charming manner. He's like a mad dog with a woman. I know this to be a fact, Summer." His hold on her forearms tightened. "Women are like so much meat to him. I won't have him near you. If he so much as touches a hair on your head, I'll kill him. I'll gun him down as quick as I would a mad dog. He may think Sadie is fair game, because of what she did in Hamilton, but while she's on my land, she's under my protection, too. Am I getting through to you, Summer? Do you understand?"

"Of course I understand. It's only . . . he was so nice today. Not only to me and to Sadie, but to the children, too."

"If he should come here again, you're to fire the signal shot." He gathered her close, pressing her wet face against his shoulder. "You're not to worry. I'll sleep in the shed, although I'd rather sleep with you." He kissed her tenderly. "We better see about getting a bunkhouse built down here, so Sadie won't be alone after you move over to the other house. Go on in now, and drop the bars across the doors."

Inside the house, she dropped the bars and went to the window. The shadow that was Slater led his horse to the back of the house and she went to the rear window to watch. The horse drank from the water trough before Slater stripped the saddle and turned him into the corral. With rifle in hand, he moved around the buildings, pausing every few feet to listen. When he returned to the shed, he stood in front of the door for several minutes before he went inside.

Summer's spirit was humbled. She had never before felt so physically and emotionally wrung. To love a man as passionately as she loved Slater, and to see him transformed before her eyes from a warm, loving, gentle man to a cold, unrelenting and violent one was heartily depressing. Her mind moved back to the hour spent in love's intoxicating completion. Never had she known such glorious fulfillment, such extraordinary satisfaction. Now, lying alone in her bed, bathing in the glow of this marvelous night, she stirred, placing her hand on her stomach just above her sex. His seed. Would she become pregnant? Possibly! She should feel disgracefully wanton; instead, she was delighted in the prospect, already perceiving a small dark boy with straight black hair, a serious face and blue-black eyes.

Chapter Ten

Summer was disappointed but not surprised the next morning, to discover that Slater had left without stopping by the house.

Sadie saw her bewilderment and sought to ease whatever disappointment she might be feeling and at the same time satisfy her own curiosity as to why the master of the ranch would choose to sleep in the shed.

"Jack said they have a few more days of rousting steers out of the brush. Slater works as hard as anyone, Jack says. Guess he's got his own reasons for stayin' the night out there, if'n he did," she added carefully.

"He did. He was angry about Travis being here."

"Angry?"

"Angry wasn't the right word. He was furious. We are to fire the gun if he comes back." She waited until she could control the slight quaver in her voice. "Oh, Sadie, Slater will kill him! Travis is bad with women, he says, and he doesn't trust him near us. I can't believe

Travis would hurt us, but Slater is so sure, he's going to sleep in the shed until he can build a bunkhouse."

"Let him kill him!" Sadie's face and voice betrayed her desperation.

"Sadie! Why do you say that? Has he . . . ?"

"He's bad, Summer. Rotten! Let Slater kill him. He's just a piece of . . . nothin'."

"You're afraid of him! What did he say to you out there in the yard? You're trembling. Is it because of him, or are you getting sick?"

Sadie fought the conflict raging within her. Travis would surely kill her and Mary if she told Summer of his threats. All night long, she had wrestled with the problem of what to do. Now, if Slater should kill him, her troubles would be over.

"Why should I be scared of him? I was just thinkin' that if'n he's like that, he should be shot. I guess what's wrong with me is I miss town!" Spots of color showed vividly on her cheeks as she tilted her head rakishly. "I ain't never been away from town for a long time, so how's I to know I'd miss it?" Her pert nose elevated to a saucy angle.

Staring at her, Summer tasted a draught of disappointment.

"You want to go back to town?" Her disbelief betrayed itself in a voice trembling with concern. "You said you liked it here."

Sadie whirled away, unable to bear the bafflement on Summer's face.

"I ain't said I want to go back to town," she flung over her shoulder. "I like it here. I was just a wonderin' how it would be when you and John Austin go over to live with Slater. There wouldn't be no need for me stayin'." She laughed scoffingly. "'Sides, I wouldn't stay down here by myself if Slater'd let me." A flush burned her cheeks. "I'd have to find me a man, and there ain't many to choose from here."

At twenty, Sadie had evolved something of a philosophy to assist her through difficulties: hide your feelings, smile over a hurt, pretend, pretend . . . pretend. But her heart rebelled: she wanted to scream and stamp her feet and pound her head against the wall, but it would do no good. No good at all.

There was a long, troubled silence. Summer had turned equally red in the face. She gazed at Sadie, then away.

"You and Mary are welcome to stay here as long as you want, Sadie. Even when John Austin and I go over to Slater's." Summer watched Sadie's face anxiously, astonished at her change of attitude. Since the day they'd left Hamilton, she had been so cheerful. Now, suddenly . . .

"Oh, I ain't goin' no place, Summer." Sadie's voice was light. "I just wanted to know if you was planning on me staying. Course I ain't if there ain't enough for me to do to earn our keep." She laughed nervously. "Speaking about workin', I'd better get along with makin' up that soap. We got a heap of ashes saved up, and I found a crock of grease."

They carried bucket after bucket of water to pour over the ashes that had been scooped into a wooden trough. The potash water dripped into a bucket through small holes in the ash trough, and when Sadie pronounced it ready, she poured it over the grease that Summer had been rendering in the iron kettle over an open fire.

When the soap mixture boiled to pudding thickness, they strained it into a large flat pan and added salt to harden it. The soap had a strong lye smell, but when used in the wash pot, the clothes would come out clean, and after being rinsed and dried in the sun, they would be sweet-smelling.

They worked silently, each wrapped in her own thoughts. The only sound that broke their silence was Sadie's scolding of Mary. She wanted the child to stay in the house. Summer was puzzled, at first, but decided

Sadie was fearful of her being near the boiling pot. Mary cried and fussed. Finally, in desperation, Sadie wrapped a spoonful of sugar in a cloth, tied it securely, and gave it to the child to suck on.

"I shouldn't do it," she grumbled. "I shouldn't let her think she'll get a sugar-tit every time she throws a spell."

They had finished the soap-making and were cleaning up, when John Austin called out that someone was coming. Both girls looked toward the creek and the trail to the Keep, and seeing no one, swung around to face the trail leading north to Hamilton: that also was empty. To the south were the hills, covered with thick brush and trees. The two riders had come from that direction and were rounding the end of the corral and almost in the yard before they were seen.

A man with a black beard, wearing a flat-crowned, Mexican-type hat, was leading a brown and white pinto pony that carried an Indian with long, straight black hair, a red band wrapped around his forehead, his hands bound behind his back and a rope about his neck. He was slumped forward, his chin resting on his chest.

Summer watched them approach, her mind numb. Sadie moved to stand in the doorway leading to the kitchen, but Summer stood rooted to the spot and steeled herself to meet the strangers.

The man rode his horse up to within a few feet of her.

"Howdy. Hot, ain't it?" He took off his hat and wiped his face with the sleeve of his shirt. His eyes moved restlessly over the corrals, the shed, swept the entire area before coming back and boldly eyeing her. He grinned, showing stubs of teeth through his black beard. "I'd be obliged for a cool drink."

Summer nodded toward the bucket. "Help yourself."

He wrapped the pony's lead rope and the rope looped about the Indian's neck to his saddlehorn and eased himself out of the saddle. He glanced at Sadie then his eyes came back to Summer. Water ran down his beard and onto his shirt as he drank, and Summer made a mental note to scrub out the dipper before it was used again.

"Mr. McLean here?" The man moved back toward his horse. His eyes roved the yard and outbuildings again.

Summer shook her head. "No." Somehow she knew he was referring to Travis.

"Suppose ta meet up with him back thar a ways. Thought he could of come here, seein' as ta what's here." He grinned, and his eyes switched from one girl to the other.

The look angered Summer.

"That man needs water, too." She indicated the sagging Indian. The edge of her voice sharpened even more. "You're not leaving without giving him water?"

He spat between his feet. "He don't need no water. 'Paches go days without none."

Fury boiled up within Summer, and she took a step toward the water bucket. Her eyes met those of the bearded man, and she read the threat in them. She glanced at the Indian, noticing that the flesh had sunk in between the cheekbones and jaws, and the rope about his neck was so tight that his mouth was open as he sucked air into his lungs. He was watching her with dull, lifeless eyes.

A commotion behind her drew her attention. Sadie was blocking the doorway, preventing John Austin from coming out.

"Can I see the Indian, Summer?" He tried to dart beneath Sadie's arm, but she drew him back.

"Stay inside, John Austin," Summer ordered sharply. Anger stiffened her back and she dipped the dipper in the water pail and went toward the Indian, who leaned toward her with open mouth.

The black-bearded man moved fast, and the dipper went flying from her hand.

"Hold on. Ain't nobody a givin' that 'Pache no water."

"He needs water badly, and he shall have it!" Summer's heart pounded heavily. She picked up the dipper and returned to the bench, refilled it, and started toward the Indian again.

"Got grit, ain't ya?" The man grabbed her close to his foul-smelling body, his hand coming around her to cup and squeeze her breast. "Ain't nothin' I like more'n a spunky woman."

Summer swung the dipper at his leering face. The blow was light and the water spilled over him. He laughed and fastened his hand in the front of her dress, holding her away from him. Summer's knees shook and she went rigid with terror.

It all happened in a moment.

"Let go! Let my sister go!" John Austin shouted, and threw himself in between Summer and the man, his fists pounding. The man laughed again, loudly, and with one sweep of his arm sent the boy rolling in the dust.

Rage and fear mixed in Summer. Her fingers formed talons and reached for his eyes, missed, and raked his face.

"You . . . bitch!" he snarled and slapped her with an open palm. Her head jarred, and only the hold he had on the front of her dress kept her from going to her knees. She vaguely heard the sound of hoof beats. Then, close to her, a young, excited voice.

"Get away! Leave her be!" Pud jumped from his horse and threw himself at the man, who easily shoved him to the ground while still holding Summer. Pud bounced up and launched himself again at the burly figure, flaying him with his fists.

"Keep away, boy. I don't aim to tell ya again." He flung Pud from him a second time. The boy went staggering before falling heavily.

Bouncing up, Pud lowered his head and charged. With a vicious oath, the man loosened his hold on Summer's dress, drew his gun, and fired.

Summer screamed.

Pud's footsteps faltered and he sank to the ground. There was another shot, and the man staggered back against his horse, his eyes seeking, his mouth open in surprise, a blossom of bright blood covering his chest. Sadie stood in the doorway, both hands holding the six-gun, waiting. . . . The man tried to raise his arm, but the gun slipped between his fingers as he began to vomit blood and collapsed in a heap between his horse's legs.

The frightened horse shied, the rope about the Indian's neck pulled taut and jerked him from the pinto.

Summer ran to Pud. He lay deathly still, and his blood poured out onto the ground. Instantly, Sadie was beside him, tearing open his shirt and stuffing the cloth from her skirt into the gaping wound to stop the bleeding.

"Summer! The Indian!" John Austin's screams reached her consciousness.

The frightened horse was backing away, dragging the Indian by the rope looped about his neck. He was choking to death! She ran to the horse, but he turned as if to bolt. Desperately, she grabbed one of the trailing reins and pulled up, hard, turning the animal around. Frantically, she sought to unwind the rope from the saddlehorn.

The Apache was almost unconscious by the time she loosened the rope. She fell on her knees beside him and worked, frenziedly, crying in her frantic effort to pull the rope through the slip knot so he could breathe. He was bucking and thrashing and she placed her knee on his chest to hold him while her fingers pulled at the heavy rope. At last, it came free, and he lay there sucking in great gulps of air. His eyes had rolled back in his head, and his swollen lips were pulled back over his teeth while his tongue protruded.

"Bring water! Wet his tongue," she commanded John Austin. "Don't let but a trickle go down his throat, or he'll choke."

She hurried to where Sadie bent over Pud.

"Is it bad? Oh, God! Tell me it isn't bad!"

"I don't know. I'm a feared of taking out this wadding. Somebody's comin'. Hurry! Hurry!" she shouted.

Summer only had time to register the sound of the rapidly nearing horses when Bulldog and Raccoon yanked their mounts to a halt and leaped to the ground. The old cowboy's eyes took in the scene at a glance, pausing momentarily at the crumbled heap that was the dead man. Seeing the danger was over, he knelt beside Sadie.

"Here, now, let me see."

"Is he . . . ? Is he . . . ?" Summer whispered on a sobbing breath.

Bulldog gently moved the wad of Sadie's skirt and the wound rapidly filled. He pressed it back and got to his feet.

"Ya done good, Sadie. Ya done real good, girl. Summer, get some cloth to plug the hole and we'll get him onto a bed." He glanced at the dead man. "Who shot him?"

"Sadie," Summer sobbed. "If Sadie hadn't a shot him, I don't know what he would have done."

"Yer a good woman, Sadie. Yer a good, strong woman." A compliment from Bulldog was something to be treasured, but Sadie disregarded it. Her small, pert features were tight, her eyes cold.

"T'was no more than killin' a . . . varmit!"

Summer gazed down at the boy and swallowed hard. A stray breeze ruffled his sandy blond hair, blood from his wound stained the ground where he lay.

"Will he . . . ?" She could hardly bring herself to say the words.

"Ain't nobody a knowin' that," Bulldog said abruptly. "Move gal, we ain't got no time for jawin'."

Pud was moved, with the least amount of jarring possible, to the bunk in the kitchen. The wound in his side was cleaned, and a quantity of whiskey poured into it before clean bandages were wrapped tightly around his body. The bullet had gone into his side and out his back, miraculously missing ribs and vital organs. He remained unconscious, but Bulldog, who seemed to be an authority on gunshot wounds, said that was due to shock and loss of blood. They were to keep him covered, and as soon as possible give him several spoonfuls of honey.

Summer felt a tremendous amount of guilt. Her agony of regret was eased somewhat by Slater when he came. After hearing her tell the story over and over, he finally convinced her that she had no way of knowing the outcome of her effort to help the Indian.

"I blame myself, sweetheart, for not having a man down here. You'll not be left alone again."

Evening came before Pud finally opened his eyes. Jack was sitting beside him.

"Miss Summer . . . ?" he whispered.

"Jist fine. Everybody's jist fine," Jack answered, his voice soft, sure.

"Did he . . . hurt her?" he asked anxiously. "Did . . . he?"

"No, boy. She's fine."

"I ort to of . . . had a gun."

"Wouldn't of helped, son. You did good. Real good. Saved Miss Summer."

"What . . . where is . . . he?"

"Dead. Sadie killed him with that old six-gun they keep for firing a signal."

"Sadie done . . . good."

"Yup. She shore did."

Pud's eyelids fell and the grip of his hands on the covers relaxed. Jack touched his head; it was slightly moist. He leaned back in his chair and breathed a sigh of relief. Now, barring a fever, he believed the kid would be all right.

John Austin was fascinated by the Indian. He had hardly left his side. The man was so weak from starvation and thirst that he hadn't stirred from where he sat leaning against the house. At first, he drank sparingly and ate very little. The boy couldn't understand his lack of appetite, and brought more and more food to tempt his new friend.

"His stomach is so shrunk up he can't take up but a little bit at a time, boy," Bulldog explained. "If'n he filled it up too fast, he'd throw it up."

John Austin sat beside the Apache. He studied everything about him, from his moccasins and fringed leggings to the rag wrapped about his head. After a while, he tried to engage him in conversation, but the Indian ignored him. Finally, he got a stick and drew pictures in the dirt. The Indian was interested, and although the expression on his face didn't change, he watched, and when the boy looked up and smiled, he nodded.

The afternoon passed. The Apache seemed to get his strength back. He stood up several times and flexed his muscles, walked a few steps, but always returned to the spot beside the house and sat down. His pony and the dead man's horse had been turned into the corral. The dead man's body was taken out behind the outbuildings and buried.

When evening came, Slater came and sat down, cross-legged, beside the Indian, and talked to him in the Apache tongue.

"I am the one your people call Tall Man."

The Indian looked at him without a flicker of surprise. "I know of you, Tall Man. I am Bermaga."

"You are welcome here. Stay until you are strong."

John Austin's eyes went from one man to the other. Slater was talking Indian-talk! He had to know how to speak like that. His cunning little mind plotted a course. He wouldn't bother Slater now, but later. . . .

"I will stay, then go soon," Bermaga said in his guttural tone. "My people are in the hills. The white man take our young men, our women. I look for my sister." The flat black eyes made no change. His face might have been hewn from wood.

"Have many of your people been stolen?"

"Two warriors, one woman, since one moon pass."

"These men are my enemies. I do not want them on my land. I watch. I guard our women."

"I do not know how we come here." He bent his head and spread his hair, showing a clot of blood. "I come on pony." He touched his stomach with his hand.

Slater nodded his head thoughtfully. "I will tell my people to give you safe passage back into the hills. Stay, my brother, until you are strong, but when you go, I will send gifts of food to your people, and you must take the horse of the man who did this thing to you."

The Apache's eyes turned toward the corral and the handsome animal standing beside his pony, then swung back to Slater. He held his gaze and nodded.

"Your woman, the one with eyes like the mountain flowers. I owe her my life."

"She only wants your friendship and that of your people," Slater said gravely.

Again the Indian nodded, and looked off into the distant hills.

For over a week, Pud lay in Sadie's bed. For the first few nights, someone sat beside him. Jack had come to stay in the shed until the bunkhouse could be built, and he and the two women took turns by the bedside. Summer insisted on Sadie and Mary taking her bed, and she took the extra bunk in the loft with John Austin. Both women spoiled and coddled Pud shamelessly. Sadie busied herself making puddings and chicken broth for him, and Summer read to him during her spare moments. The boy loved every minute of it, and Jack vowed he was playing possum, deliberately staying abed.

The fact that Slater assured them a tighter guard had been put around the house raised Sadie's spirits. That and the fact that the men considered her somewhat of a heroine, applauding her bravery and teasing her about being afraid to get her riled. She went about almost as cheerful as she had before Travis's visit, and it played on her mind to tell, now, about his threats, but for some reason she held back.

Slater worked hard during the day. His mind was easier about the women, now that Jack, Bulldog or old Raccoon spent their days at the 'little place'. At night, no matter how tired he was, he rode over to spend an hour alone with Summer. They would walk down by the cottonwood tree, and as soon as they were out of sight of the house she would go into his arms.

"My God, you are sweet," he murmured. "You are a thing of beauty, my summertime girl."

She was filled with love for him, and passion, and when his lips touched hers she drew hungrily on them in return. Strength seemed to ebb from her limbs and her heart careened when he whispered passionately:

"I love you . . . I love you. I would say more convincing words if I knew them. You are my life . . . my soul. . . ."

She did not need to reply. She offered him herself, and although his strength was ten times hers, he handled her gently, stroking and kissing her until she felt half-unconscious.

In the weeks that followed, when they felt they would burst with the terrible pressure of wanting each other, they would hide away and come together in the final act of love. Each time, it was as if they died just a little and were reborn together. Summer was wildly excited about the love she shared with Slater, but yet, at the same time, a new peace was born within her. She had given Slater her love unashamedly from the depths of her heart, and now life without him would be intolerable.

It didn't take long for the days to roll into weeks. The Fourth of July came and went without a celebration, due to Pud's slow recovery and the men working sixteen hours a day.

It was the first part of August, a hot afternoon, when Jack rode in to tell the girls that a troop of soldiers had come into the valley and were on their way to the ranch.

Sadie and Summer were in the midst of grinding corn. It had been through the grinder once, but needed to go through once again to be right for bread. Corn-grinding was one of their hardest jobs, and they both wanted to get finished with it. The cornmill was fixed to a post under a shade tree and had two cranks on it. The mill would hold about a peck of corn, and during the grinding the air was full of chaff that stuck to their damp skin. They were not in the mood to greet visitors and told Jack so.

Summer looked down at her arms covered with the fine corn powder.

"They're not coming here?" Her voice was almost a wail of despair.

"Not fer a spell anyhow." Jack's face broke into a grin at their sudden panic.

"Jack, you are the beatenest man I ever did see!" Sadie scolded. "Why in the world didn't you come and let us know sooner?"

"'Cause I didn't know sooner, that's why." He threw his leg over the saddlehorn and watched with amused eyes. "But don't get in no twitch. They'll bivouac down thar a ways, but I 'spect the captain and Jesse will come to supper if'n they have an invite."

"Jesse?" The name came from Sadie unexpectedly.

Jack's eyes narrowed, and for a moment he looked steadily down at the white face until her lips tightened and she tossed her head in irritation.

"Jesse Thurston is with the army."

"Well, why didn't you say so, 'stead of sittin' there like a wart on a hog's ass?" Her green eyes met his squarely without flinching.

During the past weeks, Sadie had become more withdrawn. She was increasingly irritable with Mary, and at times unreasonable. The child was not allowed to play in the yard unless Sadie herself was with her, and her eyes constantly roamed the hills. Summer put it down to reaction and fright after she shot the badman, but it had gone on for weeks now. In the evening, she sat on the porch in brooding silence, staring out over the hills. Once or twice, she had mentioned leaving the ranch when Summer and Slater went to town, but she still worked hard. She was up early in the morning and did her chores and most of Summer's. Although she was pleasant company, Summer suspected she held back a large part of herself and didn't share her secret thoughts with anyone. Sadie's attitude was the one blight on Summer's happiness.

"More'n likely Slater'll have Teresa set up a feed," Jack said. "Ya know, get out all them fancy do-dads. Its 'bout the only time they gets to be used. All you gals will hafta do is get all shined up and come to supper."

"I ain't goin'."

In the silence that followed Sadie's blunt words, Summer wondered once again at the change in her friend.

"Of course you'll come, Sadie. Slater will insist on it, and so will I."

"I ain't goin' and that's that."

"Why not, may I ask?"

"Course you can ask, Summer. It just ain't fer the likes of me to be sittin' down at no fancy supper with no army captain."

166

"Well, I never! Sadie Irene Bratcher, you make me so mad! The likes of you, indeed! If that high-up captain doesn't wish to sit with our friends, he can eat with his men."

"Ah . . . it's sweet of you to say such, Summer. But I ain't got no good dress, and what if'n he'd seen me in the dance hall?" She said the word and tilted her chin to look defiantly at Jack.

"Well, you ladies sort things out. I gotta go find Slater." Jack touched his hand to the brim of his hat and wheeled his horse around.

Sadie stuck with her decision not to go to dinner at the Keep, although she pressed Summer's dress and insisted on helping her with her hair.

"Me and the kids will do just fine, Summer. There ain't no need for old Raccoon to come down. Jack said he wasn't a goin' if'n somebody didn't come to stay, so I says all right, me and old Raccoon will have us a good visit. I know Jack wants to hear all the talk." She cocked her head, the saucy grin that Summer had seen so seldom lately on her face appeared. "You're just goin' to be so pretty, Summer, they ain't goin' to be doin' no talkin'. I reckon Slater's gonna be proud as punch."

Basking in her new-found happiness, Summer radiated a beauty that caused Slater, when he came for her, to pause and stare. His hungry eyes devoured her, drinking in her beauty. His laugh was all pride and tenderness.

"I'm not sure I want Captain Slane and Jesse Thurston to see you. They'll want to steal you away."

"I'd come right back," she said simply, and reached to caress his face with her fingertips. The joy of being in love had smoothed the stern lines from his face, and he looked years younger. The men on the Keep were amazed at his even temper and easy camaraderie.

Slater lifted her carefully and set her sideways in the saddle, then sprang up behind her.

"Wait until we get away from those watching eyes on the porch," he said, with a hint of menace in his voice. "I'm going to kiss you and kiss you."

"You'll muss my hair. It took Sadie ever so long to fix it."

Being careful not to wrinkle her dress or muss her hair, he put his arms around her and turned the horse toward the Keep.

"I don't understand why Sadie was so obstinate about not coming over." Slater had become fond of the spunky girl, but her moodiness was getting to be irritating.

"I'm worried about her," Summer confessed. "Something has happened to make her want to go back to town. She was so happy here, at first. Now, she's worried and I almost think . . . frightened."

"Jack admires her."

Summer's dark head swung around so she could face him. "You mean he's in love with her?" Her eyes sparkled with pleasure. "How do you know?"

"I didn't say, 'in love with her'. I said 'admires her'."

The smile flickered off her face. "Oh, I thought. . . ."

"Sweetheart, it's not for us to worry about. It's for them to know if they want to be together." He kissed the side of her neck. "I don't like having to be so careful not to muss you. You know what I'd really rather be doing."

She laughed softly and turned to kiss him on the lips.

"Later," she whispered.

Captain Kenneth Slane and Jesse Thurston were waiting on the porch with Jack and Bulldog. Slater led Summer forward with a possessive arm about her narrow waist.

"This is Miss Summer Kuykendall, soon to be my wife," he announced. "Captain Slane from Fort Croghan, and you've met Jesse."

The captain's eyes brightened in appreciation and he

clicked his heels together and gave her his most formal bow over the hand she extended.

"I must congratulate you, Slater." His eyes drank in the perfect features; the nose, straight and finely-boned, the dark brows arched away from eyes that were clear and violet against the thick fringe of jet-black lashes. They stared back at him, vaguely smiling. Under his warm gaze, the creamy skin flushed slightly.

Summer held her hand out to Jesse. "Nice to see you again, Mr. Thurston."

"Nice to see you, ma'am." The steely-gray eyes looked from her to Slater as he grasped her hand firmly.

"If you gentlemen will excuse me, I'll help Teresa with the supper."

She escaped into the coolness of the house and stood for a moment trying to still her racing pulses. She wasn't accustomed to being the center of so much male attention. She headed for the kitchen and Teresa. She was fond of the Mexican woman who had lived so many years on the ranch, who had known Slater's mother and cared for her.

This was the first time Jesse had been to McLean's Keep ranch house, and he looked around apprecia-tively. The place was solid, permanent, and he had to admit much more to his liking than the fancy frame house at the Rocking S. He had fully expected to see Sadie Bratcher arrive with Summer. The red-haired woman had been in his thoughts of late, and he needed to see her again. He had to get the shadow of her small, frightened face out of the back of his mind and convince himself she was just a woman he felt pity for because she had almost been one of Travis's victims.

"I'm convinced the robbings and killings are not being done by Indians, especially because a dead Apache is left every time. There's just too many loopholes." Captain Slane paced up and down the veranda as he talked. "They're not very smart, or they would know Apaches never leave their dead if they can possibly take them away."

"I'm sure you're right," Slater said, and told them about the man Sadie shot and about his Indian prisoner. "They're taking those poor devils alive and killing them at the scene of the robberies. That's not all, they're stealing women, too. The Apache that was here had been out looking for his sister."

The captain paused in his pacing. "You say Mrs. Bratcher killed the man that shot the boy?"

"She shore did." Jack spoke up. "Killed him deader than a doornail."

Jesse almost chuckled. Why, that . . . spunky little devil, he thought before he asked:

"What did the man look like?"

"Black beard, black hair, teeth broke off in front, riding a red sorrel, carrying a rifle and a six-gun, but no tucker. Told the women he was lookin' fer Mr. McLean."

Jesse and the captain exchanged glances.

"Did he have a heap of hair, but a bald spot on top?"

"Yup. He shore did."

"That was Black Bealy, a drifter, outlaw. A no-good bastard that would do most anything for a dollar. He hung out for a while in Hamilton, then came out to the Rocking S looking for work. I sent him packin'. Guess he found him a job after all." Jesse's mind was racing to a time he had seen Travis ride away with the man. There was no doubt in Jesse's mind that Travis was the one he was looking for. There didn't seem to be any doubt in the captain's mind either.

"We're making a sortie into the hills, Slater. We'd be glad to have you come along." Captain Slane's sharp eyes had intercepted the glances exchanged between Slater and Jack.

"As much as I'd like to, captain, I'll have to decline. We're cutting out steers, and after that Summer and I are going to town to be married." The hard planes of his face relaxed when he grinned. "If we finish in time, I want to take a jaunt into the hills myself for a few days. I don't like the idea of that bunch coming and going on my land."

"Wal, now, Jack and I can do that," Bulldog snorted. "Take that lit'l gal and go on and get hitched up. Ya ain't gonna be worth a pinch of snuff till you do."

Jesse felt a stab of envy. Slater had found his love and he had the affection and loyalty of his men. Ellen had been so sure Summer would never marry Slater. But even she would have to see the rightness of it. As far as he was concerned, he was glad a nice, gentle girl like Summer had escaped a life of hell with Travis. Each time he caught the intimate glances exchanged between her and Slater, a tide of loneliness swamped him. Behind this, he also felt a stab of regret, so strong that his stout heart almost stopped beating. A love such as they had, one that would result in a family, was not for him. He was committed to Ellen, and after twelve years of constant companionship, he knew her well enough to know she would never share his time or his loyalty with anyone, not even children. Besides, her childbearing years were likely over. And yet . . . the old yearning held a tight grip on his heart. His life, of late, had become strange and empty.

Later, Jesse excused himself, tightened the cinch on his saddle and rode toward the creek.

Chapter Eleven

~~~~

There was a clammy, sick feeling in the pit of Sadie's stomach. It had lain there now for the past weeks, sapping her strength, eating away at her self-esteem, controlling her thoughts to the extent that she realized her actions were often unreasonable. For the first time in her life, she had been happy, felt she could make a permanent place for herself and Mary, something she had not known before or after she married. She knew when she married Harm Bratcher that he was a devil-may-care drifter, a gambler, a man who was content to live from hand to mouth. He was good to her in his own way and his way was an improvement over her pa's. Pa had thought women were good for nothing but to work in the fields and produce more babies to grow up to work in the fields.

The weather was hot and sultry. Not a breath of air circulated to stir the grasses or rouse the drooping leaves on the gigantic oak trees. The silent heat lightning flashed the promise of a storm. Thoughts ran rampant through Sadie's mind as she watched the rolling thunderclouds. At least a storm was out there in the open, and you knew it was there. Not like Travis McLean, lurking in the hills, waiting to kill a baby because he had a powerful lot of hate for its mother.

The excitement she felt on hearing Jesse Thurston had come to the Keep had passed. The brief encounter she had with him down by the swing had been crowded from her mind by other worries, although for days after he was gone, she could recall every single word that passed between them. At night, while she lay beside Mary, she fantasized what it would be like to be loved by such a man . . . to couple with him. He would be demanding, she knew, yet gentle; giving thought to her pleasure as well as his own.

When the rider rode into the yard, Sadie thought it was Jack returning early so Raccoon could go to bed. The man tied his horse to the rail and came to the end of the porch. When the lightning flashed and she saw who it was, she got to her feet and stood on unsteady legs, her heart suddenly galloping in her chest.

Jesse could see only her blurred outline in the dark. He took off his hat and fumbled in his pocket for his tobacco and felt the peppermint stick. He drew it out and moved toward the white blur.

"Evening, ma'am." He held out the slim stick. "I thought your little girl would like another sweet, seeing she's so fond of them."

"Thank you." Sadie accepted the candy, then asked politely, woodenly, "Won't you sit down?"

Raccoon let the chair he had tilted against the wall come down with a thump.

"How you be, Jesse?" He got up and held out his hand.

"Fine, Raccoon, just fine."

Raccoon settled back down in his chair, wide awake now, and curious as to why Jesse would ride over when all the talk was going on at the other place. He didn't have to wait long.

"Jack said you were keeping Mrs. Bratcher and the young'uns company. I thought I'd ride over and give you a break till Jack gets here." Jesse didn't add that he had overheard a certain conversation between Jack and Bulldog.

"Ah . . . well. . . ." Raccoon said, and a silence followed. In that silence, it suddenly occurred to him that Jesse had come to call on Sadie. "That's real good of ya, Jesse. I am a mite stoved up. I'll jist wander on over to the Keep, then, and turn in. It's been good ta see ya again, Jesse."

"It's been good to see you, Raccoon. Looks like those clouds up there are stirring up a storm."

"Yup, sure do. But we need the rain."

Events were happening so fast that Sadie's head was spinning. She wanted Raccoon to go and she wanted him to stay. What she really wanted was for her crazy heart to settle down so she could gather her thoughts into some kind of order before she made a fool of herself.

"Thanks for staying, Raccoon. I told Jack that we'd be all right, but he wouldn't hear of it. I'm making doughnuts tomorrow. Come on over and get a batch."

"Wal, I reckon I'll be here if'n I have to swim fer it. And it looks like I jist might hafta. Its looks like its a rainin' pitchforks up in the hills yonder, and if'n it is, that creek thar will rise quicker'n greased lightning."

Not a word was spoken between the two left on the veranda until after Raccoon had splashed across the creek. Sadie's tongue was stuck to the roof of her mouth and she kept her eyes on the clouds that were rolling in now, and on the brief forks of lightning that were growing brighter.

"Storm coming up," Jesse said. "Acts like a bad one."

A backlash of lightning showed momentarily against the overhead blackness, and in that instant Sadie turned her eyes toward him. He was looking at her with deep intensity. She flushed and caught her lower lip between her teeth to stop its trembling.

"You afraid of storms?" The voice that beat against her eardrums was the well-remembered one from the brief encounter under the cottonwood tree.

"Not of storms. I'm scared of cyclones, though." Her voice, coming out of the tightness in her throat, sounded better than she expected, so she added, "I was in a bad one once."

Lightning now flashed almost continuously, lighting up the sky weirdly. The bulging clouds were lower and the wind had commenced to stir. Sadie felt detached from the approaching storm. The enchantment of being alone with Jesse Thurston consumed her.

"I didn't come just to bring candy." His voice seemed very near. "I wanted to see how you were doing."

"I'm doin' fine."

"Still glad you came here?"

"Yes. Only. . . ."

"Only . . . what?" Jesse asked. She had known he would, drat it.

"Nothin'. I don't know why I said it."

"I like to think of you being here." He said the words quietly, and she peered at him in the darkness, trying to see the expression on his face. At that moment, a dazzling flash lit up the area, followed instantly by utter darkness and a tremendous clap of thunder that left Sadie with her hands over her ears.

"Oh . . . the kids will wake up and be scared!"

Jesse went to the end of the porch and scanned the sky. Without warning, the wind swept through and a few big drops of rain hurled down, plopping on the stone floor. Sadie dashed to pull the flower box, that was full to overflowing with bright marigold blooms, up against the house. Jesse came to help her.

"I'll put my horse in the shed."

"You better hurry up, or you'll get a soakin'."

Jesse took off at a run, and Sadie watched the wind tearing at his hair and remembered to pick up the hat he'd left lying on the chair. Her heart was singing as she went into the house, fumbled in the darkness for the lamp, lit it, and hurried to the mirror over the washstand. After patting her bronze curls in place, she whipped off her soiled apron and stuffed it under the bunk, pulled the curtain that separated her sleeping quarters from the kitchen and quickly glanced around to be certain everything was neat. Trying to keep the smile off her face, she shook down the ashes, filled the stove with kindling to make a quick fire, and set the coffee pot on to boil.

She peered out the window. A blaze of lightning showed Jesse racing toward the house. She flung the door open as he got there. He ducked inside just as the storm struck. The rain came in a tremendous sheet and, driven by the powerful wind, hit the side of the cabin with a force that shook the walls.

Happiness bubbled up in Sadie and she laughed up at Jesse. He laughed with her, and the change in his face was astonishing.

"Yore all wet! I'll get you a towel."

His gray eyes clung to her face. "I'd a been wetter if you hadn't a had the door open." He wiped his face and hair on the towel. At the washstand he washed his hands and used the comb that lay in the comb case attached to the wall. His hair was surprisingly thick and curled back from his forehead in deep waves.

"I'm surprised the young'uns are still asleep after all that racket the thunder made, but they play so hard they're wore out by night-time. You know how kids are, got more ginger than brains." She moved quickly and set two cups on the table after whipping away the cloth that covered the caster set. "That's a fierce storm," she said after another particularly loud clap of thunder. "I was in one once in a covered wagon and, I tell you, there ain't nothin' scarier." Pinching the doughnuts in the warming oven to test their freshness, she wished they were a day newer and said so. "If'n I'd a cooked doughnuts today like I was goin' to, they would be a heap better. The men on this place! Land-a-goshen, how they eat doughnuts. They'd eat 'em if'n they was a month old and the crows had been at 'em."

She set the plate on the table and looked at Jesse. His face was relaxed and his usually grim mouth was slightly parted and tilted at the corners. His eyes . . . how could she have thought they were cold? They were warm and bright and . . . twinkling! Color came slowly up her neck and turned her cheeks crimson. She put her palms against them.

"I'm a talkin' too much!" she wailed.

Jesse put his head back and laughed out loud. The sound startled her. He got to his feet and reached her in one stride. He pulled her hands from her face.

"I was hopin' you wouldn't stop." He released her hands. "Sit down. I'll pour the coffee."

Sadie sank down in the chair and stared straight ahead, her face red, her hands dug deep in her lap. She sat there, feeling an aching torment. Why had she made such a jackass out of herself by rattling on like that?

Jesse was on his second doughnut and she hadn't said another word.

"You're not all talked out, are you?" His voice held a tinge of amusement.

Her green eyes lifted from her cup and dejectedly gazed into his. "Sometimes, my mouth works and my brains don't."

He laughed again. "You still make a mighty good doughnut."

From the laughter in his eyes, she knew he was teasing, and her pounding heart released a flood of happiness that reflected in her brilliant smile.

The thunder rolled and the wind-driven rain lashed the house. A small puddle of water began to form under the door. Sadie placed a rag rug against the door, stepping on it so it would absorb the water. Jesse refilled their cups and it gave her a chance to look at him without his steady gray eyes on her. He was as tall as Slater and slightly heavier. This was the first time she had seen him without a hat. His hair had silver strands at the temples. She suspected he was the type of man whose hair would be completely gray before he was very old.

Jesse sat down and stretched his legs out in front of him.

"Mama . . . pee, pee." Mary came out from behind the curtain. Her bronze curls, so like her mother's, were tangled, her small face flushed with sleep. The nightdress that ended halfway between her knees and ankles was an old, cut-off shift of Sadie's.

Sadie went to her quickly. "Are you sure, Mary?" The whispered words sounded choked in her throat.

"Pee, pee," Mary said again, and Sadie groaned inwardly. Why did she have to say it so loud? She drew her behind the curtain and pulled the chamber pot from beneath the bunk, lifted the child's nightdress, and set her on the rim. As Mary let the water go, the tinkling sound caused Sadie to grind her teeth. Replacing the lid, she slid the pot under the bed, and lifted Mary back on it.

"Go to sleep, baby." She leaned over and kissed her cheek, ignoring the green eyes that stared at her in the semi-darkness, and went back into the kitchen, keeping her own green eyes turned from Jesse.

She had no more than sat down and lifted her cup to her lips, when Mary came out from behind the curtain and made a beeline for Jesse.

"Mary . . . baby . . ."

Mary ran the last few steps and crawled up on Jesse's lap. He lifted her up and cuddled her against him. Sadie reached to take her.

"Let her stay," Jesse said, stroking the curls back from the child's face. "I don't get to hold such a pretty girl very often."

Sadie stood uncertainly beside the chair, and an emotion rose up in her as acute as pain. A longing to be held, cuddled, protected and cherished was so strong in her that she felt weak and sat down, but not before Jesse's sharp eyes caught the look of yearning on her face.

He lifted the child up closer in his arms, liking the feel of the small, warm, trusting little creature clinging to him. God . . . what must it be like to have one of your own?

"Where did you live before you came to Hamilton?" He wanted to hear her voice. It had a light, musical quality to it.

"Just about all over. Georgetown, Austin . . . even Waco." She lifted clear eyes to his. "My . . . husband was like a skeeter. He flitted around a lot."

"Did you love him?"

"No!" Her voice was almost angry, then softened. "No, but he warn't so bad."

"Why did you marry him?"

Sadie shrugged the question off.

"Did you have to marry?" Jesse persisted.

Her nostrils flared, angry lights flashed in the green eyes, and she said through tight lips:

"No, I didn't! If you got to know why, it was cause I ain't built to pull no plow, that's why!" She tossed her head and glared at him. "Why do you do what you do?"

In Jesse's mind a thousand thoughts clashed in riotous confusion. Why did he do what he did? Because he had found a niche for himself, that's why. He had

Ellen, a job, responsibility. It was enough reason for any man.

"I do what I do because I want to." He hadn't meant the words to sound so harsh.

It was as if cold water had been thrown in her face, but her reserve of strength came to her rescue, and she looked straight at him, studied his broad, long eyebrows, his rather long, straight nose, the strength of his jaw and his stern mouth. She watched his hands and saw that they were big, and how ridiculously small her own were in comparison. She knew now that those big hands would never hold her, reach out to her in tenderness. She might as well "throw in the cards", as Harm used to say.

"Don't get yore back up, Mr. Thurston, I ain't askin' you nothin'!" she said scathingly.

A bolt of lightning flashed, even as she spoke, bringing the room to brilliant brightness. Long before the lightning died, the house was filled with a stunning crash of thunder. It was still echoing when another bolt rent the air outside, and in its deathly light Sadie's face showed stark fear. A fierce gust of wind struck the house, sending sheets of rain against the windows.

"My name's Jesse." The quiet face studied her, as his hand continued stroking Mary's hair.

Minutes passed. The storm raged outside, and Sadie put more rugs by the doors to keep the water out. She lit a candle and went into Summer's room. Water was coming in the window and under the door. She laid rags on the window sill and more rugs in front of the door.

Jesse was standing when she went back into the kitchen.

"Little gal's sleepin'." He held the child as if it was the most natural thing in the world for him to do, and his smile made her heart lurch. Her voice stuck and it took effort to bring it out matter-of-factly.

"I'll put her to bed."

"Show me and I'll do it."

She pulled the curtain back and Jesse lowered the sleeping child to the bunk. He pulled the quilt up over her and stood looking down at her for a moment. A picture of the big four-poster bed with its thick mattress and soft down pillows in his room at the Rocking S flashed through his mind. His quick glance took in two dresses hanging on the wall and a well-worn valise beneath them.

Sadie saw the look on his face and yanked the curtain shut.

"You don't have to be a feelin' sorry for me!"

"You jump right in with both feet, don't you, Sadie?" His eyes held hers for several seconds, and some of their hardness left. Her heart kept thumping in her neck. Jesse's mouth twitched, broke into a slow, uneven smile. He cupped one big hand under Sadie's chin, gave it a shake and said, "You didn't get that red hair for nothing."

His low, chuckling voice surrounded her and warmed her. Entranced, she stared at the transformation of the stern-faced man before turning away to hide her confusion.

She struggled for something to say. "If John Austin can sleep through this storm, he could sleep through a stampede."

"There'll be no crossing that creek tonight. The water must be halfway up to the house by now. They won't worry about you and the young'uns. They'll know I'm here. Let's get those rugs wrung out and put back . . . or better yet, come hold the lamp and I'll wring the rugs."

Later, after they had talked of Summer and Slater's approaching marriage, Jesse asked her if she planned to stay on here in the cabin.

"I . . . don't think so. I can't do enough to earn my keep."

"You could marry. Has anybody come courtin'?"

182

"I ain't takin' no man to take care of me if'n there's any way a'tall I can take care of Mary and myself."

"Has Slater said anything about you leaving?"

"No! They ain't did nothin' like that. They're the best folks I ever knowed. I just can't stay on here, and I don't want to talk about it no more. You ask an all-fired lot of questions."

A long quiet slipped past following her outburst. Sadie leaned her head against the high back of the rocker. There was almost a domestic tranquility between them. Finally, after what seemed an eternity, his hushed voice came to her ear.

"It took a right smart amount of spunk to shoot that man."

Sadie's head turned and her chin raised. "He warn't no man . . . a buzzard's what he was."

"Did Travis bother you when he came to the house?"

In spite of herself, she gave a shudder of revulsion. "No!"

"Did he catch you away from Summer and threaten you?"

Wide, frightened eyes swung back to him, and she pressed her lips tightly together.

"Why are you askin' me? You wouldn't believe me no more than anybody else if'n I told you."

"I'd believe you, Sadie. I know Travis. I know what he uses to get what he wants. He blamed you for the beating he got, didn't he? He had to have revenge, and because he isn't man enough to stand up to me, he came to you."

"Ain't nothin' you can do."

"Tell me and let me decide."

He said it so kindly, so sincerely. His steel-gray eyes between the sun-bleached lashes watched every expression that flicked across her face. She wanted to tell him, wanted to unload the heavy burden of fear that had been eating away at her. The picture of Ellen smiling up at Jesse, her hand constantly on his arm and the vision of him tenderly lifting her into the buggy as if she were made of china, caused her to squirm. And because she was suddenly disillusioned with him, rage bubbled up inside her like a fountain.

"Yore . . . lady wouldn't take it kindly if'n you took my side against her darlin' boy! You saw what she thought of the likes of me. She'd not ever let you help me, so why are you askin'? I ain't got no one to depend on but myself, and I'll tell you, Mr. Jesse Thurston, 'n you can tell that fancy woman of yores, if that low-down polecat son of hers comes near me or my baby, I'll gun him, that's what I'll do. I'd think no more of it than if'n he was a rattler, 'cause that's just what he is, a belly-crawlin' snake. Come to think on it, he's lower than a belly-crawlin' snake, 'cause a snake's got other things to do 'sides fornicatin' and a threatenin' to kill little babies. He's a buzzard, that's what he is!" Tears gushed into the wide green eyes. "I just wish he would come back, I'd take that gun and I'd give that fancy woman somethin' to look down on me for . . . and that ain't all of it, neither. I'd . . . oh, you'd not help me. You ain't nothing . . . you're . . . you're as thick with her as eight in a bed! Her lap dog's what you are!" She choked on a mouthful of words and tears blinded her.

Suddenly, gentle hands lifted her from the chair and strong arms drew her against a warm, comforting chest. Her face found refuge in the hollow beneath his chin, and the sheer luxury of being held, consoled, caused the floodgates to break, and she cried as she had not done since she was a small child and her mother had died.

When it seemed she had cried herself dry, she found herself cuddled in his lap. He sat in the big chair and he was smoothing the bronze curls back from her face as he had done with Mary. The place where her face was pressed against his throat was wet with her tears, and although she wanted to wipe her nose and dry her eyes she also wanted to stay nestled against him for just a moment longer. The sheer heaven of it made her feel as weak as a kitten, but never in her whole life had she felt so safe, so at peace.

Jesse's voice against her ear roused her.

"Feel better?"

She bent her head almost to her knees so she could wipe her face on her skirt and made a move to get up, but his arms refused to release her. He pressed her head down on his shoulder.

"Use my shirt. It isn't often I get to hold such a pretty girl and . . ." She could feel the chuckle vibrate in his chest. "I don't know if I ever saw a prettier one."

She was almost lightheaded. It was as if her tears had washed away her strength. Closing her eyes tightly, she reveled in the smell of his shirt, the tobacco smell of his breath, the steady beating of his heart against hers.

"I don't know what got into me. I ain't much given to bawlin'. I'm sorry I said them things 'bout you and Mrs. McLean. It ain't no business of mine." The words were muffled against his chest. It was heaven being so close to him, his hand stroking her head. She prayed silently: Don't stop. Please don't stop, just yet.

"It's all right. I know what's said about me and Ellen."

"I still don't have no right."

"I want to know about you, Sadie." His voice was low, gentle. "I want to know all about you. We're much alike, I think."

"There ain't nothing much to tell 'bout me, Jesse." She felt as if she had known him forever.

"Tell me," he said and leaned his cheek against the top of her head. His hand traveled down her back. He could feel every rib, every vertebra in her small body, yet her hips were well rounded and the breasts pressed tightly to his chest were full and warm and tempting.

The storm outside had moved away, leaving only a

steady downpour of rain. Inside the cabin, in the glow made by the flickering lamp, Sadie nestled in the arms of the big, frightening, sometimes violent man, and related the details of her struggle to survive from the time she was old enough to hoe cotton and carry water to the day she rode away from the dirt farm on a mule behind Harm Bratcher.

"He didn't really want me, 'cept for . . . you know. He wanted to play cards and get drunk. Mary was born in a wagon outside of Waco. He never ever really looked at her, poor little mite." She talked on, leaving nothing out. "I never went to bed with any men." She tilted her head back so she could see his face. "After Harm was killed, I worked hard to keep me and Mary. I ain't any of them things Travis said. I ain't a whore." There was pleading to be believed in her voice.

"I know that." He cupped her head with his hand and pressed her closer. "Tell me about Travis."

Halfway through the telling, she commenced to tremble and her voice started to break.

"And when he said that . . . about shootin' Mary . . . I know he'd do it, but Summer wouldn't of believed it. She thought he was nice and she was put out at Slater because he was mad 'bout him comin' here. I thought about tellin' Jack, but if'n Jack had rode out there he'd just a got killed, then sure 'nuff Travis would have hunted me down and done somethin' bad to the baby." She paused to still her trembling lips. "I don't know why I told you, you can't do nothin' if you wanted to, 'cause of Mrs. McLean. And I ain't blamin' you. Just a tellin' him to leave me be would be like puttin' a torch to a dry prairie. He'd come for me sure."

"I know that, Sadie. I won't do anything to put you and Mary in more danger."

Jesse sat quietly. The rage he had felt when she told him of Travis's threats had simmered down to calm planning. He would have to be away from her to think clearly. Holding her was too distracting. He could feel the warmth of her body through her thin dress and the steady beating of her heart against his. Abruptly, he knew why she had haunted his thoughts, drifting in and out of them like a strange, sweet dream. In his heart he had known that he could not rest until he had seen her again, held her in his arms like this, comforted her, protected her. He was conscious of a desire to face Travis, force him to draw, and kill him. Yet . . . he knew he couldn't do it, no matter how badly Travis needed killing. Her son was the center of Ellen's life. She doted on him. No, he couldn't kill him if there was any other way.

A half-hour passed while his hands stroked and caressed the woman in his arms and his mind groped for answers.

Sadie turned her head and looked full at him.

"I ain't askin' you to do anything. I ain't a puttin' my troubles off on you. I just feel better for the tellin' about it. I ain't told nobody else."

He felt indescribably moved at the calm way she said that, and it showed in his face. Her hand stroked his arm with a little comforting gesture. He was acutely aware of her slim figure against him, of the warm flush of her skin, the soft sweetness of her mouth. It was like coming home. This woman and her child were like coming home! His eyes wandered over her upturned face, then found and held hers. They were full of concern now, for him. His arms tightened and slowly he lowered his lips, giving her the chance to turn away if she didn't want his kiss.

Sadie lifted her face to meet his, trembling lips slackened and parted as his mouth possessed hers. Happiness engulfed her like a tidal wave engulfing the shore, and any doubt of his response to her was dispelled by the shaking of his body against hers, and the insistent pressure of his mouth, which demanded and received a response she had never believed herself capable of giving. Clasped tightly to him, as if he would draw her into himself, Sadie felt the thunderous beating of his heart and heard his ragged breathing in her ear.

Almost instantly, he was calm again. She stared into his eyes, glorying in the tender regard she saw there. Happiness sang out like a bird in her heart, and she lifted her hand to stroke his cheek. His brow furrowed. She gently rubbed her fingers across the harsh lines of his frown, smoothing it away. His eyes searched her face. Their gaze warmed and played within the depths of each other's eyes.

At last, his lips came to rest on her forehead and he kissed her as if she were a child and tucked her face once again into the curve of his neck. His voice, when it came, was firm.

"You must stay here for a while. You and Mary will be safe here. I'm going south with the army troop for a few days, maybe more than a few days, but when I get back we'll plan what we're going to do." When she shook her head in protest, he stilled it with his hand. "Trust me. I'll speak to Slater. He'll see that you're not left alone."

"No. Summer is gettin' married. This is her happiest time. She won't want to go away and leave me if she knows. 'Sides, I still don't think they'd believe it."

"Slater will believe it, and so will Jack. Stay here and I'll figure out something. You'll be safe here until I get back."

Sadie remained still. Reality was coming back. There was a long silence before she spoke.

"You won't come back." Her voice held a queerly resigned, almost laconic note. "You won't come back, 'cause Mrs. McLean won't let you. She's pretty and rich and has nice manners. I don't blame you, Jesse, for wantin' to be with her." The eyes she lifted to his were those of some stricken little animal caught in a trap and surrendering to its fate. "Mrs. McLean won't let you come back," she repeated. "She'll . . . not ever let you go."

"We'll not talk of Ellen now. Close your eyes and get some sleep. It'll be dawn in a couple of hours, and I suspect Jack will find a way to cross the creek." He held his palm against her cheek. "You're awfully pretty, Sadie." He smiled gently. "Awfully pretty and . . . sweet."

At McLean's Keep, the wind tortured the heavy branches of the oak trees and hurled the rain against the glass window panes. The two figures that lay pressed closely together in Slater's bed were unmindful of the raging storm.

Summer sighed contentedly and kissed the side of Slater's neck.

"This is a wonderful soft bed," she murmured drowsily. Her hand searched for his face in the dark, touched his lips before slipping about his neck as he leaned over her.

"I thought you were asleep, you've been so still," he whispered, his lips playing on hers.

"I don't want to waste time sleeping," she replied softly, wistfully. "Dawn comes so quickly."

"Never thought I'd be grateful to the creek. Think I'll name it Witch's Creek, for this beautiful witch in my arms."

She drew him to her and closed her eyes in ecstasy as his kisses came upon her mouth, warm, devouring, fierce with love and passion, then traveled lower to spread their heat over her quivering breasts, which thrust forward in eager anticipation.

Passion spread in the heat of their touch. His caresses were searching, and Summer opened her legs to his questing hand, rolling her head in bliss. His wandering fingers brought soft, breathless whimpers of trembling joy. She felt the hard, manly boldness of him against her thigh, and then the flame was within her, consuming, searing, setting fire to every nerve, flaming, filling her with an almost unbearable pleasure. His heart beat wildly against her naked breast, and beneath her hands the hard muscles of his back tensed and flexed. She heard harsh breathing in her ear, and hoarse, whispered words of love. Then they were riding high on the surging, swelling tide of rapture.

The wind howled and the rain pounded against the windows, but in the aftermath of their own storm, Summer and Slater lay peacefully content, legs entwined, slender fingers gently interlaced in a knot of love. Slater's lips nibbled at the soft flesh of her shoulder, paused to take her earlobe into his mouth, then sucked gently at the flesh of her slender neck.

Summer wiggled away, laughing softly. "You'll make a mark for all to see!"

"They'll wish they were me."

"Slater, darling." The corners of her mouth curved softly. "I love you."

Slater smoothed her tumbled hair and nuzzled his face into its fragrant mass, breathing in the sweet scent of her.

"I think I've loved you forever."

Summer giggled and nestled closer. "You haven't known me forever." Then, suddenly serious, she murmured, "You're sure no one will know I spent the night in your bed?" Her hand caressed the ridge of scars on his chest before moving to the ones under his arm and over his rib cage.

Slater leaned on an elbow. "Don't worry, love. Jack and Bulldog went to the bunkhouse and the captain brought his men up to the shed by the blacksmith. Raccoon is with Sadie and I suspect Jesse is, too. He was asking questions about Sadie. Actually, one question, but that was a lot for Jesse." He laughed and pressed kisses on her face. "Don't feel guilty, sweetheart. Love me. Just love me."

His lips pressed hers gently, tenderly, and Summer gave a quick, warm answer, returning fleeting kisses. All the qualms she had expected, all the quirks of gnawing guilt she had imagined would torment her, were not there. She had given herself out of wedlock, had sinned in the sight of God, and yet there was a strange sense of rightness being here in his arms, as if here was where she was meant to be. Then contentment prodded her mind along a different path. She laughed teasingly, lightly nibbling the lobe of his ear, touching it with her tongue.

"The night won't be over for a couple more hours, my sweet love."

Chapter Twelve

The last thing Slater saw as he put his heels to the tall black gelding and rode toward the hills was Summer standing in the yard waving to him. A half-mile from the house, he slowed the horse to a canter, then to a walk.

The cattle had all been moved into the lower pastures along the creek, and there wasn't too much to do now except guard the herd until roundup and branding time. McLean's Keep and other ranches in the area, including the Rocking S, made one big drive each fall up the Chisholm Trail, across Indian Territory to the rails in Kansas. Each ranch furnished men according to the size of their herd. Slater had made the trip many times, but he wouldn't be going this year.

His face gentled when he thought of the reason why he wouldn't be making the trip. Summer. Her name slipped unnoticed from his lips, and he gave himself up to his favorite pastime—daydreaming about her. Summer, soft and yielding; Summer, lovely and proud across the table; Summer, beautiful and tempting in a faded dress with her arms buried deep in soapsuds. He was ever conscious of her. She could not guess the depth of his feeling for her or how his life had changed and become suddenly precious to him. His pa would have loved her! He wished Sam could know there would be another generation of McLeans at the Keep.

Slater had given himself three days to scout the hills surrounding his land. He had moved his lookouts in to watch the herd and the buildings, posted a guard at the entrance to the valley, and assigned several men, including Jack, to guard the "little place".

It was late afternoon. He had made a big circle and now pointed Estrella toward the boundary line camp where Sam had been killed. Drawing up at the crest of a low hill, he scanned his back trail. He sat his horse for a moment, studying the terrain before and behind him with a careful eye. There was nothing on the trail, no dust, no movement. It was growing late and the sun was already behind the mountain. The softness of the hill evening was settling over the densely-wooded trail, and the air was cooler.

The big horse, restless for home, moved off of his own volition, and Slater let him go. Taking his time, he worked his way around a boulder. A wild turkey gobbled and scurried into the underbrush, then the night was silent, carrying no sound except for Estrella's hoofs. Slater drew cool air deep into his lungs, air touched with the faint scent of sage; it was as refreshing as a drink of cool spring water.

Suddenly, a distant sound, foreign to the evening, caught his ears; he drew up sharply against the black clump of mesquite, listening, his hand on the butt of his gun.

Each boulder, pine or clump of brush was a spot of darkness. The floor of the hillside was covered with a thick cushion of pine needles and profuse stars blos-

somed in the clear field of sky overhead. Slater waited
patiently. Each rock, each tree, each shrub was studied
with particular care, making allowance for the darkness, contours, distances, but there was no further
sound. Slowly, his hand came away from the butt of his
gun, and the horse walked on.

After several minutes of slow progress, the gelding's
ears began to twitch, then stood straight. At that
instant, Slater heard the click of metal, saw the flicker
of a darker shadow among the mesquite clumps. He
threw himself flat along the horse's neck just as he was
struck a wicked blow on the shoulder. Searing pain tore
through him and he grabbed wildly at the saddlehorn
and clutched it with a desperate grip. He heard the
other shot as it struck him, and he seemed to go
tumbling forward, over and over, round and round in
the velvety darkness. His fingers clung to the one real
thing in his tilting world: the saddlehorn. Estrella was
running smoothly. With all his will, he held on, through
the heaving, roaring blackness. Behind him, there was
another sharp, splitting crack. The shot tore the hat
from his head. Silence, except for the sound of Estrella's hoofs on the pine needles and his own hoarse
breathing.

It seemed an eternity before he pulled the horse up.
Fighting to stay conscious, he relaxed the death grip he
had on the saddlehorn, kicked his feet from the
stirrups, and slid to the ground. He crawled into the
underbrush. His last thought was of Summer. I can't
die . . . I can't leave her.

He fought his way back to consciousness in broad
daylight. He lay in a nest of dried grass, flat on his back,
half under a bush. The sky beyond was blue and
spotted with fluffy clouds. He lay very still, afraid to
move, trying to locate where he was. He could hear
Estrella cropping grass nearby, and he moved his head
carefully until his eyes found him.

Memory returned. Memory of shots out of the

darkness. He cursed himself for a stupid fool. He had
let himself be bushwacked! Yet . . . how could that be?
He scowled. Who had known he would be on the trail?
It was no accidental meeting. The place had been
carefully chosen, and the dry-gulcher there well ahead
of him. The trail he had used was well-known to his
own men, but to few others.

Now the pain made itself felt. It was his left shoulder.
Two bullets had hit him, one had gone through his
shoulder below the collarbone and the other skidded
off his hip-bone, ripping the fleshy part of his side.
Son-of-a-bitch, he cursed. An inch or two and either
one would've killed him. He rolled over carefully, using
his right hand to push himself up into a sitting position.
He looked around, turning his head carefully on his stiff
neck.

He wasn't far from the place he had planned to
camp. He must have had some grip on that saddlehorn.
Undoubtedly, he had lost a lot of blood, his thoughts
were hazy and he couldn't bring his eyes to focus clearly
on any object. He lay back and stared up at the sky.

Knowing he was hunted quarry prompted him to
move. He sat up again, let the world stop swaying, then
struggled to his feet and staggered to the horse. He
tried to mount, but his weakness was too great, and he
went sprawling on the ground. Bright lights flashed
before his eyes, his head seemed to explode, and he
sunk down into a pit of blackness.

It was sunset when his eyes opened again. The air
was cool and a slight breeze was blowing. He lay there
in the grass. His shoulder was on fire and his head
pounded. A long time later, his right hand searched the
grass beside him for the canteen. His thirst seemed
without end, and he remembered from somewhere that
thirst usually accompanied a heavy loss of blood.
Thank God he was near the stream.

The pain in his head was agonizing, and his shoulder
burned like fire. He tried to decide what to do. He'd

not make it into the saddle, but he had to have food, water. His stomach rumbled and he dug into his saddlebag for biscuits and meat and ate hungrily. While untying his blanket, his mind dully remembered that this was the second night he had been out . . . or was it the third? He had to get his strength back and get on the horse. Summer would be worried.

It was night. He settled himself in the grass and pulled the blanket around him. His mind told him that he must do something about his shoulder before the fever that he knew was coming set in. He crawled to the stream, made a poultice out of the wet biscuits, refilled his canteen and crawled back to the blanket. His head throbbed with slow, heavy throbs, his shoulder felt as if someone had put a torch to it. He kept flexing his fingers, turning his stiff neck, afraid of stiffness, knowing that if he was found by the bushwacker, he wouldn't have a chance if he couldn't use his gun.

He awoke with a start and glanced quickly at the sun. He had slept well into the day. His face was hot and his mouth dry. After drinking deeply from the canteen, he ate beef jerky, deciding to leave the biscuits for another poultice. Gathering the blanket around him, he lay back in the warm sun.

Night came while he slept. He awoke in complete darkness, shaking with a chill despite the blanket. He crawled to the stream, drank, changed the poultice and drank again. The water was cold and went down his throat like intoxicating wine, giving him strength and new life. After he finished drinking, he lay wrapped in the blanket, his head throbbed and his shoulder and side tortured him with every beat of his heart. Drifting in and out of sleep, the day passed and night came again. The sun was directly over the tree tops when he awoke. He dozed, and when he next opened his eyes it was dusk.

His mind told him that he must move, but his muscles refused to obey. God, he was weak! He had to get on the horse . . . Summer would think he was dead. The days had floated by, he couldn't remember how many.

Getting first to his knees, then to his feet, he looked around for Estrella. He was not in sight, and Slater felt a quick prick of alarm. He whistled and waited. Whistled again. Relief fell over him like a cloak when he heard the soft nicker and the horse came toward him.

"Good boy! God, you're a good horse!" Slater hung his right arm about the horse's neck and leaned on him while his heart pounded in his head. It seemed hours before he got the strength to thrust his boot into the stirrup, but mounting was easier than he thought it would be.

Night comes quickly to the hills, and it was dark when he touched his heels to the horse and said: "Let's go home."

He sat in the saddle like a drunken man. Exhausted, almost sick to his stomach from the effort of climbing on the horse. His head felt heavy and part of his mind dwelled on Summer. The other part dwelled on the thought of what had been done to him and the driving urge to fight back, to slash back, to kill . . .

Slater knew himself well, and the anger he was feeling gave him strength. He was actually a man of violent and explosive temper, and his usual quietness was a coverup for what lay under the surface. Seldom did he lose control, but occasionally, under exceptional strain, he had given way to outbursts of fury.

Unfortunately, the shortest route back to the ranch would mean he would travel the boundary line for several miles. In his present condition, he realized he wasn't worth much, but on the other hand there was not much of a chance of anyone riding by this way at this time of night. He checked his weapon to be sure he was prepared to defend himself. The next thing he had to do was stay in the saddle. He thanked God again for a good horse.

Reaching the lower fork of the creek, he waded the horse through the stream and up the bank. He was shaking with pain and fury, no longer conscious of the cool night because the fever was on him again. A steady beat of agony pounded in his wounds.

Suddenly, Estrella's ears came up. Instinct snapped Slater to awareness, his inborn will to survive alerting him to danger. He drew up, listening. He heard nothing, but the ears of his horse told him there was something. He moved only a few feet and pulled up again. It was then he smelled the woodsmoke. He urged the horse along a flat boulder. At the end of the boulder, which was at least twenty feet high, Slater could see that it overlapped another boulder of equal size and shape. Between the two was a passageway that would easily be overlooked if not for the pause beside the boulder. The path was large enough for a horse and rider to pass through.

He could hear voices. One sounded strangely familiar. He moved the horse into the passage and the voice that reached his ears was unmistakable. Travis.

"What's the matter, kid? Don't you have a stomach for real sport?"

"It ain't that, Mr. McLean, but . . . ain't ya already done a'nuff to 'er?"

"There's never enough, kid. Never enough you can do to a woman. And an Indian woman ain't worth the sole on my boot. Now, you're going to have to learn that, if you're going to join up with me. Men, real men, got to take their pleasure where they can get it. You're not one of those that like men, are you?"

"Well . . . no, Mr. McLean, but . . . " The young voice was hoarse, strained.

"Then what are you balking for? Come on, get on her. Or can't you get it up no more?" Travis's voice was scornful.

"I already been on her once . . ."

"Once! Hell, boy," he said the word insultingly, "I

been on her three times and I'll be on her three more. Come on, now. I want to see you hump her."

"I . . . don't think I can, Mr. McLean. I think she's swooned or . . . dead."

"She's not dead. Only playing possum. Here, I'll show you."

An agonizing wail of pain jarred the stillness of the night, followed by convulsive laughter.

Something inside Slater welled up and burst. Wild with fury and pain, he dropped his hand to his gun and put his heels to Estrella. The horse leaped around the boulder, through the narrow passageway and into the firelight.

A naked Indian girl lay staked out, her arms above her head, her legs spread; her anguish and the marks of recent torment were obvious.

Slater's blazing eyes took in the scene in a second.

"My God, Travis! Have you gone mad?" He swayed in the saddle.

Travis smiled. The malevolent look on his face caused frenzied rage to explode in Slater's head. He lifted his six-gun as another explosion in his head sent him tumbling off the horse and into oblivion.

When he came to, his mind was a blur. He lay a few feet from the Indian girl, his feet bound and his hands tied behind him. The agonizing pain in his shoulder made him wish for pain-free oblivion. His head felt as if all the blood in his body was there, pulsing, throbbing, protesting.

Three men sat beside the campfire. Travis, a young kid with a fuzz of a beard on his face, and Armando, the Mexican from his own ranch. It was he who had knocked him from the saddle and it was he who had ambushed him. The bastard must have heard him tell Jack or Bulldog where he was going and rode out and waited for him.

Now Slater realized the gravity of his situation. They would never let him live. He would die without having made Summer his wife. And the ranch would go to the next living McLean, which would be Travis. He gritted his teeth in frustration.

"How'd you like to be the ramrod at McLean's Keep, Armando?" Travis was saying. "Soon as this bastard is dead, the ranch will come to me. You know what that'll make me? The largest landholder in the state of Texas. My old man had it fixed so I won't get the Rockin' S for another year, but I can take the Keep any time I want to. We can just ride in and take over. The soldiers are over east. Jesse's with them. You can forget about that son-of-a-bitch. The first time I set eyes on him, I'm going to gun him down. He's been a fly in my craw long enough. Mama'll just have to find herself another boy!" He threw back his head and laughed. "What we ought to do is ride down and get Bushy Red and the boys . . . they ought to be in on this. There's quite a few men at the Keep. If we kill off the stubborn ones, the rest will fall in line as soon as they see who has hold of the handle. There's two split-tails at the ranch. A black-headed one that thinks she's so nice her shit don't stink." The men snickered. "And a red-headed bitch I got a score to settle with. Men," Travis announced proudly, "we'll have us some nice women to diddle with."

Slater squirmed, his guts tied in knots. Travis was insane, there was no doubt about it. And here he lay, trussed up like a hog about to be roasted!

Travis had seen the movement as Slater writhed in anguish. Taking a stick, he flipped a glowing coal from the campfire into one palm of the hands tied behind Slater's back. Slater felt the pain shoot through him, smelled the burning of his own flesh, but he clamped his teeth shut and not a sound escaped his lips. The only movement he made was the jerking of his body as he cast the coal from his hand.

Travis came to stand over him and Slater looked up at him with hate-filled eyes. The pleasant, boyish grin was still on his face as he drew his foot back and kicked Slater in the ribs. The breath went out of him, and he was barely aware when the other booted foot reached over and nosed its way between his bound arms. Shoving him over to the fire with his other foot, Travis held the bound hands over the flames.

The sound that was torn from Slater's lips was like something he had never heard. He wasn't even aware that it was his own voice. The searing, burning flesh on his hands was the only thing in the world. He heard only a few words before he fainted. They came from the boy.

"Mr. McLean . . . don't!"

He could hear Travis's voice as he drifted in and out of consciousness.

"Got to be a man, Lonnie. There's no room in my outfit for a chicken-livered boy. Get the horses, Armando, and try and catch that black of Slater's. Can't have him going back to the Keep before we get there. It'll take us two or three days to get Bushy Red and the men."

Slater faded away again, but when he came back he knew he had but a few minutes to live. Armando having failed to trap Estrella, held the other horses. Travis walked over and poured the remains of the coffee on the fire. It sizzled, flickered and went out.

"I'm going to let you kill 'em, Lonnie. It's got to be done. You been holding back, boy. It's time you jumped in and got your feet wet. First time's a little scary, but after that, there ain't no more to it than crookin' your finger." Travis mounted his horse, and the spirited animal danced around in circles. The voice came from farther away when he spoke again. "Shoot 'em, Lonnie. Shoot 'em and come on."

The boy came to stand over him, and Slater looked squarely into his eyes, determined the boy would remember that stare until his dying day. The boy had a pleading look on his face and his lips trembled. Slater continued to stare.

"Are you going to kill him . . . or look him to death?" Travis taunted.

The boy made a movement with his mouth, then put the gun down beside Slater's head and fired into the ground. He raised up slowly, his eyes begging. Slater's body had jumped at the sound of the explosion and lay still.

"Now the girl."

"I think she's already dead, Mr. McLean. She ain't moved . . . or nothin'."

"Well, shoot her and make sure."

The sound of the second shot rebounded between the boulders. Lonnie hurried to his horse. Travis's voice continued, laughing, teasing.

"Now, don't you go and get sick. You done it, boy. I'll make a man of you yet."

In spite of the searing pain, Slater felt such relief that weak tears filled his eyes. He was alive! He would see Summer again! He didn't know if the boy had killed the girl, but guessed that if she was dead Travis had killed her with his torture. He lay still, not daring to move lest they come back. After a while, he began to shake, his teeth chattered so that at first he wasn't sure if they were making the noise he heard. Luckily, he was lying on his right side and not on his wounded shoulder. He tried to edge closer to the warm ashes of the fire, seeking some relief from the cold that penetrated his bones and the scorched flesh of his hands. The effort was too much. He sank into a black pit where it seemed demons, howling with glee, played on his body with torches and pitchforks.

When Slater opened his eyes, he was staring into a campfire. His brain was too numbed to know or care where he was. Fog drifted before his eyes and his body felt suspended in a vacuum. He felt no pain and moved his arms, thinking he might be dead. At the end of each of his arms was a bundle of cloth, and he stupidly wondered where his hands were. He was covered and he was not cold. Curious now, his eyes searched. Three Indians sat cross-legged beside the fire. One of them came to him, knelt down.

"Tall Man. It is I, Bermaga."

Slater's mind cleared for a moment. "The girl," he croaked.

"My sister. She will live."

Slater closed his eyes in relief, opened them again. The Apache was still there.

"How?" It was one word, but it was enough.

"We see horse. Know it is horse of Tall Man. We follow."

"Thank God!"

Slater knew they had given him a pain-killing drug. Apaches were masters at living off the land, knowing the effects of the leaves and the berries, the roots and the dried pods on the bushes. With supreme effort, he forced himself to stay awake.

"Bad white men come to take woman who helped you." Slater thanked God, again, for his knowledge of the Apache language. "You must go. Tell men to keep watch for Mexican who betrayed us. They will know of whom you speak. Take my horse and go swiftly. Two days before they come."

Bermaga nodded gravely, and turned to speak rapidly to the other warriors. They got swiftly to their feet and began scurrying around. It was all too much for Slater to understand. He sank back and let the darkness envelop him.

Chapter Thirteen

Summer stood on the porch and waited for the approaching buggy to reach the yard. She didn't smile. She would rather Ellen had come to visit at another time. Slater had been gone three days longer than he'd said he would be, and the acute fear that something had happened to him had her nerves strung almost to the breaking point.

The drovers who escorted the buggy swung off toward the corrals, and the handsome animal pulling the buggy came on to halt beside the rail that protected Summer's flower beds. An older man, with iron-gray hair, tied the reins to a post before going back to help Ellen down.

"Thank you, Tom. You've been ever so nice to drive me. Hello, Summer. Are you surprised to see me? I couldn't stand that ranch another day. Jesse has gone trekking off with the army and Travis is heaven knows where. He'd rather be out in the line shacks with the drovers than at home with his mother." Her trilling laughter was soft, feminine. "So I decided to call on you, the next-dearest person to me in the whole world."

"It was nice of you to make that long, hot ride to see me, Ellen. Won't you come in?" Summer tried to put enthusiasm into her welcome.

"Yes, it was a long, dusty ride," Ellen said, taking off her hat, "but knowing you'd be at the end of it made it worthwhile."

Summer took her hat and small bag and opened the door leading into her bedroom. Sadie had screeched when she saw who was coming. She grabbed Mary and went out to the bunkhouse to wait for Jack, who was sending men out to look for Slater.

"I've come to take you home with me. Please, don't say no! I thought of it just last night. I thought: If I don't go over to the Keep and bring you home with me, the summer will be gone. Time passes so quickly. Seems only a week ago I drove over to see your mother." She patted her high-piled hair in place and dabbed daintily at the moisture on her face with a lace-edged handkerchief.

"Let me get you a cool drink, Ellen. Or would you rather have a glass of cold buttermilk?"

"Buttermilk sounds marvelous, dear, but don't fuss. I'm just so happy to be here with you. We can have a nice chat. Where is that little brother of yours?"

"He spends most of his time with Jack and Pud when Slater isn't here. He's learned a lot this summer. For the first time in his life, I'm not afraid to take my eyes off him."

"That's nice."

Ellen's lips smiled sweetly, but her eyes didn't match her lips. They were busy taking in everything about Summer, from the top of her shiny black hair to the soles of her high-laced shoes. The girl had changed, matured, become a woman in every sense of the word. Lord, she was in love! She couldn't have fallen in love with Slater! Travis had said she was friendly with him and seemed to welcome his visit. And he'd also said he was sure he could win her. Well, if the little fool had fallen for Slater, she was in for a bad jolt. Ellen was immeasurably glad she had tucked the letter into her bag at the last moment.

Summer returned with the buttermilk.

"It's freshly churned, Ellen, and should be cool."

"Thank you, dear. Come and sit with me. You seem to be worried. Is anything wrong? Have you found the ranch too isolated for you? Some women can't take the loneliness, you know. Slater's mother couldn't."

"Oh, no, it isn't that. I love it here. It's just . . . I'm worried, Ellen!" she blurted out suddenly. "Slater went out along the boundary line six days ago. He had an idea the outlaws the soldiers are looking for are using the hills as a hideout. He was going to look for sign and meet the army men back here. It was something he wanted to do before we went to Hamilton to be married. He's three days overdue, Ellen. I just know something has happened to him." Tears sprang to her eyes and her lips trembled uncontrollably.

For once, Ellen was speechless. She didn't allow a flicker of expression to cross her face. All she could think of was that this was something she hadn't counted on. Her sharp mind clicked into gear.

"Slater's able to take care of himself, dear. Don't worry. He's come through some rough scrapes." She said the words, but her thoughts were: I hope to hell the bastard is dead! If he is, the ranch will come to Travis, and I'll not show her the letter. If he's not dead, I'll tell her . . .

"Bulldog had already gone to town to see about a preacher." Her lips quivered. "Slater would have been here if he could. We planned to leave yesterday. Jack sent men to look for him and would have gone himself, but Slater told him not to leave the ranch no matter what happened." Summer wrung her hands in the handkerchief she was holding and tears rolled down her cheeks. "Ellen, I just know he's hurt . . . he couldn't be . . . dead! I'd just not be able to bear it if anything happened to him."

Ellen leaned forward and clasped Summer's hands.

"Did it occur to you, dear, that Slater might have gotten cold feet about getting married? It isn't unusual for a man." Summer was shaking her head vigorously, but Ellen continued. "The McLean men are like that. My dear Scott loved to play around . . . I kept a loose rein on him, knowing that he'd always come back to me. And Sam. Oh, that Sam! He always had a woman. Libby couldn't understand that. It was one of the reasons . . . well, we won't go into that. I'm telling you this to make you understand that Slater might just have decided to stay in the hills and think about it—think about how tied he will be if he marries."

Summer pulled her hands away. She was calm, suddenly.

"It's nothing like that, Ellen. You're mistaken about Slater."

"I hope so, dear. Oh, how I hope so!"

They sat in silence for a moment.

"Did you have a noon meal, Ellen?" Summer finally asked.

"Well, no, but don't bother. I don't want to burden you when you have so much on your mind."

"It's no bother and I'd rather be busy. We have fresh-baked bread and meat. And we have strawberries."

"The strawberries sound delicious. Sam always had a gift for growing things."

"These are wild ones, but quite good." Summer was suddenly irritated. "With cream and sugar, they can't be beat."

Ellen sat at the kitchen table eating daintily.

"Is the woman you brought from town still working for you?"

"Sadie doesn't work for me, Ellen. She's my friend. I don't know what I would have done without her these last few days."

"Of course, dear, I understand. This has been a dreadful time for you. And I also understand that any other time you would have picked your friends more carefully. You were alone in Hamilton, needed another woman, and she was handy. Travis told me about her. I didn't really believe all he'd heard about her was true, so I asked Jesse. Jesse gets around and in his quiet way knows . . . everything. He assured me that what Travis said about the woman was true. He was terribly sorry for the scene he made when we were leaving that morning. He said what really made him angry was that Travis would speak so in front of me. Jesse is so protective, and gets so violent sometimes that he frightens me." Ellen gave a little laugh and watched Summer closely.

Summer looked away from her and out the window, her mind churning . . . Jesse said that about Sadie? Doubts about Ellen entered her mind and not for the first time. Slater had said . . . Oh, darling, how could I have doubted a word you told me? Summer sighed to herself. The wide violet eyes swung back to Ellen.

She had paused with the spoon, holding it just outside her open mouth. Oh, Jesus! Ellen thought. Had she gone too far? The girl wasn't in the mood for a rebuke. From the look on her face, she resented it, too.

"I'm sorry, dear. I'm terribly sorry. I shouldn't have repeated gossip. I'm grateful the woman is here. I'm sure she's taken a load of work off your shoulders."

"Yes, she has," Summer said quietly. "I don't care what anyone says about her. She's good and sweet and I'm proud she's my friend."

Ellen lowered her eyes and let the expression on her face reflect the possibility that she had been wrong about Sadie.

Summer heard John Austin calling her. She went to

the door and out to the yard. He was racing toward the house.

"Summer! Summer! That Indian's comin'! He's leading Slater's horse. Luther has got a gun on him." John Austin sped across the yard and down the track. He had talked of nothing but the Indian since he was here. Paying no attention to Summer's call, he ran on until he reached the spotted pony, shouting, "Hello, Bermaga! Hello. What are you doin' with Slater's horse?"

The thing that Summer had feared was turning into reality. She thought her heart would burst. Dread kept her rooted to the spot in the yard, but her eyes went from Slater's horse to the Indian to Luther bringing up the rear, his gun in hand. She was scarcely aware when Jack, Sadie and Ellen joined her.

"Caught this 'Pache ridin' in, bold as ya please, Jack." Luther spat in the dust. "Almost killed him when I saw Slater's horse, but he kept on a jabberin', a tryin' to tell me somethin'. I don't know 'nuff 'Pache to know what he was a sayin'. I got one word—woman—so I figured. . . ."

The Indian slid off the pony and came to within a few feet of Summer. When she had seen him last his face had been drawn, his eyes dull, his body weak. Now, he walked proudly, his head held high, his eyes sharp and piercing. He commenced speaking in an even tone. He would say a few words and stop.

"What is he saying, Jack?"

"I don't know much Apache, Summer, but it's something about Slater." Jack said a few phrases in an Indian language. The Apache didn't understand. He shook his head vigorously and frowned. He spoke again, more slowly.

Summer thought she would scream. She shrugged off John Austin's tugging hand. The boy's eyes went from the Indian to Summer and then back to the Indian. He dashed away and came back with two sticks.

"Bermaga." He thrust a stick into the Indian's hand. "Slater told me some Apache words, Summer," he said, still looking at the Indian. "I'll tell him to draw." He said the guttural word, then said, "Tall Man . . . Tall Man."

The Apache walked a few steps to a smooth, bare spot on the ground, stooped down and began to draw. The figure that emerged was a man lying down.

"Tall Man?" John Austin asked. The Indian nodded. John Austin screwed his face up in a grimace of pain, staggered a few feet and fell down. All eyes were on the Indian to see if he understood. He nodded and put his hand to his shoulder, then to his side and doubled over as if in pain. Then he stood and touched both his hands.

"He's been hurt," John Austin said. "Hurt in the shoulder, in his side and both hands."

"How bad? Find out how bad." There was almost hysteria in Summer's voice.

The boy lay down on the ground and closed his eyes, then got to his feet and waved like a bird. The Indian shook his head, then held out his hand drawing his thumb and forefinger slowly together.

"He isn't dead, but almost," John Austin announced.

"Oh, God! Oh, God! Where is he? Find out where he is."

Bermaga was drawing again. First it was a crude but recognizable horse. The straight lines he added brought a word bursting from the boy.

"A travois! Travois!" He said a variation of the word to the Indian and he nodded. John Austin ran to the cabin and patted the walls. The Indian nodded again. "They're bringing him on a travois, Summer. That's a thing they drag behind a horse."

Summer was never more thankful for her little brother.

Bermaga went to Jack and touched him on the chest. With his stick he commenced to draw men. At first, he

211

drew two men, then a third, from there on he held up his fingers one at a time so Jack would understand many men. Jack nodded. The Apache went to the cabin and patted the wall, as John Austin had done, then he went to Summer and touched her lightly on the shoulder.

"Many men are coming here to get Summer, Jack. That's what he's saying." The boy's grave face went from one to the other.

"That couldn't be right, John Austin. Who would want to get me? Ask him again."

"It is right, Summer," Jack said slowly. "There's been woman-stealin' goin' on. Try and find out when, John. See if he knows when they're comin'."

The boy drew a flat line, added a house and trees, then a sun and an arc. Bermaga watched him closely, and after he completed another house, he tapped him on the shoulder and with his own stick drew two lines, then rubbed out one of them.

"In two days, or maybe one day, Jack." John Austin proudly grabbed Bermaga's hand. "Slater said the Indians were real good people. I like him." Bermaga loosened his hand and touched the boy's head.

"Ride out and watch for the Indians bringin' Slater, Luther," Jack ordered. "For God's sake don't let anybody shoot 'em. Pud, you go on out and tell Arnie and ol' Raccoon what's happened, and tell 'em I said to keep their eyes peeled and to draw in a mite closer. Fire three quick shots if'n they see anything."

Tom Treloar, the cowboy from the Rocking S and the three escort riders had joined the group.

"We're here, Jack, we're dealin' in. Tell us where we'd be of a help." The cowboy had turned his back to Ellen as he spoke. "Ain't no question of us takin' Mrs. McLean back till this is settled."

"Thanks, Tom. If you're of a mind to, spread out and stay here near the women. I'll go over to the Keep and have the Mexican women brought in. Teresa'll look after 'em, she's done it afore."

Bermaga jumped to the back of the spotted pony and followed Luther.

"Bermaga." Summer ran after him. He wheeled the pony and waited. "Thank you, thank you," she repeated, knowing he didn't understand the words. The Apache looked deeply into the violet eyes before he bent down and touched the top of her head, much the same as he had done to her brother. He kicked the pony and raced after Luther.

Sadie, holding tightly to Mary's hand, put her arm about Summer's shoulder. "It's goin' to be all right, honey. It's sure a lot better than I feared. Jack, too. Indians know about doctorin'."

"I know, Sadie. I'm relieved he's alive, but he's bad off. Bermaga would know."

"Come on, we'll walk out a little ways. They'll be comin' from that way, the same as the Indian did. Jack said for us not to go past the cottonwood tree, so we'll wait there, less 'n you want to go back and wait with . . . her."

Summer hadn't given Ellen a thought since the Indian rode to the house. She glanced back. Ellen was sitting on the porch.

"Let's walk," she said to Sadie.

Ellen had stood in the background, taking in every word and gesture during the meeting with the Apache. She understood one thing. Slater wasn't dead yet. She'd have to wait and see how bad he was before she decided if she would bring her ace out of the hole now or wait until later. She had been completely ignored, disregarded, during the whole thing. It rankled. One thing was sure, none of her men would ever turn their back on her again and offer their services to someone else. When Jesse got back, Tom would go. He would go even if he had been on the ranch longer than any of their other men. She didn't believe for one minute the story about a gang of outlaws riding on this ranch. There wasn't a gang that big around here. If there

were, Travis would have heard about it and told her.
The idea was ridiculous. That little idiot Summer had a
nerve walking off with that dance-hall girl and leaving
her sitting alone. She wouldn't forget that, either. It
was going to be a pleasure breaking down her dream
castle. Of course, if Slater died, she wouldn't tell her.

The afternoon dragged on. To Summer and Sadie
waiting beneath the cottonwood it seemed forever.
This was the place, Summer thought, where Slater and
I first . . . It would be the place where . . . She
wished she had told him what she suspected. What she
was almost sure of. He would have thrown back his
head and laughed, picked her up, whirled her around
and around and said this was the first of a dozen. Dear
God, don't let it be that he'll never know.

When the horses were first sighted, Summer wanted
to run to meet them, but Sadie held her back.

"Jack's goin', honey. Save your strength."

When Summer first saw Slater it took all her
willpower to keep from crying out. The man who lay
there looked nothing like the one who had kissed her
and smiled and said he would be back in a couple of
days. His eyes were sunk back into his head, his lips
were puffed and parched, and the week's growth of
beard on his face did nothing to keep the hollows in his
cheeks from showing. He was tied to the travois with a
blanket, and in his delirium waved his arms and rolled
his head from side to side.

"We'd better take him to the Keep." Jack spoke
calmly and his unruffled voice had a soothing effect on
Summer.

She glanced back toward the house. Ellen waited on
the porch.

"Yes. Let's take him home, Jack."

Tom and one of his drovers came to take the ends of
the travois.

"We'll spell ya to the creek," he said.

Summer walked alongside the stretcher.

"I'll do more good stayin' with . . . her," Sadie said.

"I know how you feel about Ellen. You can come with me."

"No. Me and the kids will stay here. You go on and don't be worryin' 'bout a thing over here. And . . . Slater'll be all right." She squeezed Summer's arm. "I just know it!"

Tears filled Summer's eyes. She stumbled on the rough ground, but kept going.

When they reached the ranch house, Teresa came to meet them. The Mexican woman's face showed her concern. This *gringo* was as dear to her as her own children. She had nursed him through childhood illnesses, and injuries she couldn't even remember. Now he needed her again. She issued crisp orders to a girl, then sent for her son-in-law, who spoke the Apache language.

Slater was taken to his room and lifted gently onto the bed. When all had left the room but Summer and Jack, Teresa went to work. Summer stood helplessly by, until a girl came in with a basin of hot water followed by another with a stack of clean bandages. After that, she and Teresa worked together, first washing and bandaging the wounds after they had been smeared with a smelly salve, and then washing the rest of him.

Summer squeezed water from a cloth onto his dry lips and into his mouth. Hoarse sounds came from his throat as if he were reliving the cruelties that had been done to him.

Bermaga and Teresa's son-in-law, Santi, came to stand at the foot of the bed.

"Bermaga say the *sēnor*'s hands are burned. Bad white man hold them over fire." A cry came from Summer's lips before she could stop it. "Pulp from healing cactus is under cloth. Say burns are mostly on back and sides. Bermaga say leave cloth until he can bring more cactus in two days." Santi listened to something Bermaga was telling him. "He say hands will be good again."

Teresa nodded her approval. "I have heard of the healing cactus. Tell him I would like to have a plant."

Santi talked to the Indian. Bermaga listened, but didn't take his eyes off the still form on the bed. When he spoke, it was slowly and in an even, dispassionate tone.

"He has named you Healing Woman, *Madre Politica,* and will bring plant. He says ribs are broke and he wrap tight."

Teresa nodded knowingly. "He did right, we will do the same."

"He brought powder to take away the pain and make fever go away."

Teresa now looked at the Indian with more respect, and said something rapidly in Spanish to Santi, who translated to Bermaga. As they started to leave the room, Summer called out to Santi:

"Santi, tell Bermaga thank you. Tell him if we can ever help him or his family to come to us."

Santi spoke the guttural words and Bermaga listened, his face, as usual, expressionless. When Santi finished, he gazed for a long moment at the slender girl beside the bed, then turned and went out of the room.

Summer pulled a chair close to Slater's bedside and sat down. She could hear their voices in the hallway talking in hushed tones. Slater moved restlessly on the bed, and she leaned over and kissed his forehead and commenced to talk to him.

"You're home, darling. You'll be all right. I'll take care of you, not leave you, ever. Lie still, darling. Please lie still." She stroked his bare arms and smoothed the hair back from his face. Dipping a cloth in the cool water, she placed it on his hot forehead. "There, there," she crooned. "Is that better?" Her voice seemed to have a soothing effect. His head ceased to roll. She lay her head on the pillow beside his and talked softly into his ear. "I'm here with you, darling. Your summertime girl is here. I love you so much. You've got to get well, so I can tell you my wonderful news. I am so happy about it and I know you will be, too. I don't care if we're not married yet, darling. We belong to each other, that's all that matters. Please get well. Please open your eyes and look at me. I want you to know that I'm here."

Teresa moved in and out of the room. They mixed the powder Bermaga brought with a little water and spooned it into Slater's mouth. It was bitter and he choked and gagged, but Teresa was merciless and held his mouth shut until he swallowed it. After that, he was calmer, but his fever soared. Summer bathed his face and changed the wet cloths on his head every few minutes. The Mexican women kept the basin filled with the coolest water from the deep well. Finally, Teresa threw back the covers, and they covered his legs and thighs with wet towels.

It was well after midnight when Summer noticed the small beads of perspiration forming on his temples. Almost afraid to believe the fever was breaking, she removed the wet cloth from his head and waited. Soon, the forehead was damp, and she called Teresa.

"Teresa. I think the fever is breaking."

The Mexican woman bent over him and slipped her hand under the cover to feel his body. A smile lighted her face.

"*Bueno, bueno, señorita.* It is true. He will sleep now." Quickly, she removed the wet towels from his legs and dried him.

"Will he be all right now, Teresa?" Summer held her breath while she waited for an answer.

"I pray to the Madonna it is so. You rest, *señorita,* so when the *señor* wakes he will see his *bella novia.*"

"I'll sit here, Teresa. This chair is quite comfortable."

She leaned her head back and for the first time in

days let thoughts other than of Slater come into her mind. The Mexican women and children were bedded down on pallets all over the house, but only whispered sounds of them had come to Slater's room. One had brought Summer a plate of food and smiled shyly. The food was still on the bureau, she had forgotten to eat it. She wondered how Sadie had managed with Ellen. Poor Sadie. She was in love with Jesse and had promised him she would stay here at the Keep, under Slater's protection, until he worked out problems of his own. Jesse and Slater had had a long talk before Jesse left with the army. The only thing Slater had to say about it was to caution the women to take the children into the house and bolt the door if Travis should come riding in. When Summer questioned Slater, he kissed her and told her to do as she was told.

Sadie, on the other hand, was eager to do whatever Slater suggested, and her old, bubbly spirit returned, causing Summer to wonder, more than ever, if her depression of the last few weeks had anything to do with Travis. She had been so ecstatically happy since the night of the storm that Summer didn't want to put a damper on her happiness by telling her she had doubts that she and Jesse could have a life together. She couldn't imagine Ellen letting Jesse go. She was too possessive, had too great a hold on him, whatever it was, and the bond between them was strong. Summer was afraid Sadie was in for a disappointment.

Summer's thoughts drifted to John Austin. How proud of him she was! He had been able to communicate with the Apache when the rest of them couldn't. He had a new hero now. With a start, she realized that she hadn't even thought of him since Slater had been brought in. Jack had promised to look after him, and Jack's word was next to Slater's.

Another thing Jack had told her was that he was going to invite Bermaga and his people to come onto the ranch land and stay as long as they wished. It's what Slater would do, he said. Summer was glad that Jack had thought of it.

If Slater was better by morning, she thought drowsily, she would go back to the "little place" and get clean clothes and apologize to Ellen. There was the matter of the outlaws . . . and she still had to hear the story of how Slater got away from them and how he happened to be with the Indians.

Hours passed. She didn't move. She kept her eyes on Slater's face. She must have dozed, because suddenly she realized his eyes were open and he was looking at her.

"Slater? Darling," she breathed, and slipped to her knees beside the bed. "Darling, you're awake!"

"Summer . . ." His voice was the merest of whispers. "Kiss me."

"Kiss you? Yes, darling . . . yes, yes, yes."

She placed small, feathery kisses on his mouth, his cheeks, his eyes.

"I'm not dreaming?"

"No, darling, you're not dreaming. You're home and you're going to be all right."

"I thought I'd never see you again." Weak tears fell from the corners of his eyes and rolled across his temples to the pillow. She kissed them away and murmured to him.

"Sleep, darling, and when you wake we'll get some food into you. You must be starved."

"Water."

She spooned water into his mouth from the dipper. After a while he closed his eyes wearily.

"Go to sleep, sweet darling," she crooned in his ear. "You'll feel much better when you wake again."

Morning came and Slater slept on. Teresa was sure now, barring infection, he would recover.

"He may sleep all day, *señorita*. When he wake he will be hungry as a bear."

Summer went to the veranda at midmorning. Santi, whose real name was something longer that no one could pronounce, waited there.

"Is Bermaga still here?"

"No, *señorita*. He go."

"I wanted to talk to him. Do something for him."

"He take nothing but tobacco."

"We'll never be able to repay him."

"Bermaga say his life belong to *señorita* with eyes like the mountain flower. He be her friend and blood brother to Tall Man."

To Summer, the day was exceptionally beautiful. The sky was a brilliant blue, with mounds of huge white clouds scattered about. The baskets hanging on the veranda were bursting with blossoms, honey bees buzzed, bluejays scolded, mockingbirds sang, muffled sounds of children playing came from the back of the house. Everything was wonderful! The tight hold she had kept on her emotions for the past days had loosened. Slater was back, her world had stopped tilting.

Warm, friendly violet eyes smiled at Santi.

"I need to go over to the other place."

Santi took off his flat-crowned sombrero and smiled broadly.

"Santi will see the *señorita* there. Teresa, she say: . . . ." He rolled his eyes.

Summer smiled. She could imagine what it would be like to have the capable Mexican woman for a mother-in-law.

As they rode down the path toward the creek, they passed a drover armed with a rifle. He didn't seem to notice their passing. On a rise above the creek, another man stood, motionless, looking toward the north, his weapon cradled in his arms. Until now, the threat to the ranch had been pushed to the back of Summer's mind.

"Santi, are they expecting the outlaws to come here?"

"*Si, señorita*. We watch. We wait. Every man has a post. Bad man come—we kill!"

The viciousness in his voice caused her to look at his face. It was cold, set, determined.

Chapter Fourteen

The house was quiet when they reached it. Summer dismounted and Santi took the mare down to the corral. Several men were talking by the new bunkhouse. Most carried rifles, all had six-guns strapped about their waists.

When Summer went into the kitchen, she could hear Sadie and the children in the loft. She called out, and Sadie came down the ladder.

"I want to see Summer." John Austin stuck his head down through the opening.

"Stay and watch Mary like a good boy, please, John Austin. If'n you do, we'll play us a game after a while." To Summer, Sadie said, "He's been just as good as gold. I'll swear to goodness, he's a perfect angel when he puts his mind to it. He's kept Mary up there and out of the way. Jack told us we got to stay in the house and I thought I'd just lose what few brains I got a tryin' to keep her quiet." She pressed her lips together and jerked her head toward the bedroom. Then, "Jack says Slater'll be all right."

"Teresa thinks so. We haven't taken the bandages off his hands yet, but she says there's nothing we could have done that would be better than the cactus pulp Bermaga used. I can't bear to think of the horrible things they did to him."

"Don't think about it, honey. You must be tired. Have you been a sittin' up all night?"

"I'm too happy to be tired. I want to get clean clothes and go back if you can handle things here. Is Ellen sleeping?"

"I'm not sleeping, Summer." Ellen stood in the doorway. "Did I hear you say that Slater will recover?"

"Oh, yes! I'm so relieved. You should have seen what had been done to him." Her eyes went from Sadie to Ellen in a stricken way. "The Indian saved his life. It's just so wonderful that he's still alive!"

"Yes, wonderful," Ellen said without enthusiasm.

"I want to go back to him, Ellen. I realize I'm not being very polite to you. I hope you understand. Did you sleep well? Is there anything I can do to make your stay more comfortable?"

"Endurable you mean, don't you?" she said dryly; then, briskly, "I want to talk to you, Summer. It's quite important. I plan to leave as soon as I get word to Tom. I'll swear, I think he's taken leave of his senses. He's off somewhere with that man . . . Jack. The whole idea of outlaws riding on this ranch is ridiculous. We never saw a single soul on our way here, except those fools of Slater's who were guarding the trail like it led to a gold mine. I can't understand why everyone got so worked up. Travis says the only outlaws around here are on the other side of Spider Mountain, and there aren't nearly as many of them as people believe."

"It would be foolish not to take precautions, Ellen. It could be a misunderstanding, but then again, it may be true." Summer spoke calmly, pleasantly. She wasn't going to let anything or anyone spoil her day.

"It isn't about the outlaws that I wish to speak," Ellen said coolly.

"I'll go on back up to the loft and look after the kids," Sadie said. "I'll talk to you before you go?"

"Of course."

Summer followed Ellen into the bedroom. She longed to have the room to herself so she could wash and change her limp dress for something cool and fresh.

Ellen sat down on the bed and patted the place beside her.

"Come sit beside me, dear." Her voice held none of the sharpness of a moment ago. "You're quite sure Slater will recover?"

"We can't be certain, Ellen, but all the signs point to it. Slater is a strong man." She tilted her chin proudly.

"Well in that case, I have no choice." She shook her head sadly. "No matter how painful this is for me, it's something I must do." She stopped and searched Summer's face. "I would never have told you this if . . . well, if Slater had . . . died. I would have spared you the hurt, but. . . ." She sighed and reached into the pocket of her skirt and brought out a letter. It was folded, the edges of the envelope well worn.

Summer's face paled. A premonition closed a cold hand of fear around her heart.

"You don't know, dear, how sorry I am that I didn't bring this letter to you sooner. But then, I didn't have any idea . . . I couldn't imagine you becoming fond of Slater. He is so scarred, so difficult. Well, I had better start at the beginning. About five years ago, I received this letter. It had come in care of the fort. One of the officers brought it out to me thinking it was for my dead husband, Scott. You can see that the name on the envelope is smeared. It was an easy mistake. I opened it at once. It was then I realized it was for Sam, and

from your mother. Would you like for me to read it
to you, dear? Would you rather I tell you what it
says?"

Summer swallowed drily, feeling the frantic clamor
of her frightened heart even as hidden strength prodded her to say:

"I'd rather read it for myself, please." The color had
drained from her face and her hand trembled as she
took the paper.

There were two pages to the letter. Summer recognized the paper because paper had been scarce in their
home, and her mother's handwriting because it was
neat and beautiful. She turned her back to Ellen and
began to read.

May 14, 1847

My dearest Sam,

I take pen in hand to acquaint you with the news
that J.R. met with an accident and is dead. I
suffered an injury to my back and am confined to
my bed. No, no, dear Sam, I do not want you to
come or be concerned for me. J.R.'s pension cares
for our needs. J.R. and I had a son. He is three
years old now. A bright little boy, who reminds me
so much of Slater. But this is not my reason for
writing. I have wondered all these years if I did the
right thing by not telling you the news that I feel I
must tell you at this time. At the time Summer was
born, I never knew what day or what hour J.R.
would come for me. I had hoped our going would
be easier for you if you didn't know. You have a
beautiful daughter, Sam. There is no way she
cannot be yours. I was not with J.R. for more than
a month before Ovalee and I came west. As you
know, Ovalee was killed days later, and as you
held me in your arms to comfort me, our love
grew, and we couldn't hold ourselves from each

other. Nine months later, Summer was born. I see you in her every day, Sam. Her hair is black, like yours. She tosses her head, like you do. I think J.R. suspected, but he never showed it. He loved her and was a good father to her. She is a good girl, Sam. And beautiful. You would be proud of her. I am telling you now because I feel my time here is short. I will not tell Summer. I couldn't bear for her to think her mother was sinful, a loose woman. The summer we spent together before she was born was the magic time of my life, and not a day passes that I don't think of you. I pray Libby has recovered and you have been able to live a fruitful life. I fear my sins of that wonderful summer are catching up with me. Don't mourn for me, dear Sam. Rejoice that a part of you and I lives on in our daughter.

> God bless you,
> Nannie Kuykendall

Summer was stunned. Her eyes were no longer seeing the words on the page. The full import of the shocking news had not yet reached her dulled brain.

"It can't be true," she whispered.

"It is true, dear. You've got to face it." Ellen's voice came strangely to her ears. "You understand, now, why I was so shocked when I heard about you and Slater. I thought he knew you were his sister. I was sure he knew. I can't, for the life of me, understand why Nannie didn't tell you."

Summer looked at her dully. Her face felt wooden, then a trembling set in. The letter dropped to the floor.

"You couldn't have fallen in love with Slater, dear." The now-hated voice droned on. "He's your brother, just as John Austin is your brother." She paused, then hurried on. "I was going to send the letter on to Sam, but before I could find someone to deliver it, he was killed. And Slater . . . well, Slater acted like a mad dog every time I came near. I'm glad I kept it, for your sake, dear. What if you had married Slater? What if you had a child by him?" The horrified note that crept into her voice was not lost on Summer. "Why, dear, children from such a union are deformed, idiots. . . . You know, the ones with the big heads. How glad I am that I came at this time! There's no telling what horrors I've saved you from."

"Shut up! Shut up!"

Summer leaped to her feet shouting, and then her hand went to her mouth and she bit hard at the knuckles on the back. Anger and grief were tearing her apart. Unable to look at Ellen's beautifully-composed face any longer, she let out a pathetic cry, dropped her hand, and threw herself face-down on the bed.

Her body convulsed as she began to sob hysterically. It couldn't be true! It was a mistake! It couldn't be true—but it was! Her mother's words, her mother's continual talk of Sam McLean. Her mother saying that all McLeans named their children names that started with the letter S. I gave you the name Summer, she had said, because it reminded me of something beautiful. Her heart ached with a physical pain almost too hard to bear. She continued to tremble violently, both inside and out. Please, please, her inner voice cried, let this be a nightmare. Let me wake up and everything will be all right. But she knew that everything would not be all right, that this was no nightmare, and she cried all the harder.

Thoughts crowded into her mind. The hands that had caressed her so intimately were those of her . . . brother! The lips that kissed her so passionately and had carried her to the brink of rapture and beyond were those of her . . . brother! The child . . . oh, God, the child was her brother's child! Dear, merciful God, she prayed, please let me die! Don't make me live to face this . . . hell!

She cried bitterly. Cried until her mind was drugged with grief and remorse. Covering her face with her hands, she shrank deeply into the pit of her misery, accepting the most crushing blow she had ever known.

Ellen would not allow her to escape into unconsciousness. She shook her shoulder. Gently at first, then harder.

"Summer, you must get hold of yourself, make plans. You'll make yourself ill carrying on like this. Summer, listen to me. Have you been to bed with Slater? Have you?" Ellen shook her shoulder again. "Answer me." When Summer didn't answer, she said with finality, "You have. This is much worse than I thought. Do you know what that means, Summer? It means that you have committed incest! You and Slater . . . Good heavens, if the men should find this out! And, heaven forbid, if you are pregnant! They would hang Slater, sure as the world, Summer. Texas men can get pretty riled up over something like that. They wouldn't stop to think that maybe Slater didn't know you were his sister. Do you want to see Slater hanged?"

Summer rolled over and sat up. Ellen's words had reached into the deep recesses of her dulled mind. She couldn't let any harm come to Slater. He had not known, any more than she had, that he . . . that she . . . She couldn't bring herself even to think the words. Ellen was right. She must leave before anyone suspected. She and John Austin would go back to the Piney Woods. Almost as soon as the thought came to mind, she rejected it. No! She had to go someplace where Slater couldn't find her. Some place where he wouldn't even think of looking.

"I've given this thought while you were coming to grips with the truth, Summer. I'll help you get away from here. It's essential that you go. You understand, don't you, dear?" She peered into the tear-swollen eyes. "There's a Mormon settlement about eight miles out from Hamilton. I know the leader quite well. He is a good man. I have bought a lot of furniture from them, and he owes me a favor. If I ask, he will take you with them when they leave to join a larger colony in Utah. For all their goodness, they are mercenary. You will need money." She reached into her valise and pulled out a bag.

"No," Summer said hoarsely. "No. . . ."

"Yes. Take it." Ellen put the bag in her hands and closed her fingers over it. "You can repay me if it will make you feel better about taking it. I'm doing this for you, Summer, for your mother . . . and for Slater. The Mormons will take you to Utah and Slater will never know, will never have to suffer the disgrace of knowing that he impregnated his own sister."

Summer let the bag of money fall to the floor. Ellen reached for it and the letter. The bag she placed on the bureau, the letter in her pocket.

"I'll take the letter." Summer's voice was bitter. "It's my mother's letter. You opened it, read her secrets." She held out her hand.

Ellen shrugged indifferently, and handed her the envelope.

"Is there anythin' wrong, Summer?" Sadie stood hesitantly in the doorway.

"Sadie! Oh . . . Sadie!" Summer scrambled to her feet and ran to her friend. She threw her arms about the startled Sadie with a force that almost tumbled her over. She kept repeating over and over: "Oh, Sadie! Oh, Sadie!"

"What's wrong? What's she done to you?" Sadie held the wildly sobbing girl and tried to keep her balance.

"I haven't done anything to her. She did it to herself." Ellen's voice was coldly aristocratic once again. "I've given her proof that she's Slater McLean's sister. If you're a friend of hers, you'll help her to pack her trunk so she can get away from here. If it's

230

discovered she's slept with her own brother, she'll be an outcast. No decent person will have a thing to do with her, and Slater will be hanged! I'll leave you to convince her. I'm going to the porch to take some air."

Summer sobbed out the story in Sadie's arms. Afterwards, she lay on the bed, flat on her back, staring at nothing, as if her eyelids were paralyzed. Sadie brought a wet cloth, wiped her swollen face, and smoothed back her tangled hair.

"I don't believe it." She sat on the edge of the bed holding tightly to Summer's hand and desperately trying to find a reason to believe the story was not true. "I ain't never met nobody like her. She makes me feel like I'm a nothin' when she turns her eyes on me. Couldn't she of wrote the letter?"

"No. It was my mother's paper and my mother's handwriting." The violet eyes that looked at Sadie were dry but puffed, and showed the effects of her violent weeping. "It's true, Sadie. No amount of wanting it not to be is going to change things."

"What'll you do, Summer? Will you tell Slater?"

"I'm pregnant, Sadie." She paused at the look of astonishment on Sadie's face. The words were incredible and voicing them aloud put a permanence to them. "I can't let Slater live with the bitter fact he made his . . . sister pregnant."

"Oh, Summer! Oh, you poor girl!" Her own tears swamped her throat, almost smothering her words.

"I've got to go away, Sadie." She leaned on her elbow. "Ellen has offered to help me." She clutched Sadie's arm. "It's John Austin I'm worried about. Will you take care of him for me, Sadie? Please, do this for me. I'll send for him as soon as I can."

"Why, don't you worry none about John Austin. But, but why can't me and Mary go with you? We could all manage somehow. We could go off somewhere and I'd get work. We'd get by." Sadie's face was troubled. "I don't want you to go off with that woman, Summer.

Please don't do it. Somethin' bad will happen. I just know she ain't no good!"

"I won't stay with Ellen. Promise me you'll stay here and take care of John Austin and that you'll not tell anyone that I'm pregnant."

"Course I promise. I'd do anythin' you'd want me to do. But what's Slater to think when you just up and go?"

"He's too sick to be told now. He'll be hurt, but it's better this way. In a few weeks, or a month, I'll be far enough away that it will be safe for you to show him the letter. He'll understand then."

"I don't know, Summer. He's goin' to be powerful mad when you leave without tellin' him. I don't know if I can wait a month."

"Wait as long as you can, Sadie. Even if he knows, he won't be able to ride for quite a while."

After that they were quiet, each lost in their own thoughts, but holding tightly to each other's hands. Ellen paced back and forth on the porch, looking in through the open door from time to time. From an unsuspected source within her, Summer had summoned the strength to think calmly. A line from her mother's letter staggered grotesquely across her mind: "I fear my sins of that wonderful summer are catching up with me." Like my mother, Summer thought. I'm like my mother. But my sins caught up with me sooner, and I'll pay for them longer.

Sadie took Summer's small trunk from under the bed and started filling it. Without asking, she lifted the bag of money from the bureau and tucked it inside, along with the box that held the hair necklace and the money Slater had given her to buy her wedding dress. It was a large sum of money; more than Sadie would dream of having. She was glad that Summer, at least, wouldn't have to worry about money for a while.

John Austin and Mary came down from the loft.

"I'm tired of staying up there, Summer," he complained. Then, seeing what Sadie was doing, he asked: "What are you packing Summer's trunk for? Slater can't go to town now. Jack said he couldn't go for a long time. Jack said that he was going to go to town and drag that preacher out here if he had to scare the sh—" His eyes darted to his sister. "Jack said he'd be damned if he'd. . . ."

"Jack said, Jack said!" Impatience made itself known in Sadie's tone. "Summer's goin' to go visit Mrs. McLean. Slater's goin' to laid up for a long time and Summer's goin' to go with Mrs. McLean . . . to make her wedding dress."

"What's she on the bed for?"

"She's tired, that's what for. She's been up all night. Now skee-daddle and read your books or somethin'. Mary, you come and sit here on the floor and I'll let you hold Summer's lookin' glass."

Summer lay motionless on the bed, staring at the ceiling. Sadie worked and talked softly to Mary, her own problems forgotten now, in the face of the blow that had been dealt her friend.

When John Austin appeared in the doorway and told her Jesse had returned, the news didn't make her as wildly happy as it would have done a few days ago, or even one day ago.

"The soldiers are back, too. I wish Jack would let me go talk to them. Do you think he would, Sadie?"

"You'll have to ask him, but not now. Jack said for us to stay in the house, and that's what we got to do." Sadie walked to the door.

Jesse was standing beside his horse, and in spite of herself, she couldn't control the sudden leap of her heart. Ellen stood close to him, her arms about his waist while he patted her back.

The sight of the two of them together aroused anger in Sadie. Anger at herself for being so stupid as to think that she had a chance with him. She watched them, fascinated, as Ellen worked her wiles. She stroked his cheek, smiled up at him, laughed at what he was saying without taking her eyes from his face.

"Men are dumber than sheep," Sadie muttered, trying to keep the tears of disappointment from her eyes, "and sheep ain't got no brains a'tall!" She turned from the doorway in disgust, looked at Summer to see if she had caught the significance of the soldiers being back, but Summer lay as before, still staring at the ceiling.

Jesse and Ellen moved to the porch and their voices drifted in through the open door.

"I want to go home, Jesse."

"We'll have to wait, Ellen. Captain Slane is taking his troop out in hope of bottling up that gang before they come in here. I'm to stay here in case some of them get through. They are a bad bunch, Ellen. About the worst bunch this part of the country has known. This is the captain's chance to get them. So we'll sit tight until it's over."

"I've got something to say about that, Jesse. While you were chasing around with Captain Slane, your own men were here taking orders from Slater's foreman. There are four men here who work for us. Tom has ignored me ever since we got here. When we get home I want you to get rid of him. Travis said he was always a taking too much on himself. And from the way he has been acting, I can certainly believe it."

"We'll talk about it later, Ellen."

"We'll talk about it now."

"Later. You're tired now, and frightened." Jesse's voice was firm, then gentle, patient.

"I'm not frightened!" Ellen's voice rose angrily. "Don't you be telling me I'm frightened when I'm not! Another thing, Jesse, don't you forget you work for me, too. You work for me and Travis." There was a long silence, then Ellen's voice, soft, wheedling. "I'm sorry. I didn't mean that, darling. You know I didn't.

You're my mainstay, my strong one. I couldn't possibly get along without you. You know that."

"I know. It's all right. We'll go home just as soon as. . . ."

They moved away from the window and Sadie's stomach did a slow turnover. Her dreams were slowly floating away.

Chapter Fifteen

When Jesse appeared in the doorway, Sadie looked at him with hostile eyes. He came into the room, glanced at Summer, who ignored him, at the open trunk, then at Sadie with questioning eyes, but didn't voice the question. Mary ran to him and wrapped her small arms about his legs.

"Hello, punkin. How's my girl?" He lifted her up into his arms for a moment, then gently set her on her feet. "Is this what you're after?" He handed her a stick of candy after carefully picking off the fragments of tobacco that clung to it. Mary looked at him adoringly.

Jesse looked at Sadie for a long while before he spoke. It was still there . . . the wanting to hold her, protect her. She was holding herself away from him . . . forcing herself to be cold. He understood. It was Ellen.

"I came to tell you that Travis is riding in." Sadie seemed to freeze. Her green eyes grew large and frightened. "Jack and Tom and two strangers are with him. You'll be all right. Stay out of sight and keep Mary and the boy away from the doors." He glanced at Summer again. "Is she sick?"

Sadie shook her head. "Just tired."

"And you? You been all right?"

"Course." She tried to stop her eyes from looking in his direction, but she was helpless to control them. She was too nervous to say more, her throat dry. The silence seemed to elongate.

He continued to look at her until outside sounds reached them. Jesse stood back from the door and looked out. He didn't want to bring his quarrel with Travis out in the open at this time: Better for the two of them to settle it alone, with Ellen out of the way.

The men halted their horses back from the porch, well behind Summer's flower beds. Jack and Tom moved to the side and slightly in front of the other three. All had somber, quiet faces, except Travis. He was the only one that dismounted.

Ellen, with her arm wrapped about the porch post, called out to him.

"Travis, darling. Have you come to take your mama home?"

He grinned at her, but didn't answer. He had pushed his hat to the back of his head and his face wore that devilish, reckless expression that said his blood was high and he was in one of his devil-may-care moods. He swaggered to the front of the horse, the reins dangling carelessly over his arm, stood with straddled legs and rolled a smoke.

To Ellen, who knew him so well, he was putting on a show. She smiled indulgently at him. He was so handsome, this boy of hers. Someday, he would be the richest, most important man in Texas.

"What makes you think that, Mama?" He scraped the head of a match on his boot heel and let the flame flare for a second or two before holding it to the end of the smoke. "I didn't even know you were here." His voice was lazy, his attitude confident. He was very much the man in charge and he was enjoying it.

Ellen laughed. "Well, you know now." Her eyes narrowed as she looked at the men with him. They were strangers and didn't look like the sort of company her son would keep. A little prickle of uneasiness came over her. "Tom," she called, "hitch up my buggy. Travis and his friends will escort me home. I knew that was a bunch of hogwash about a band of men riding on this ranch. You didn't see them, did you, Travis?"

Travis flipped the half-finished smoke into the dust, looked up at the two men who sat their horses, silently, expectantly. Confidently, he crossed his arms over his chest and rocked back and forth on his heels.

"Yes, I did, Mama," he announced. "But I don't think they're going to ride in here. There's no need for it." He waited a moment. His eyes shifted from his mother to Jack. "All of a sudden, there's been some changes made around here." His eyes moved back to Ellen and he grinned broadly. "You see, Mama, the Keep belongs to me now." The grin left his face and he snarled at Jack. "You got no more to say. You can either ride out on that horse you're on, or you can ride out a laying across the saddle. Makes no difference to me."

There was silence. Jack never moved nor showed the least expression. Ellen took a deep breath and clung tighter to the porch post. Jesse, listening in the house, felt his muscles tighten.

Travis continued. "Got nothing to say, Jack? Don't you want to know how come the Keep belongs to me? No? Well, I'll tell you anyhow." His eyes swept from Tom to Jack to his mother. He was enjoying this. He felt stimulated, his pulses raced as they did when he was subduing a fighting woman. He let a minute go by, while the tension mounted. Then he laughed.

"What's bad news for you is good news for me, Jack. A day or two ago we come onto old Slater's body up in the hills. He'd been done in by the Apaches. Looked like he'd been dead for a day or two. The buzzards had already picked his eyes out." He paused and looked at his mother's shocked face. "You know what that means, don't you, Mama? McLean land goes to blood McLeans. The Keep belongs to me. Slater's got no other blood kin. Ain't that right, Mama?"

Ellen's face turned deathly white, her breath almost left her. She clung frantically to the porch post as her suddenly limp legs refused to hold her. Oh, my God! she thought. Oh, Travis, my darling boy, you didn't finish the job. We've let him live, again! Her head buzzed and her eyes refused to focus. She wasn't sure if she had uttered the words aloud.

"Jesse!" she screamed. "Jesse!" She looked frantically around. Jesse would know what to do, he would make things right. Jesse always took care of things.

Jesse came out the door the instant Ellen called him. She ran to him and clutched at him, her face a mask of anguish.

"Jesse! Do something!" she sobbed.

The hate he felt for Travis boiled up in his throat like bile. He was rotten to the core, he had known it for years, and now, at last, he had tripped himself up. He put Ellen from him, moved over a pace, and faced Travis.

"What the hell are you up to?" The cold voice whipped Travis like a lash.

The question that was posed in that confident, hated voice, was the key that opened the coffer of feelings that had been building inside Travis for years. The rage, humiliation and resentment for all the times he had come out second best to this man foamed up inside him. This was the moment to end it. It had to be now. He couldn't live another day, breathe the same air, walk on the same earth as this arrogant bastard. His nostrils flared and his heart pounded. Hell, he could beat him at a draw. Hadn't Bushy Red said he was pretty good? What was Jesse, anyway, but a stray pup his mother had picked up.

Ellen read the expression on her son's face and called out frantically.

"Travis! No! You behave, now!"

"Shut up, Mama!"

"Move out of the way, Ellen," Jesse said calmly.

"No, Travis! You mind me!"

"I said to shut up, Mama!"

"Jesse will fix it . . . please, Travis!"

Travis took a step forward, his eyes glued on Jesse. "You bastard! You goddamn bastard!" The words were a strangled snarl.

His head suddenly thrust forward and his right hand dropped. At that instant, Ellen sprang in front of Jesse. Jesse's own gun was up, but Ellen was in the line of fire. He saw her body jerk as the bullet hit her, spinning her around. A second shot was fired a split second after the first. Jesse didn't see Travis's body fall or Tom Treloar's smoking gun swing to cover the other men. He caught Ellen's falling body.

He stood numbly, holding Ellen in his arms. Travis lay sprawled on his back where Tom's bullet had slammed him. The blond hair was gone from the top of his head, blood and brains drained out onto the ground.

Summer and Sadie had run out onto the porch. They stood there in horrified silence.

Ellen lifted her head from Jesse's shoulder and looked down at the front of her dress.

"Am I hurt, Jesse? I don't feel anything."

For an instant, he rested his cheek against her forehead, then looked anxiously into her face. Her eyelids drooped.

"Ellen?" he whispered hoarsely. Then louder, "Ellen?"

Ellen raised dull eyes to his. "You do love me, don't you, Jesse? You won't leave me?"

"No, Ellen, I won't leave you." His voice was thick and hoarse with anguish.

Summer and Sadie stood as if paralyzed. Sadie finally let the air escape from her lungs. Ellen was dying!

She followed Jesse into the house and threw the quilt back from the bed. Gently, he lowered Ellen down. The wound was high up in the middle of her stomach, her blood a bright blossom beneath her breast. He unbuttoned her bodice while Sadie went to fetch bandages.

Summer stood at the end of the bed holding tightly to Mary's hand on one side and John Austin's on the other. For once, the boy was awed into silence.

Jesse placed the wad of cloth on the wound and almost immediately it was soaked with bright blood. He placed another cloth on top of the first one and bent to remove Ellen's shoes.

"I couldn't let him shoot you, Jesse." Ellen's voice came suddenly. "He had a little temper fit, but he'll get over it. He needs you, Jesse. He needs you to look after him. You'll make things right, won't you?"

"Yes, Ellen. I'll make things right."

"He didn't make sure of Slater. He didn't make sure he was dead. If only he'd let me help him plan things. But he's a McLean and proud and stubborn and didn't want his mama helping him." She looked appealingly up at Jesse. "You're not mad at him anymore?" Jesse shook his head and she tried to smile. "He's a handsome boy. I've always been so proud of him."

Sadie looked down on Jesse's bent head and could hardly hold back the retort that came to her lips. She longed to shout that Travis was nothing to be proud of. In fact, he was nothing but a rotten. . . . Tears filled her eyes. She went to the head of the bed, where Ellen couldn't see her, and placed a hand on Jesse's shoulder. Maybe her touch would tell him that she cared.

"He's not as strong as you are, Jesse. Not as strong as

his mama, either." Ellen's voice had surprising strength. "When I want something, I fight to get it. The only thing that I ever really wanted that I didn't get was . . . Sam." Her lips trembled and her face puckered as if she would cry.

She looks old, Sadie thought. She looks twenty years older than she did this morning. Her soft skin was almost yellow, her lips thin, and wrinkles creased the corners of her mouth. It was as if before she had kept herself young-looking by sheer willpower. She didn't look cold and haughty like she did. She looked . . . pitiful.

"I did everything to win him. He'd tell me to go home to Scott. Scott was so dull and . . . adoring. He would forgive me anything." She closed her eyes and each time Sadie wasn't sure she would open them again.

Jack came in, stood silently looking down, then laid his hand on Jesse's shoulder briefly and went out.

"It was that Nannie!" Ellen's voice was weaker, but there was no mistaking the venom in it. "I was prettier and had a finer bosom. She was scrawny and backwoodsy." Her face crumbled, tears slid out of the corners of her eyes. She lay quietly while Jesse wiped them away with the bed sheet.

Sadie put her lips close to Jesse's ear. "Do you want me to go?"

He said just one word: "Stay."

She touched his cheek with her hand and backed into the shadows. They were alone with the dying woman.

Summer fed the children their supper in the kitchen. She gave them cold mush and milk, and for a treat she let them smear the last of the honey on their cornbread.

Evening finally came. Sadie lit a lamp and set it on a shelf so only a dim light shone on the bed. Ellen talked in snatches. Sometimes it was to Jesse, other times to Travis or to Sam, as her mind wandered.

"When I got the letter I cried and cried. He had been to bed with . . . her. Gave her a child! He wouldn't have me, but took her. I hated him! I wished he was dead a million times. I planned what I was going to do, Travis. Your mama can plan things." It was difficult for her to breathe, but she continued to talk. "Jesse went off to get lumber for the new house and you, dear boy, were sporting with those vulgar women in town. I dressed up in your clothes and rode out with some men I hired. It was the grandest feeling!" She giggled, and blood came from her nose and streaked her cheek. Jesse gently wiped it away. "You should have seen Sam's face when they shot him. I wish he'd known I was watching, that I had planned and waited for my chance to kill him. Only . . . I wanted Slater dead, too, but he didn't die." She looked pleadingly at Jesse, her eyes beginning to cloud. "Slater just won't die, Jesse."

She closed her eyes and almost immediately they flew open. "You won't let me die, will you, Jesse? You . . . always take care of . . . me." A great gush of blood came up and out of her mouth, soaking her, the bedclothes and Jesse's hands clutched tightly in hers. She looked at him with startled, accusing eyes just before the second gush. The staring eyes remained open.

Minutes went by. Jesse loosened his hands from her death grip and took the wet cloth Sadie offered. After wiping his hands, he gently closed Ellen's eyelids and washed the blood from her face and hands. That done, he stood looking down at her.

"I'll take care of her, Jesse." Sadie stood beside him. "She has a clean dress in her valise."

"I'll thank you for it."

Tom got to his feet when Jesse came out onto the veranda. Night had come and Jesse wasn't aware of it.

"Is it over?" Tom stood, awkwardly, twisting his dusty hat round and round in his hands.

"Yes, it's over." Jesse was dog-tired, and his voice showed it.

"If'n I'd just been a mite sooner, Jesse. . . ."

"You couldn't of known, Tom. I thought it would be me and Travis."

"Yes, but. . . ."

"It's over, and I thank you for what you done. If you hadn't of, I'd of had to do it." Jesse rolled a smoke with not quite steady fingers. "What's the word from Slane?"

"They killed a few of them and the rest gave up when they saw what they was up against. They got 'em hog-tied fer the night and 'll start out with 'em in the mornin'." Tom went to the edge of the porch and spit. "I knowed Travis was runnin' with a wild bunch, but didn't know he'd got in so deep."

"I knew it, Tom. So did the captain."

"He had a cruel, mean streak a mile wide. Showed up when he was no bigger than knee-high to a jack rabbit. Guess his ma givin' him everythin' he wanted didn't help it none."

"Guess not."

Tom stood silently, then said: "The boys has hammered up two real nice boxes, Jesse." He paused. "Good, clean wood."

"It was good of them. I'll get a wagon from Jack and we'll head for home come daylight."

When Sadie finished with Ellen, she drew a clean sheet up over her face. It had been a distasteful job, but one she wouldn't have shirked for anything. It was for Jesse, she kept telling herself. *If I only get the chance to make it up to him,* she prayed. *I'll make him feel happy and wanted and loved.*

Whispering instructions, because Summer sat at the table sleeping, her head on her folded arms, she sent John Austin up to bed and undressed the protesting Mary. The child wanted to see Jesse. Sadie promised that maybe, just maybe, Jesse would come in and say something to her. That satisfied the little girl. Sadie fervently hoped she would go to sleep and it wouldn't be necessary for her to ask Jesse to do such a trivial thing.

Later, she went out onto the porch, balancing a plate of food in one hand and a cup of coffee in the other. Jesse got up and came to her, taking the cup from her hand. She stood hesitantly.

"Sit with me." He sounded bone-weary.

"If'n you eat this."

"I'll eat."

She sat beside him. He ate the food quickly and emptied the cup.

"Guess I was hungry. Any more coffee? Sit still, I'll get it."

When he returned, he sat quite close to her and, to her surprise, picked up her hand and held it enfolded in his. After a while he spoke.

"Guess you're wondering about me and . . . Ellen."

"Well . . . I. . . ." His words had taken her by surprise.

He set his cup down and took her hand between both of his, playing with her fingers.

"I don't know if anybody would understand it but me."

"I'll . . . understand." Sadie held her breath. Was she too bold? Had she lied? Could she understand?

"It's a long story. Maybe too long for one telling, but I want to tell you about it. I never told it before and I'm not sure I can make anyone understand how it was. You'd of had to lived like I did to know how it was." He leaned over with his forearms on his spread thighs, her hand clasped in both of his, and began to talk.

"I'm from over around Nacogdoches. I never did know how I come to be dropped off with folks that worked on Ellen's grandpa's place. They were the white trash that worked alongside the slaves and had a whole houseful of kids. One more didn't make no never mind." He drew in a deep breath and leaned his head back against the house. "When I was real young, a woman used to come to see me. I can just barely remember. She was pretty and smelled nice and I'd sit on her lap. It was the bright thing in my life. It didn't last. She stopped coming. I looked and waited for her until I started looking and waiting for Ellen. I can't remember when I first saw Ellen. She lived with her grandpa in a great big fancy house. They were among the uppity-ups and didn't have no truck with the likes of us, but Ellen took to coming down to the shanties. She would smile at me, pat my head, and soon her visits were all I lived for. She got to bringing me a treat once in a while, and I longed to think she was coming to that dirty place just to see me, but I knew she wasn't. She was coming to see the older boys, and I think now some of the men. I was about ten years old, and doing a man's work, when I found this out. I tried to beat the kid to death that told me and got a whipping from the old man that put me on my stomach for days. Ellen came storming into the shack when she heard I had got a beating for fighting for her, and threatened to tell her grandpa if I was beat again. It was the most wonderful thing that had happened to me. Ellen stood there protecting me, standing up to the old man, then washing and dressing my sore back. I loved her from that moment on.

"It wasn't long after that that Ellen stopped coming to the shanties. I didn't see her again until I was about fourteen. I'd left the shack where I was raised, but strings pulled me back to the only home I'd ever known. The old folks were gone, the kids scattered, and the shack was burned. Ellen's grandpa was dead, and she was a rich lady and married. When I heard she had come back to sell the property I waited beside the house for two days just to get a glimpse of her. I couldn't believe it when she walked up to me, remembered my name and talked to me. I thought she was the prettiest thing I'd ever seen. To me she was an angel, everything my heart desired. She filled my thoughts so completely, I would have died for her had she asked me. Well . . . she sold her property and went away again. I went to drifting. It's a hard life, drifting, when you're a kid. I had hell beat out of me so many times that it got to be a regular thing. I finally got big enough and tough enough, so I was able to fight for myself. But just being able to make my way wasn't enough. It kept eating at me that I had nobody. Nobody, but Ellen." He lit a smoke and Sadie wondered if he was finished, but he started talking again.

"I got mean. I got mean as hell. Got to where I'd fight at the drop of a hat. People kind of backed off from me, tried not to rile me. I kept to myself; driftin', always driftin'. Looking for God knows what.

"It was about five years before I saw Ellen again. She was in a carriage and had a young boy with her. I'd just come into Nacogdoches after working on a riverboat, and I went charging down the road after her. The driver was going to use his whip on me, and if he had, I'd of killed him on the spot. Ellen knew me right away and asked me to come to the hotel to see her." Jesse gave out what was a half-laugh and half-snort of disgust. "I was in heaven. I got myself all slicked up. Had a bath at the barber shop, spent my last dime on new clothes and boots. The room she was in was the fanciest room I'd ever seen, and Ellen was the prettiest woman I'd seen. Just as pretty as I remembered. She had supper sent up for just the two of us and told me her husband was dead. She told me about the Rocking S and offered me a job. That was twelve years ago. I've been with her ever since." He let go Sadie's hand and rolled another smoke. "I know what folks said about me and Ellen. I didn't care. Ellen had strong . . . desires that most women wouldn't understand. She needed me, just as I needed her when I had no one who cared if I lived or died. She wasn't perfect, but I loved her." He was quiet and finished the smoke, flipped it out into the night and said with wonderment, "I never had any idea she'd do what she said she did. Guess I was about as blind about Ellen as she was about Travis."

Sadie sat spellbound while he talked. She understood his feelings. They reflected her own longing, the yearning for something permanent, the wanting to belong. Her compassion made her bold.

"You've got me now, Jesse. If you want me." She could feel his sharp eyes searching her face in the darkness. She waited in agonizing silence for his answer.

His arm came around her and pulled her tightly to him.

"I want you, Sadie." The words were whispered against her ear. "Oh, God, yes. I want you."

"I love you, Jesse," she said, with tears in her voice. "I ain't much, but I love you so much it hurts me . . . but it's a hurt I like."

"Sadie. . . ." He raised his head and looked at her. "Sadie, you're everything. You and Mary are everything. I've saved my wages, and it'll give us a start."

He kissed her gently, lovingly, yet possessively. His arms held her protectively and she snuggled against his chest. She had come a long, lonely way through the years, as Jesse had done, but now she had found home, safety, someone to love and someone to love her.

Summer awoke. Night had come. She came awake fully aware of the events of the day. The house was silent and dark except for the low burning lamp on the mantel. Ellen was dead, she knew it at once. No sorrow touched her heart for Ellen, and no regret for Travis. He had done that terrible thing to Slater . . . Slater! Oh, God! How can I ever think of him as . . . brother?

Her face was wet with sweat where it had rested on her arm. She washed it matter-of-factly and tidied her hair from habit. Her stomach protested the fact she had not eaten all day, and propelled by yet another habit, she went to the warming oven for cornbread and to the crock for milk. The food went down automatically. She looked behind the curtain. Only Mary was there. Taking the lamp, she climbed the ladder until she could see into the loft room. The small shape of her brother was on the bunk.

At that moment, the reality of what she was doing hit her. She was leaving her little brother! He was her child in every sense of the word except by birth. He was her reason for coming here. Since the day he was born she had cared for him, taught him, never stinting on love and devotion. Here, in this place, he had grown wings, learned to depend on her less, expanded his knowledge by leaps and bounds. This was the place he should be. Slater would see to his education. Someday, he would be in a great university, teaching others. At that time, she would know she had done the right thing by leaving him behind.

At the door of her room she paused, holding the lamp out to the side so she could see. Ellen's body lay on her bed, the outline clearly visible beneath the sheet. Ellen had been going to take her with her in the morning. Now she would go alone.

Calm and dry-eyed, she was returning the lamp to the mantel when the door opened. She turned quickly, guiltily, suddenly fearful of whom she must face. Sadie came in, followed by Jesse. Jack followed close behind. Summer avoided his eyes and looked at Sadie.

"Is your head better? You was sleepin' so sound I was a hopin' that when you woke up your head wouldn't a be a killin' you like it was."

250

Summer looked from the men to Sadie and understood her line of talk. She was helping her to produce an excuse for her absence.

"It's not much better, Sadie, but the sleep helped." It astonished her that she could speak so calmly. She looked directly at Jack. "Did Slater sleep most of the day? Teresa said he would."

"Off and on, I guess. Teresa said he et stew like his stomach was stuck to his backbone. He was frettin' if'n things was all right over here. Ain't tol' him the whole of what's happened yet. Reckoned tomorry would be soon e'nuff."

"He should be much stronger tomorrow."

Jack stood first on one foot and then the other.

"You told him about the soldiers?" Sadie broke in speaking fast. "You told him they corralled the whole wild bunch? That ort to make him feel just jim-dandy, considerin' t'was them that did that to him."

"Yup, I told him and he swore he was goin' to kill Travis. I had to tell him it was already done. He swore again. Now all he talks about is Miss Summer and why she ain't over there."

"Well, she's dead tired, is what she is. She didn't get no sleep a'tall last night, with all that's been goin' on. Well, for land's sakes, she ain't strong as no ho.se. I. . . ." Jesse placed a hand on Sadie's shoulder and stopped her sputtering words.

Summer smiled wanly, tiredly. "I feel better now, Sadie." She suppressed the shiver of dread as she met Jack's eyes. "It's too late to go over tonight, Jack. Tell Slater we're all right and to stop fretting. Can't Teresa give him Bermaga's powder?"

"Wal, yes, but he be buckin' and not wantin' to take it."

Summer managed a small laugh and watching her, Sadie thought her heart would break.

"Tell him I said to take the powder and quit being so mule-headed."

"I'd better be gettin' back. I'll tell him what ya said. Kind of want to hit the bunk myself. Anythin' I can do for you, Jesse?"

"No, but thanks, Jack. We'll be leaving at first light. I'll bring the wagon back first chance I get."

"Ain't no hurry. Ain't no hurry a'tall. Need any help with . . . Mrs. McLean?"

"If it's all right with Summer, I'll leave her be till morning."

"Of course it's all right, Jesse. And Sadie and I will do the box real nice."

After Jack left, the tension eased somewhat. Summer stood holding the back of the chair. The new intimacy between Sadie and Jesse had not gone unnoticed. Summer was aware that Jack noticed it, too. Jack had been on the verge of falling in love with Sadie. She hoped he wasn't hurt by this sudden turn of events.

Sadie was nervous. She moved too fast, talked too fast. She was as easy to read as a book. She sped around the kitchen, first filling the stove and putting on the coffee pot. Summer stood by the chair and waited. Jesse sat at the table. Finally, it came out.

"I had to tell Jesse."

"Sadie! You promised. . . ."

"I had to, Summer. There ain't no way you can leave here in the morning without Jesse's help. You know you can't go a ridin' off by yourself." Sadie's pixie face was twisted with a plea for understanding.

Summer put her arms around her and Sadie hugged her in grateful relief.

"You're right, as usual, Sadie." She sat down at the table and looked into the steely-gray eyes of the man who had always frightened her a little. He looked like the same man, but somehow his eyes were kinder. She had expected to see censure, rebuke, disgust or pity. None of those things were there. "I'll be grateful for your help," she said simply.

"I'll drive you in the buggy. We can say you're going

to the buryin'. It's the only thing I can think of. We'll leave an hour before dawn. It'll give us time before they're all a stirring."

"I'll be grateful," she said again. "I want to be gone and get it over with."

"It'll make it easier on you."

Long after the stove had cooled and the coffee pot was empty, they sat at the table and talked. Summer was reassured by Jesse's attitude. She was doing the right thing, he said. He only wished she had family or friends to go to. He promised Sadie he would see her safely to the Mormon settlement. Summer promised Sadie she would write. Both women cried.

At the ranch house Jack gave Slater Summer's message. He had been forcing himself to stay awake until Jack returned.

"She's all right?"

"Yeah, just tired. Had a killin' headache accordin' to Sadie. She'll be over first thing tomorry. You better let Teresa give you that powder like Summer said."

"Tell her to get it," he said dejectedly. "Might as well sleep."

He closed his eyes and Jack tiptoed out. A feeling that things were not quite right settled on him, but he was too tired to think about it, and headed for the bunkhouse.

Chapter Sixteen

Summer never looked back once she climbed into the buggy. She sat in the corner of the soft, leather seat, keeping her eyes straight ahead, and was only vaguely aware when the buggy springs yielded to Jesse's weight and he was beside her. He flicked the reins and they moved out. The wagon carrying the bodies of Ellen and Travis fell in behind them, Tom's and Jesse's horses tied to the tailgate.

Leaving had put such a strain on Summer that she felt faintly ill with weakness. Sadie had burst into tears at the last minute, and begged to be allowed to come with her, and John Austin had come down the ladder to stand mutely perturbed. Watching her with solemn, puzzled eyes, he made no attempt to approach her.

Summer had awakened her brother and explained she was leaving. She didn't say how long she would be gone, but that it was necessary for her to go without him. He was to mind Sadie and do the lessons Slater would assign to him. She would write to him, she said, and he was pleased that he would be getting a letter. When she was about to leave him he almost dumbfounded her by asking:

"Have you got trouble, Summer? If you have, me and Slater will take care of it."

Summer laughed before she would cry. "Of course not. But thank you." She hugged and kissed him and instead of wiggling away as he usually did, he returned her kiss and clung to her for a moment.

It was going to be a warm day. That was only one of the reasons Jesse wanted to get an early start, another being he wanted to be well ahead of the soldiers when they headed out with their prisoners. And foremost, he wanted to leave before it was necessary to explain why he was leaving with Slater's intended wife.

It seemed unreal to Summer that she was sitting in Ellen's buggy, leaving McLean's Keep. She tried to keep her thoughts away from Slater. She needed time to get used to the idea that she couldn't love him. A few months ago, she would have been delighted to know she had a . . . relative. A lump rose up in her throat that she found difficult to swallow. She wouldn't think about it now! She would think of something else, anything. See the beautiful sunrise, she told herself. There's a rabbit, and isn't that a mockingbird that's singing?

Before she knew it, her thoughts were back at McLean's Keep. She wondered if Sadie would be convincing when she announced that she had gone to attend Ellen's burial, she wondered how long she would wait before she gave the letter to Slater. She had promised to give her time to be far, far away. Oh, Slater, dar—No! No! I can't think it, I can't say it, anymore. I must not think of him . . . that way!

A shiver passed over her when she realized how alone and unprotected she would be once Jesse left her. It seemed that McLean's Keep and everything dear and familiar was dropping away into the distance behind her, and the more it receded, the more vulnerable she felt. Soon, she would have no one at all. Soon, she would have nothing except her own strength and wits to aid her.

The sun was up, and neither Summer nor Jesse had said a word. By the time they left the hills and were on the plain, the sun was far above the horizon. The trail was overgrown and full of holes and jagged pieces of sandstone, which Jesse skillfully avoided. The horse plodded on into the heat of the day. A dead possum lay beside the trail, its body grotesquely bloated. A snake slithered into the grass in front of them with startling speed and disappeared. Summer could not still the revulsion the scaly, diamond-patterned creature aroused in her. The only sound to disturb the eerie peace of the prairie was the jingle of the harnesses and the thump of the horses' hooves.

Sitting beside the silent Jesse, Summer stared up into the sky. It soon split into layer upon layer of floating white clouds, and she could feel them enveloping her. It was a familiar feeling, like a summer day of her childhood. It was a time for not being attached to anything.

"Better put your hat on. You'll get a touch of sun."

She wished Jesse hadn't spoken; it spoiled the silence. Obediently, she put on her hat and, as if suddenly remembering he was there, turned to look at him. His eyes were squinted against the sun's glare and his face was wooden. Her heart and mind had room for compassion. Poor man. Enslaved by his love for Ellen all these years. He must have known the kind of woman she was. Yet he loved her and accepted what crumbs of affection she chose to give him. Now, he was free to love Sadie, and she, Summer, was the one enslaved by the results of love.

Midmorning, Jesse stopped to talk to Tom and to tie his horse to the back of the buggy. After that, Tom veered the wagon off onto another trail and they continued on toward Hamilton.

"It's good of you to do this," Summer said. "I know you want to go on—want to get on with the burying."

"Tom will start things and I'll be there by evening. We'll go on to the Mormons."

"Ellen said they were good people and would take me west with them."

Jesse was silent, then said thoughtfully, "I'm not so sure this is the place you should go."

A flutter of apprehension stirred her. "Ellen said if I had money, they would take me."

"We'll see."

Because she must, she believed Ellen had been speaking the truth, and sat silently, her face a blank, but surging inwardly with uneasiness.

As the buggy approached the Mormon settlement, Summer had an ominous feeling in the pit of her stomach. The women were washing clothes and didn't raise their heads as the buggy swept by. The children were not running and playing as children usually do, but stood silently beside their mothers with averted faces. Men, who were working at various chores, neither looked up or offered a greeting. Most depressing of all was the silence. The ring of a hammer, the buzz of a saw were the only sounds.

Jesse stopped the horse and wound the reins around the brake.

"I'll see what I can find out. You stay put."

Summer watched him leave. She tried to catch the eye of one of the women so she could give her a friendly smile, but there was not a single woman who did not have her eyes averted. The children were all being forcibly made to look elsewhere and were uncommonly hushed. The sight of this universal snub caused Summer to grind her teeth. They were peaceable people, Christian people. Why were they ignoring her? It was almost as if they knew!

Jesse spoke to a man working on a wagon wheel. The man had not turned from his work, but gestured toward a rear building. After a quick glance around, Jesse went behind the building.

Summer sat in confused silence, her heart racing even thought it felt heavy as lead. When Jesse returned a tall, thin carrion of a man walked beside him. He was wearing a black frock-coat and a straight-brimmed black hat. A long, flowing beard rode majestically on his chest. When they reached the buggy, Jesse climbed in and picked up the reins.

The man's pinpoint-hard eyes fastened on Summer. She felt the color drain from her face and wanted to move closer to Jesse, wanted to leave this place, wanted to cry.

"Ain't ya gonna talk it over with the woman?" The voice was deep, booming and full of self-righteousness.

"Hell, no." Jesse flicked the reins and the horse moved ahead. As they circled to return the way they had come, the man stood in the road, his arms raised, his powerful voice reaching them.

"I am a devout Mormon," he shouted. "Our Prophet, Joseph Smith, was a divinely-inspired man. His vision of a modern Zion in the west has been realized. We go to join him. It is God's will that woman be used to procreate so we may multiply and spread across the land. We preach that the wages of sin are death!"

"What you want is to satisfy your own filthy lust, old man!" Jesse shouted, and to the horse, "Heee . . . eee yaw!" The animal responded with a burst of speed.

Jesse allowed the horse to run until they were out of sight of the settlement and pulled him up to a walk.

"Goddam crazy old fool!" Jesse's face was red and sweat ran from his forehead. "Goddam crazy old fool," he said again.

Summer's head was spinning. She had been holding tightly to the side of the buggy but she let go now to fumble in her pocket for something to wipe her face.

What could she do now? Willing the tears not to come, she glanced at Jesse and found him looking at her.

"What did he say?"

"He said you'd have to marry him, be one of his wives before he'd take you with them."

Summer gasped, tears forgotten in her sudden anger. "No! Never!"

"That's what I told him," Jesse said drily, "along with a few other things."

Her anger died as quickly as it came. What could she do now? What in the world was she going to do? Tears would have started had she been left to her own thoughts, but Jesse was speaking again.

"I've met Bible-spouting lechers like him before," he bit out. "Had my doubts about takin' you there in the first place." He turned to face her, and for the first time she saw him smile. "When he clapped his eyes on you, they almost laid out on his face. He thought he was about to get hisself a real choice little bit of woman."

In spite of herself, Summer smiled in return. Then, as if she had no right to smile, she sobered.

"I'm imposing on you, Mr. Thurston, and I feel badly about it. I think it's best for me to go to Austin. I can get a teaching job there." She stopped, then forced herself to go on. "I can drive the buggy on into Hamilton and leave it at the livery stable, if you want to take your horse and go on to the Rocking S."

"I'm not in that big of a hurry, Summer. Nothing at the ranch that won't keep till night. We'll go on into Hamilton and see when the stage runs to Austin."

"Thank you, Mr. Thurston."

"Name's Jesse. Just plain old Jesse," he said with a sigh.

Summer shivered. "I can't help thinking about that old man, and what I'd have done if you were not with me."

"Don't think about him. He ain't worth a plug of tobacco."

"But those poor women. They all seemed so sad."

"That's how he keeps 'em with him, cowed and afraid."

Hamilton's street was teeming with several times its normal population when Jesse drew up beside the stage office. He wrapped the reins about a post and disappeared inside. He didn't need to tell Summer to stay put this time. She sat quietly, eyeing the jostling crowd. There were drovers in their drab work clothes, former easterners in dark suits, soldiers in pieces of uniform and the usual amount of strutting cowhands laden with pistols and Bowie knives. What Summer didn't know was that the army troop had arrived with their prisoners, and the crowd had surged into the street to watch their passing and to linger to talk about this exciting event that had jarred their usually monotonous existence.

The last time. . . . For a moment, gripped by a rush of savage emotion, Summer thought she would scream. She closed her eyes and willed herself not to think of the time she and John Austin had arrived at this stage stop, and when she opened them again, Jesse was climbing into the buggy.

"Friday. The stage goes on Friday."

"Friday? That's . . . five days. I can't wait five days."

"Yes, you can," Jesse said gently, but firmly. "You can stay at the hotel." He was turning the buggy around in the middle of the street.

Summer's lips trembled. She wanted to protest, but didn't feel she had the right to burden him further.

"It'll be all right," Jesse said, seeing her stricken look. "It won't be very comfortable, but you can stay in the room. I'll come on Friday and put you on the stage."

At the hotel, he helped her down. She could feel the stares of the men lining the benches as she stood waiting for Jesse to lift her trunk from the back of the buggy. The hotel lobby was stiflingly hot, and the odors

261

of highly-seasoned food, beer, tobacco juice and sweat mingled.

Graves, the hotel man, got up from a cot where he lay fanning himself.

"Well, well, well, Miss Kuykendall."

Jesse drew the soiled register pad forward and scribbled something.

"This lady will take that front room with the windows on the south." He spoke in a clipped, no-nonsense tone. "You'll bring her meals over from Mrs. Hutchinson's place three times a day. And you'll keep your mouth shut." Quick as lightning, he reached across the counter and grabbed the front of the man's shirt, pulling him almost off his feet. "If any harm comes to her or if she's bothered in any way, I'll stomp you to death." He gave the man a vicious push. "I'll be back, and she better have no complaints." He picked up Summer's trunk, and with a hand beneath her elbow ushered her up the stairs.

At the door of the room he left her with the promise to return the day after tomorrow. The room was not the one she and John Austin had shared. For that she was thankful. She wanted no reminders of a time when she was full of hope, confident that she and her brother would be happy under the protection of Sam McLean.

Sam McLean! The name lit some flame that had never been lit before. Such a burning hate and fury took hold of her that she shook with the fever of it, and every vestige of self-control went up in a white blaze of emotion. With a terrible little sob, she pummeled her stomach with her fist, blind to everything but the fact that her brother's child grew within her.

When the storm passed, she was quiet, head bowed, a little dazed by the evidence of her own feelings. She suddenly felt terribly sick, her stomach convulsed and she removed the lid from the chamber pot just in time for it to catch the vomit that gushed from her mouth.

Weakly, she leaned against the wall and wondered numbly if her face had gone as white as it felt.

Slowly, she stumbled toward the bed, walking as if she carried a heavy load, undressed, and lay down.

With extraordinary clearness of mind, she seemed to see the entanglement clearly. Her mother had fallen in love with Sam McLean while her husband was away fighting the war, but when he returned she went back to the Piney Woods with him because it was her duty to do so. But Papa had loved her, she almost cried aloud. He loved her dearly. Sometimes, he'd pull her down on his lap and whisper to her. How could Mama have done this to him? To me?

For hours, Summer lay awake staring into the sunlit room, then into the shadows and finally the darkness that was no blacker than her own thoughts. And every minute, her despair and apprehension grew deeper. A few short months ago, she had not even known Slater existed. And then her mother had died, and by an utterly unexpected chance she was here. He had woven himself into the very fabric of her life, befogging her judgment so she could not help herself when he kissed and caressed her. And because of her wild infatuation for him—Summer's mind stumbled over the word "love"—she had turned her back on her Christian teaching, her moral obligation to keep herself pure for her husband. She had imagined that together they could make a world of their own, a family out of their love for each other.

It is strange, she thought painfully, that God's punishment is so vicious. Where in the Bible did it say something like, "Thy sins shall be washed away"? Where was the all-seeing Providence that was forever leaning out of the window of heaven to put things right? Was her sin the unforgivable sin? Maybe this punishment was not to last, she thought hopefully. She had missed only one of the bleeding periods that came to her every twenty-eight days. No, she told herself sternly, that was wishful thinking. She was well into what would be the second period. She couldn't pretend that everything was all right when it was really all wrong.

She closed her eyes for a moment, and when she opened them once more it was morning, and the hotel man was pounding on the door.

"Open the door, I got yer grub."

Summer raised her head. The room swayed and her stomach turned over.

"Leave it in the hall," she called.

"I'll get yore chamber pot," he insisted.

"I'll leave it outside the door." Her voice rose in agitation.

With relief she heard him set the tray on the floor and then his heavy footsteps plodding down the stairs. She leaned back weakly, and prayed that her stomach would not heave.

Bulldog rode into town shortly before noon. He was hot and tired and mildly agitated. Waiting around town wasn't the thing he liked to do best. After he had waited for three or four days for Slater and Summer, he decided to ride up to Burleson to see a rancher who joined their cattle drive each year, thinking it would save him a trip later.

When he'd come into Hamilton almost a week ago, he had been surprised to discover the town had progressed to the extent it had its own new plank church and a skinny young fellow for a preacher. With the purpose of his trip accomplished, all he had to do was loaf about and wait for the wedding party to arrive.

Now, thinking he should check with the liveryman, he turned his horse toward the stable and inquired if anyone from McLean's Keep had come to town.

"No, but Jesse Thurston brought that fancy buggy of

Mrs. McLean's in." The liveryman looked expectantly, waiting for a sign to continue.

"I ain't a carin' 'bout Mrs. McLean or her goddam buggy," Bulldog retorted. "I'm a waitin' for Slater and his bride to come in to be married."

The liveryman couldn't believe that here was someone who hadn't heard the big news and joyfully launched into the long story.

"It was one of the troopers what told me. Said Travis shot his ma. Said he come in a braggin' he'd seen Slater McLean up in the hills, eyes already picked out by the crows, said Jesse dealed hisself in and the woman run betwixt 'em. Tom Treloar, Jesse's top man, shot the top of Travis's head off. There's more to it. Soldier said Slater was hurt, bad hurt. . . ." He looked at Bulldog slyly, because he was about to drop his heaviest load. "Did ya say that Slater was gonna wed up with that gal that come from the Piney Woods? Yeah? Wal . . . I wonder why she come to town with Jesse Thurston. He put 'er up at the hotel the other day."

Bulldog almost swallowed the cud he was chewing. Without a word, he turned his horse and rode toward the main street. A feeling of importance for being the one to pass along such disturbing news caused the liveryman to hitch up his britches and grin as he watched Bulldog ride away.

At the hotel, he stomped into the lobby and bellowed:

"Graves! Where the hell you at?"

The man ambled in from the back room, wiping his nose on his sleeve.

"What you want? I let yore room out."

"I ain't a wantin' yore goddam room. I'm a wantin' to know if Miss Kuykendall is here."

Graves looked uneasy. His eyes shifted toward the saloon door.

"Well, is she or ain't she?" Bulldog grabbed the

register and looked at it, forgetting momentarily he wouldn't recognize her name if he saw it.

"Her name ain't writ thar."

"I ain't carin' if her name's writ thar, ya dumb ass. Is she here?"

"It ain't none of yore business who's in my hotel."

"I'm makin' it my business, you shit-eatin' bastard."

Graves made a move to block the way to the stairs, but seeing the look on Bulldog's face, shrugged and stepped aside. He'd done what he'd been told to do. It was a toss-up which one of them gents was the orneriest. It would be a good fight ta see . . . yes, a damn good sight ta see Jesse Thurston and Slater McLean a fightin' over that lit'l bit of tail.

Summer was standing beside the window when Bulldog rode up to the hotel. She had forgotten he had come to town almost a week ago . . . come to be sure a preacher was in town, and if not to go on to Burleson or even to Georgetown to fetch one. At the sight of him, the sharp edge of terror caused her head to throb unbearably, but that was nothing at all compared to the chill surrounding her heart. She shrank against the wall, and stood there very still for what seemed an eternity.

She knew the heavy footsteps on the stairs were Bulldog's even before he commenced pounding on the doors down the hall and calling her name. Someone opened the door and cursed him. The short, old, bowlegged cowhand spewed out a reply that caused Summer to quake. Finally, the door of her own room shook from the force of his knocking. She stood still, eyes closed, her mouth suddenly full of saliva. Time seemed to stand still while he pounded.

"Summer! Goddammit, girl, if you're thar, open the door."

At last, at long last, he went away, and the breath left her tortured lungs. Hardly daring to move, she sidled to the side of the window and peeked out. He was turning his horse and riding down the street.

Tears she could no longer hold back came to her eyes, tears of fear and bewilderment. She sat on the edge of the bed, her weary head in her hands, and let the tears ooze between her slender fingers.

John Austin Kuykendall had never spent a day of his young life away from his sister. The newness of it lasted until exactly noon of the second day, and then a lonely, scary feeling came over him. What if Summer had left him here and would never come back? She had always been there when he needed her, always encouraging him to try something new, always looked after him, fixed the things he liked to eat, sat with him when he wasn't feeling well.

He sat with his back to the big cottonwood, the book about the Revolutionary War on his lap. Today, he couldn't even get interested in Nathan Hale. He kept seeing his sister's happy face when she came to tell them Slater would be all right and hearing her shouted words: "Shut up, shut up." He couldn't remember Summer ever saying words like that even when she was very mad. It had to be something to do with Mrs. McLean.

John Austin stared off into space, seeing nothing. He realized now that he hadn't appreciated his sister. Sometimes, he hadn't been very thoughtful of her. She had done most all the work, hadn't nagged him as Sadie was doing now. That was something else he had noticed . . . Sadie. She was acting flighty, like something was bothering her. He suspected it was something to do with Summer's going. He began to feel really scared when the thought entered his mind that maybe Summer would not come back, that she hadn't been going to Mrs. McLean's burying, after all. He tried to still his fears by thinking she wouldn't do that. She wouldn't go away and leave him . . . unless she was in terrible trouble.

He carefully marked his place and closed the book. On his way to the corral, he left it on the bench on the veranda. If Summer was in trouble, the one person to fix it would be Slater. Slater liked her, liked her a lot, almost as much as he did. Hadn't he said he was going to take care of them from now on, that they would all live together in the big house? He saddled Georgianna, climbed up on the fence, and jumped onto her back.

"Where you goin', John Austin?" Sadie came into the yard. "Don't you leave this place! Hear me? Come on back, I'll play a game with you and Mary. John Austin. . . ."

Paying her no attention, he rode on toward the creek-crossing leading to the Keep.

Jack's horse stood beside the house, stamping and swishing his tail to rid himself of the pesky flies. John Austin hesitated. He had an intuitive feeling that Jack wouldn't want him to bother Slater. He guided his horse around behind the bunkhouse, tied her, and squatted in the shade to wait until Jack left the house.

It seemed a long while to the waiting boy, but finally Jack came out, mounted, and rode off toward old Raccoon's garden. John Austin walked quickly along the stone wall, then darted into the coolness of the house. He could hear Teresa in the kitchen as he sidled past the door and down the hall to Slater's room. The door was open and he peeked in.

Slater lay on the bed in his drawers. He had bandages around his waist and up over his ribs. Another bandage was on his left shoulder, and both his hands were covered with strips of cloth. His right arm was raised, the forearm laying over his eyes. John Austin stared for a moment. Slater wasn't in any shape to help himself, much less Summer. He thought about it for another moment, before deciding he could at least talk to him about it.

He walked into the room and sat down in the chair beside the bed. When he next looked at Slater, he was looking back at him, the arm having moved up to rest on his forehead. The first thing that struck the boy was how awful Slater looked. He had just been shaved and had small nick-cuts on his chin. His cheeks were sunk in so that the scar stood out in bold relief on his face. Suddenly, John Austin was scared, and almost wished he hadn't come. Slater looked scary! Looked like he didn't want to be bothered about anything.

"What do you want?"

Slater acted as if he was mad at him. A part of his mind searched for a reason, the other part was deter-minded to get help for Summer.

"Are you feelin' better?"

"No. I feel like hell. What did you expect?"

"I wish you felt better."

"Well, I don't. Now, what do you want? If it's another book, go get it."

The cold tone hurt a little, but a determined look settled on the boy's face.

"I come to talk about Summer. You like her, don't you? You said you did."

Slater covered his eyes with his forearm again. He lay still for so long John Austin wasn't sure he was going to say anything. Finally, he said harshly:

"What about her? She went off with Jesse to bury Ellen, didn't she? She thought that was more important than staying here with me."

He sounded bitter and hurt-like. John Austin had heard that tone before, but not from a man.

"I don't think it's that," he said, then rushed on. "I don't think she even liked Mrs. McLean or she wouldn't of yelled 'shut up, shut up' at her."

Slater lay still for a moment, then removed his arm slowly. His eyes roamed the boy's worried face.

"When did she say that?"

"The day she come to tell us you were goin' to be all

right. She had on a big smile then, but she didn't smile no more after she talked to Mrs. McLean. She cried and held onto Sadie, and Sadie made me take Mary up to the loft. Mrs. McLean just walked up and down on the porch. That was before Travis come to shoot her." He waited to see what effect his words were having, to see if he was telling Slater something he didn't know.

"Go on, go on," Slater urged.

"Well, I've been thinkin' that if Summer was just goin' for the buryin', why did she take her trunk and why did she say she would write me a letter? That morning, she almost cried when she come to my bed to say she was goin'. I know how Summer looks when she laughs 'cause she wants to cry. She did it lots of times when Mama was sick."

Slater lay silently for a long while. John Austin knew he was thinking, because he did that himself sometimes.

"What does Sadie say?" Slater didn't act like he was mad anymore.

"She don't say nothin' about it a'tall. I tried to ask her, but she said if I loved my sister, I'd best hush up and read my books like she told me. Sadie acts flighty and scared like she did that time Travis come. I knew she was scared of him 'cause her eyes got so big and she wouldn't look at him. She never smiled or laughed and played with me and Mary after that, and I don't know why she was scared of him. I liked him."

Slater's quiet eyes studied the boy's face until John Austin began to squirm and finally his lips began to quiver and he blurted out:

"I miss Summer! I want her to come back! I think she's got . . . trouble!" He looked away from Slater and blinked to hold back the tears, but the dam broke when Slater reached out a bandaged hand. He fell on his knees beside the bed, hiding his face in the folds of the sheet. His shoulders shook with the force of his sobs.

Slater placed an arm across the boy's shoulders and let him cry.

When John Austin raised his tear-streaked face, it was defiant. He was ready to defend his right to cry.

"Summer said it was all right for a man to cry. Summer said boys and men have feelings, too. She said. . . ."

"It's all right, John. Don't apologize. Summer's right. Men do have feelings."

"And you'll get her back?"

"First, we've got to find out why she left. Go and get Sadie. Tell her I want her to come over here right now."

"She'll be awful mad at me, Slater."

"Well, in that case, go find Jack and tell him I want to see him. After that, tell Teresa you'd like to have some of that pudding she made before Pud eats it all."

That terrible heavy weight seemed to roll away from John Austin's shoulders. Things would be all right now that he'd told Slater. It had been silly of him to wait almost three whole days before telling. He was almost running by the time he got to the front of the house, then was running when he reached the yard.

John Austin was sitting in the kitchen when Jack came out of Slater's room. He was still sitting there when Jack returned with Sadie and Mary. Teresa sat Mary on a chair and gave her a bowl of pudding. Jack and Sadie went into Slater's room. John Austin could hear loud, angry voices, could hear Slater cursing, Jack's even tones and Sadie crying. He wanted desperately to hear, but Mary kept on wanting to talk to him. When Teresa wasn't looking, he slipped into the hall and stood beside Slater's door.

"It seems goddam strange to me that she'd go off without telling me." Slater was angry. His voice wasn't loud, but cold, and dripped with sarcasm.

"I only know what she told me, Mr. McLean."

"For God's sake, why the Mr. McLean now, when

I've been Slater for weeks?" There was silence. "How come she decided to go to the burying? Did Jesse talk her into it? Make her feel obligated? I suppose he wanted to give Ellen . . ." he said the name sardonically, "a decent burial, with soon-to-be family members present."

"I . . . don't know," Sadie said between sobs. "But he didn't do nothin'! It ain't his fault. None of it's his fault."

"Then why isn't she back, Sadie? Tell me that. It's been three days. Ellen had to be put in the ground two days ago, or you could smell her clear over here," he said cruelly, bitingly. "I know Summer wouldn't of gone off without John unless she was coming right back—or unless she decided she'd rather have Jesse than me! If that son-of-a-bitch lays a finger on her, I'll kill him!"

"He won't! He's just takin' her . . . cause after the buryin' she wants to go to the Mormons . . . and get chairs and things."

"You're lying!" Slater shouted, and John Austin cringed against the wall. For a terrible moment, it was deathly quiet, then Sadie said:

"Do you want me to . . . go?"

"Hell, no, I don't want you to go! But you're lying! You're lying to protect both of them! God! If I could only get on a horse. If only. . . ." Slater was really mad and John Austin was thankful the anger wasn't directed at him. "Jack, take Luther and whoever else you want and go get her." His tone was rough, commanding: then, in tones of anguish, he said, "She's slipping away from me, Jack. I'm losing her! I got to know if she wanted to go—if she changed her mind."

"We'll leave at first light, Slater. We'll find 'er and bring 'er back. She can tell ya herself why she went. Don't you worry none 'bout us findin' 'er. I ain't takin' Jesse's part, but I've knowed him a long time, 'n I'd bet my boots he's straight with womenfolks."

"He better be! By God, he better be!" Slater's voice was hoarse, strangled. "If anything happens to her, Sadie, you'll wish you'd never heard of McLean's Keep."

"Ain't goin' to help you none talkin' to Sadie that way, Slater." Jack spoke up hastily and firmly. "From the looks of things, Summer did what she wanted to do."

"Get the hell out of here! Both of you!"

When Jack and Sadie came out, Sadie's face was swollen from crying. She walked past John Austin without looking at him, went to the kitchen, thanked Teresa, took Mary and left.

John Austin stood with head bowed. He didn't want anybody to be mad at him, but if Summer came back, he didn't care! He wished she was here now.

It was dark when Bulldog rode in. The old man was exhausted and his horse was lame. He didn't believe he had ever been so worn out. He figured he must have rode sixty miles since daylight. After stripping his horse, he went to the cookhouse and bellowed for grub.

"By God, Bulldog, I ain't never seed so much a goin' on in all my born days, and ye missed it all! Jist been one happenin' after the other ever since ye went off."

"Where's Jack?"

"Dunno. Round some'ers." The cook set a bowl of stew on the table. "Ye looks like ye been squeezed through a knot-hole, Bulldog. He, he, he! Them rangers on yore tail?"

Bulldog gave him a disgusted look and began eating.

"Ain't had so much goin' on . . . since the hogs et my brother." The cook eyed Bulldog to see if he appreciated his joke.

"I didn't know you'd come back." Pud came into the cookhouse and the hand he poked into the crock came out with a fistful of dried peaches.

"Well, ya know now. Where's Jack?"

"Dunno. Round some'ers."

"Is that all anybody can say round here? Dunno! Dunno!" Bulldog gave a snort of disgust. "Get off your arse 'n find him."

Thirty minutes later, he and Jack sat in the yard, away from the bunkhouse, away from the curious ears anxious to know what was happening now. Jack did most of the talking, telling Bulldog everything from the time Slater rode off into the hills until the army troop took the prisoners to the fort. Told him about Travis shooting Ellen, told him about Travis's torture of Slater and Slater being brought in by the Apache. It was a lot for Bulldog's tired mind to soak in, but he had to know it all before he dropped the news that Summer was in the hotel in Hamilton and Jesse Thurston had taken her there. He waited patiently for Jack to finish explaining about Slater being so upset about Summer going to the Rocking S for Ellen's burial.

Jack built a smoke while Bulldog told the reason he had high-tailed it out of town and almost rode his horse to death getting back to the Keep.

"What do you make of it?" Jack asked.

"I ain't got no idey."

"Slater's beside his self a worryin'. Ain't gonna be no holdin' him down once he hears that she's in town." Jack was thoughtful for a moment. "Ain't no use me ridin' to the Rockin S, now."

"Why do ya reckon she went and did somethin' like that for? A goin' off with Jesse with Slater all stove up . . . I'd just never a thought it of 'er. I'd a swore she was solid."

"Wal, she done it, and we ain't goin' to be able to keep it from Slater much longer. If'n we could wait another day, t'would give his side and ribs a lit'l more time to heal. He's a goin' to be rarin' when we tell him. Ya know how he gits."

"I know." Bulldog grinned in spite of his weariness.

"He got a temper what matches Sam's when he gets riled."

Both men sat in thoughtful silence. They had one strong common bond between them. They both loved Slater like a son. They both had been elated when he fell in love with Summer and she with him. It seemed to them that the boy who had been alone so much, bitter over his pa's murder and his own scarred face, had found the gold nugget all men dreamed of finding.

"I think the best we can do, Bulldog, is ta give 'em another day to heal up, 'afore we tell 'em. He thinks I'll be gone tomorry so he won't be askin' and if he dunno you're back, it'll take care of some of the time. I'll tell Teresa not to let nobody near him, no matter how loud he bellers. She might could slip a bit of that Indian powder in his grub to settle him down. We can stay out a sight, but by tomorry night we'll have to tell him, and God knows what hell might break loose."

"I can't think of nothin' better ta do," Bulldog said, with a wide yawn. "I'm so all tuckered out I can't hold my eyes apart. If'n I don't wake when you think I ort to, come 'n get me."

Chapter Seventeen

Friday finally came. It followed five of the most miserable days of Summer's life. Today, at noon, she would board the stage that would take her away from Hamilton forever. By the time the first light of dawn came, she was up and dressed and sitting beside the window. Later, after she ate the breakfast left on the tray in the hall, she repacked her trunk and returned to the window where she could watch for the first sight of Jesse, who was coming to take her to the stage office.

Jesse had been to see her twice during the last five days. She thought she would have lost her mind without his visits. He was an altogether different man than what she had at first believed. He was a lonely man, she discovered. She could understand how Ellen had commanded so much loyalty and love from him. Without him having to tell her, she knew that Ellen's death freed him to love Sadie. His face took on a smiling, eager look when he talked of her and Mary.

He talked with Summer briefly about his plans for

the future. Slater, he explained, was now the owner of
the Rocking S. He felt sure that was the way the judge
would see it, as Slater was the only living kin as far as
anyone knew. When things were settled, he and Sadie
would be married and start building a spread somewhere else.

"Slater will want you to stay," Summer had said.

"It's time I start building something of my own," was
his simple reply.

Summer leaned her head against the window frame.
She knew every inch of the street below, every
knot-hole in the building across the street. She had had
nothing else to do for five whole days but stare out the
window. She had not been out of the room, had seen
the hotel man only one time and that was when he left
the tray by the door and she thought he had gone away,
but he was standing down the hall waiting for her to
come out so he could get a glimpse of her. Somehow,
his leering look had made her feel guilty and unclean.

The shadow on the building across the street told her
that it wouldn't be long until the sun would be straight
overhead. She began to feel anxious. Jesse said he
would be here and he would be, she told herself.
Nevertheless, the minutes dragged while she watched.
Nervousness made her twist her handkerchief round
and round her finger, and by the time she saw him turn
the corner and head toward the hotel, the hankie was
soaked. With a deep feeling of relief, she got up and
put on her hat, pinning it carefully to her piled hair so
the wind wouldn't whip it from her head. Jesse didn't
come up right away and she figured he was settling with
the hotel man. She got out the money Slater had given
her and waited.

"Summer?" Jesse's voice.

She unlocked the door. "Hello, Jesse."

"The hotel man's paid, put your money away. You'll
need it. I've got your fare bought to Austin, and Bill
said he would look after you. Come on, he's holding

the stage." When Summer protested about the money, he said, "We'll settle it later. Sadie and I may come through Austin. Where could we find you?"

"I've decided to use my mother's name. Wheeler. I'll leave word at the post office."

Summer tilted her chin a little higher and straightened her back when they walked out into the noon sunshine. Jesse lifted her trunk to his shoulder and put a hand beneath her elbow. As they walked to the station, she was conscious of the curious eyes that followed them, and her face burned. She forced herself to lift her eyes from the dusty street and looked straight ahead, her face calm, her feelings well bottled up inside her.

Bill, the driver who had brought her and John Austin to Hamilton, was waiting beside the stage. He took Summer's trunk from Jesse and heaved it up to his helper to secure in the luggage rack.

Now that it was time to go, Summer wanted to cling to Jesse. Reading her thoughts, the torment on her face, he squeezed her arm and bent forward to murmur reassuringly:

"You'll do fine, Summer. Remember, if things don't work out, write to Captain Slane at the fort. He'll get word to me. Now, you'll do it?"

Fighting back the tears, she nodded. "Thank you," she whispered through trembling lips.

Jesse turned and lifted her into the coach, his own face masked over to conceal his feelings. Summer sat down beside a Mexican woman with a squirming baby. The coach was full; three men and one woman beside the one holding the baby. The men looked irritable because of the delay, and stared at her resentfully. The whip cracked, the coach lurched and began to roll. Summer, sitting on the backward seat, kept her eyes on Jesse for as long as she could see him. The trail curved, a cloud of dust rolling up behind them, and they left the town behind.

It seemed to Summer that she was alone in a lonely world. In fact, she had never been as alone as she had been for the last five days. On the way out from the Piney Woods, she had had John Austin to take care of. In this very same coach they had come to Hamilton in search of Sam McLean. They had found him, all right, Summer thought bitterly.

The heat was stifling in the coach. Summer took off her hat to fan herself and the breeze it created helped to quiet the baby. She prayed her stomach would stay still. Usually, by noon it would settle down, but today she had been so nervous waiting for Jesse that she had to keep swallowing to keep her mouth from filling with saliva.

She watched the vanishing hills pick up colors of sun and sky, watched the prairie of bleached grass stretch into nothingness. She stared back over the trail until the sun's glare caused the corners of her eyes to water. An eagle spiraled in the sky, climbing higher toward the sun until he was only a speck in the vast emptiness. Oh, to be an eagle!

The worst part of her pain was buried in the back of her mind and she was determined not to let it surface. It was there all the time, on the periphery of her vision, tormenting her, reminding her.

They splashed across a shallow creek and rolled into a stage stop. Because it was so hot, Bill said they would take a few extra minutes after the fresh horses were hitched, if anyone wished to get out. Everyone did, except Summer. She sat and waited, hardly conscious that the back of her dress was soaked with sweat and that rivulets ran between her breasts. The Mexican woman with the baby on her hip brought her a dipper of water. Summer drank it thirstily, greedily, and thanked the woman with a tearful word.

Rolling again, Bill cracked the whip and shouted to the straining team to make up for the minutes lost. The afternoon wore on. No one talked. The baby slept. The coach was like a furnace. Summer felt lightheaded, like she was floating. The torturous ride was making every inch of the road known to her aching body. She leaned her head back and closed her eyes, her mind too weary for thought.

When the coach slowed and came to a stop, she didn't bother to raise her head or open her eyes until the voice of the man opposite blasted forth.

"Now what the hell's the matter? We ain't never gonna get nowhere at this rate."

Summer looked out the window, squinted her eyes, thinking she saw Jack sitting on his big sorrel talking to the driver. She blinked several times and looked again. He was still there. On this very hot day, in this steaming coach, she felt such a chill she clamped her jaws tight to keep her teeth from chattering. How could it be? He couldn't have known she was on the stage. She shrank back against the seat, holding her hat in front of her as if to shield her face from the sun. She felt the coach sway as Bill got down off the high seat, heard the man opposite her curse the delay, heard the door of the coach open.

"Miss," Bill was saying to her, "Jack here says he's come to take you off the stage."

"No! I paid my fare. I'm going to Austin."

"It's up to you, miss, if'n you go or stay," Bill said firmly, and banged the door shut.

A few minutes passed, and the door opened again. Jack stood there looking at Summer. She wanted to die.

"Summer, get on out now, 'n let these folks go on. I come to get ya, and I ain't leavin' without ya."

"No! I'm not getting out. You've no right to interfere."

"Hell, no, you ain't got no right. The gal don't have to go if'n she ain't of a mind to." This came from one of the men inside the coach.

Jack ignored him. "It'll save a heap of trouble if you step out. It's that or the folks here'll have to wait with ya."

"Leave me alone, Jack. I'm not going back, so go away and leave me alone." Anger and humiliation caused the tears to stream from her eyes.

Jack stepped back and motioned for Bill to move away from the coach. When they turned to face each other, Jack's six-gun was pointed at his belly.

"What's . . . what's this?"

"I sure do hate to do this, Bill, but it don't 'pear to be no other way. There's a man a comin' a few miles back. He's been ridin' in a wagon, a joltin' over ruts and prairie-dog holes since two hours afore daylight. He got two bad holes in him and some broken ribs and hands what ain't let him feed hisself in a week. He's comin' to see that gal and yore not movin' till he gets here."

"You know yore settin' yourself up for trouble a pulling a gun on me, Jack. My job's to take this stage to Austin. If that little gal and her man had an out, it's betwixt them. The law could come down real hard on you, Jack, for holding up the stage."

"Then it's goin' to have to do it, 'cause I'm holding you all here till Slater gets here. Won't be long. I can see their dust."

"What did you do? Come cross-country? That's a hell of a ride."

Jack grinned. "Tell yore helper to pull the coach over to the shade while we wait." With his gun, he motioned toward a spreading pecan tree that was one of several along the stretch of shadeless trail.

"Pull over under the shade tree, Gus. We'll be waitin' a spell, that is, if'n the lady ain't changed her mind. The folk can step out and stretch a spell."

The helper leaned over and called to Summer, then yelled out to Bill. "The woman says no, Bill." The coach moved to the shade.

"Goddam women! Glad I ain't married up with one." Bill cursed and took off his dusty hat and beat it against his thigh.

"It won't be long, Bill. You and Slater will have to settle it. Ain't nothing wrong with his mouth. Ain't never heard so many curses come out of it afore. He's fit to be tied since he heard it was Jesse that put her on the stage. That joltin' ride ain't done his temper no good, even if'n we did fix up a sling in the wagon and put a feather bed on it."

The three men and the woman got out of the coach, leaving Summer alone with the woman with the baby. The doors were left open and a breeze of sorts cooled them a little. Summer wiped her face on her sopped handkerchief. The woman held out a timid hand and touched her knee. The action of sympathy caused her to lift her head. Jack had no right to make them wait like this, thinking she would change her mind. She'd tell him so. She turned around so she could see him and thought she must be losing her mind. Did Jack have a gun pointed at the driver? Dear God, he did! What was happening? Had the world gone crazy?

"Jack! Jack, what are you doing?" She scrambled out of the coach, almost falling in her haste. "Let him go. It isn't right for you to hold him! Let me tell. . . ."

"Ain't no need for you to be a tellin' me nothin'. The wagon's comin'. You can tell Slater yoreself why you run off and left him and him all stoved up." Jack's voice was cold, hard, as if he were speaking to an enemy. "He's goin' to have his say . . . if'n one of them jolts ain't drove a broke rib through his lungs."

A wagon was approaching at a fast clip. Dust surrounded it briefly before drifting away to be replaced by more dust. Summer stood in numbed silence. Slater was in the wagon! She wanted to run, but even her numbed mind knew it was futile.

Bulldog pulled up hard on the team slowing them to

a walk and then brought the wagon to a halt a few feet from where she stood. Slater lay in a canvas sling in the back of the wagon. His face was streaked with dirt and sweat and his eyes blazed with anger. He raised himself up painfully and leaned on one elbow. His eyes raked her, narrowed, and his nostrils flared.

"Get in the wagon!" He spat the words. "Get her trunk, Jack."

"No!" Summer started toward the wagon. "You don't understand."

"I sure as hell don't understand! Didn't you have the guts to tell me to my face you'd changed your mind? Tell me to my ugly, scarred face?" He was shouting. "Couldn't you tell me instead of slinking off with a bastard like Jesse Thurston? Some would say I'm lucky to be shed of you, but you're going to tell me why, and you're going to tell that boy back at the Keep that's worrying and crying over your leaving him."

Summer couldn't reconcile this Slater with the Slater of a few weeks ago. He was livid with anger.

"Don't! Don't . . . please. . . ."

"Don't!" he mocked. "Get in the wagon!"

"I won't." Summer tried to firm her quivering voice. "Didn't Sadie give you the letter?"

"I don't give a goddam for a letter! Now get in the wagon or I'll let loose with this shotgun and blast those horses to hell! Those folks will spend the night out here on the prairie." He lifted the gun cradled in his arms, the muzzle pointed at the coach horses. "I still got a thumb to pull the trigger."

The tension in him was so strong that she was shaking from the impact of it.

"You wouldn't! You couldn't be so cruel."

"Cruel? You've put me through five days of hell. In about thirty seconds, you're going to see how cruel I am."

"Don't make me do this, Slater. Please, don't make me."

For the first time, she looked him full in the face. It was a face she didn't know, and her eyes widened as she stared at him. His eyes were sunken and blazed with bitterness. His cheekbones stood above hollowed cheeks shadowed with a day's growth of beard, a vein in his temple stood out prominently and throbbed with each beat of his heart. It was the boniness of his face, the wolfish snarl of his twisted mouth that held her in acute fear. The scraping of metal, as he cocked the gun, put her weak legs into motion, and she moved to the back of the wagon and crawled in over the tailgate. Almost as soon as she sank down on the plank floor and covered her face with her hands, she heard the thump of her trunk as it was dumped down beside her. The wagon lurched, the team making a full circle, before beginning a steady, rolling pace.

Summer sat crunched in the corner of the jolting wagon, her mind going in a thousand directions. How was she going to tell him? How was she going to spare him the shame and the hurt of knowing he had shared with his sister the most intimate act a man can share with a woman? How could she tell him that she was going to have his child? A human being that more than likely would be deformed, an idiot!

The sun beat down mercilessly on her head and the soft skin of the back of her neck. She was so steeped in her own misery she didn't notice. She was almost drowsy when Slater's harsh voice broke the silence.

"Put your hat on. You'll be sick from the sun."

She raised her head and groped blindly for her hat because her eyes were blinded by the brightness of the sun. After a few minutes, she glanced at him. His face was turned away from her so she was free to look at him. He lay sprawled in the sling, one knee bent, booted foot resting on the floor, bandaged hands laying at his sides. An umbrella, of sorts, had been rigged to shade the upper part of his body. He was emaciated. It didn't seem possible a person could have lost so much weight in so short a time.

The wagon was moving slowly. Bulldog was letting the tired horses plod along. Jack rode a little ahead, slumped in the saddle. It was quiet. So terribly quiet.

Evening came and it was a welcome relief from the merciless sun. An exhausted Slater had slept the afternoon away. Ignored by Jack and Bulldog, Summer leaned her head back against her trunk and tried not to think of the ordeal ahead of her.

It was still light, but a few stars had made their appearance, when they reached the stage stop by the creek. Bulldog pulled the team to a stop and said a few low words to Jack. The wagon turned and they went alongside the creek for a few rods before stopping. Bulldog climbed stiffly from the wagon seat.

"We'll camp here," he announced, to no one in particular.

Summer had sat for so long that she moved slowly at first, stretching her legs out in front of her. She glanced at Slater. His face was turned toward her and his lids were not completely closed. He had been watching her, was watching her! Her face burned with embarrassment, then resentment, for being blamed for a situation that wasn't any more her fault than his.

Bulldog led the team to water. After waiting patiently for them to drink their fill, he staked them out. They immediately rolled in the dirt and stood on stiff legs, shaking off the excess dust. Jack rode up while Bulldog was building a fire. He had borrowed a coffee pot, utensils, and bought food from the man at the station.

Summer didn't know what to do. She was sure her offer of help would be spurned, and she didn't know if she would be able to stand rejection without bursting into tears. The decision was made for her when Jack came to the end of the wagon.

"You can go down the creek a ways. Me and Bulldog got to get Slater out fer a while." He didn't speak unkindly. She was surprised.

Jack didn't offer to help her down and she clung to the end of the wagon for a moment after her feet were on the ground, allowing the numb, tingling feeling to leave her legs. She held her back stiff and her head high until she was out of sight of the camp, then walked slowly on until she found a place to relieve herself. Close by, the bank to the creek was sloping, and she sat on a rock, and dipped the hem of her skirt in the water and washed her face. The water was so refreshing that she longed to remove her shoes and bathe her hot feet, but fear of snakes stopped her. Night had come and the darkness seemed a comforting cloak. A frog croaked. It was not a loud sound, but with no other it was more obvious. A squirrel, awakened by the frog, chattered inquiringly; then there was silence.

Tired, Summer got to her feet. She would talk to Slater tonight. He would realize she could not live at McLean's Keep or at the "little place". She would make him realize it would be better for her to go where she wasn't known, where she could pose as a widow and still keep some semblance of respectability. It would be easier talking to him in the dark. She wouldn't have to see the shock of what they had done on his face.

On the way back to camp, she met Jack. The glow of his smoke alerted her to his presence.

"I wasn't going anywhere," she said drily.

"I was makin' sure."

With the help of the light from the campfire, she could see that Slater had been moved, tarp, feather bed and all, to a grassy spot beside the wagon. He lay flat on his back, arms and legs outstretched. His shirt had been removed and Bulldog knelt beside him putting a new dressing on his shoulder. She could feel his eyes on her and turned her back to fumble with the straps on her trunk, anything to be busy so she didn't have to face him.

Cornbread was cooking in a skillet and strips of meat hung from a spit over the fire. Fat sizzled as it fell, and the flames were constantly alive with small bursts of brightness.

Later, she sat with her back to a tree, where she could see only the top of Slater's head and he couldn't see her at all. The silence between the four of them was terrible, but speaking was worse. Bulldog squatted beside Slater and dropped food into his mouth from time to time. If any words passed between them, they were so low she couldn't hear them. Summer picked at her own food. The meat was too greasy and almost nauseated her. Not wanting to leave it on her plate, she flipped it into the grass when she was sure no one was looking. She ate the cornbread and drank the strong coffee, and felt surprisingly better when she had finished.

Jack came and took the granite plate from her hand. His manner was so purposeful it immediately killed her intention to offer help. Calmer now than she had been all day, she decided to wait and let Slater make the first move. It wouldn't be long, she reasoned. Part of her wished to hurry and get it over with, the largest part of her dreaded the scene.

With plates and cups in hand, Jack went toward the stream. Bulldog kicked dirt onto the fire until the blaze was small, and stalked off toward the horses. Somehow, Summer knew this was the time. She was getting to her feet when Slater's voice reached her.

"Come down here where I can see you."

Calm and resigned, she moved to stand beside him, looking down at him, but not into his eyes.

"Sit down. Here on this blasted feather bed that's been like an oven all day." Obediently, she sat down, her hands clasped in her lap. Time passed, it seemed years, but could only have been minutes. "I been thinking about that letter. The one Sadie didn't give me. What did you say in a letter you couldn't say to my face?"

It was coming sooner than she expected, and for a second she felt acute panic, her tongue suddenly thick, her breath wanting to leave her. Slater's voice crashed against her eardrums.

"Tell me! I've got the right to know! I went through hell to get back to you . . . I'd have died out there, but I couldn't die and leave you! You should be pleased to know, it was heaven when I opened my eyes and you were there. What are you? A whore? A slut to go straight from me to another man? I'll tell you this . . . I'll kill you and I'll kill Jesse before I'll let him have you!" Slater's anger, his humiliation and disillusionment were total.

Summer recoiled at the verbal assault. For an instant, she was stunned by the viciousness of what he said, until she understood how he would be driven to say such things. He was easing his own pain by hurting her.

"Don't blame Jesse. I asked for his help."

"You what?" His voice echoed through her head painfully.

She winced and repeated herself. "He'll tell you. I asked for his help."

"Goddam right he will! He'd tell me anything, when I'm fixin' to hack off his balls!" His nasty voice was blistering and her face reddened.

"You'll not blame him," she said stubbornly. "He's a good man, a friend when I needed one badly."

Hurt, anger and bewilderment surfaced in his smoldering eyes. Grim-faced and shaking with fury, he snarled:

"You needed him, but not me? Is that what you couldn't tell me?"

"The letter," she said softly; then, more firmly, "the letter was not from me." Her eyes caught his and held them defiantly. "It was from my mother."

"Your mother!" His voice dripped with sarcasm and disbelief.

"Yes, my mother." Summer's back stiffened at his scathing tone. "She wrote the letter to Sam McLean over five years ago. It came to the fort and was delivered to Ellen by mistake." Her voice sounded like that of a stranger. "Ellen read it. She said Sam was killed before she could deliver it, but now we know he was killed because of the letter. She couldn't stand the thought of Sam and . . . my mother." With determination, she stilled her trembling lips. She had to finish, had to get this over with. "The letter was in my mother's handwriting and on my mother's paper. There's no doubt in my mind that she wrote it." She looked away from him, she couldn't see him anyhow, for tears suddenly blinded her. "The letter said that I am . . . Sam McLean's daughter." There! It was out! She had said the words!

She was glad she couldn't see his face. This must be a terrible shock to him. Suddenly, she was afraid of what he would say. Her body tensed. There was a long moment while she held her breath, while her heart almost stopped beating. Then the hoarse, whispered words reached her through the silence.

"My God! I should have known."

The visions that came to her, illuminated in her mind, were of the times they had lain together, naked and desperate in their need for each other. Help me, God. Help me to help him. I've had five days to accustom my mind to this. If I could bear the pain, the humiliation he is feeling, I would gladly do so. His next words, when they finally penetrated, were as shocking to her as hers had been to him.

"I had started to suspect."

"Suspect?" She felt a terrible sinking sensation.

"Little things you did that seemed familiar."

"You suspected that you and . . . I, and yet you . . . we. . . ." The horror of it was written on her face. "You . . . how could you?" She gasped for breath, choked, made a gurgling sound in her throat. "You're an animal!"

Slater struggled to sit up, his bandaged hand reaching out to her.

"No! It isn't like that! Summer, listen! We did nothing wrong . . . darling . . . sweetheart . . . we did nothing wrong!"

If Summer heard, she gave no indication. She had clasped her hands over her ears and was shaking her head in wild denial.

"Nothing wrong?" she gasped. Dazed, confused, she had expected most anything from him but this.

"Sam was not my real father!" He shouted the words, trying to penetrate the wall of hysteria that surrounded her.

Through the storm that shook her, Summer heard the words, but couldn't comprehend them. Then the insistent pounding of the words: *Not my father . . . not my father.* Could they be true? Was he lying to cover up what they had done? The forearm of his bandaged hand was striking her arm, shaking her.

"Stop! Stop!" she cried, and jumped to her feet, tears streaming down her face and into her mouth.

"Don't go, Summer! Please, don't go! Jack and Bulldog will tell you it's true. I was going to tell you. I swear I was going to tell you. I never dreamed it would be so important." There was pain, anguish, pleading in every fiber of his voice.

"Important?" She felt as though she was about to fly into a million pieces. She sank to her knees, her face covered with her hands. She wanted to believe him. Oh, how she wanted to believe him!

"I promised Sam I would never tell. Ellen and Travis would have taken the Keep if they had known."

"You're . . . sure?" she whimpered.

"I'm positive. I've got letters my mother wrote to my father thinking he was still alive. I'll tell you the whole story. There's no doubt, sweetheart. No doubt at all. Come to me, my summertime girl. Come let me hold you. God, what I've put you through by not telling! Come to me. I'll make it up to you. I swear I'll make it up."

He lay back with arms outstretched. She crawled to him, like a small, wounded animal, and nestled against him, her wet face pressed in the curve of his neck. His arm came around her, and with surprising strength clasped her to him. The safe haven of his arms was wonderful, glorious! He murmured love-words and nuzzled his face in her hair. His heart was thumping wildly and a clammy film of perspiration covered his bare chest.

Summer didn't want to talk. She wanted only to be close to him, savor the delight and enjoy the wonder of being held by him in love. They both felt fatigued and weakened by the emotional ordeal they had been through. Minutes passed without words. Low moans came from Slater's throat as he kissed every part of her face he could reach with his lips. The sweetness of it caused the tears to come again.

"It all seems like a bad dream," she sobbed. "Tell me again. Tell me we didn't have the same father."

They lay close, lips never far apart, breathing the same air, and Slater told her the story of his mother and father and the part Sam had played in their lives.

"Sam and my pa were boyhood friends back in Scotland. They were close as brothers; closer than Sam was to his own brother, Scott. Sam came to Texas and filed a claim. Times were hard for my pa in Scotland, and Sam wrote for him to come to America. In the meanwhile, Pa had married. My ma was a gentle girl, and crossing the ocean to a new land was a frightful

292

experience for her. The ship they sailed on landed in New Orleans, and from there they took a smaller boat to Corpus Christi. At that time, Corpus was just a frontier trading post and rougher than a cob. It still is, for that matter. Sam went down there to meet them, but before he arrived, my pa, a big brawny Scot, tried to break up a fight and a sailor stabbed him to death right before my mother's eyes. She never recovered from the shock, never believed he was dead. When Sam got there, he saw there was but one thing for him to do. She was pregnant and alone. He married her and brought her back to the Keep, where I was born. No one knew I wasn't Sam's son. It was a long time after my mother died that Sam told me. He wanted me to know about my real pa. He showed me letters my mother had written to him over the years, believing he was still in Scotland and would come for her. Sam wouldn't have made such a thing of keeping it a secret, but Scott, his brother, and Ellen held that McLean land went to blood McLeans. Sam said it was true in the old country, but this was a new land. There were never any papers to make me Sam's legal son. You would have had to know him to understand how he depended on his own strength and ignored legal matters. I was his son in every way, except he didn't sire me. It mattered so little to me, that years went by and I never thought about it. It doesn't matter now. Ellen and Travis are dead. The Keep will go on just as Sam planned."

"He must have loved my mother," Summer spoke quietly. "I know she loved him even though she loved my pa, too."

"Yes, I think he did love Nannie. I can see that now. He was probably the only man that ever rejected Ellen, and her love for him turned to hate." He closed her eyes with his lips. "I love you so much. . . ." he whispered. "I wanted to die when you left me."

She kissed his neck, his chin, his rough cheek. His

head bent and he desperately sought her lips with his. The kiss lasted a long time and was full of sweetness.

She whispered endearments and sighed his name.

"My darling summertime girl, the time went so slow. I waited and waited for you to come. I hungered for the feel of you. I need your love. Don't leave me again." His humbled voice vibrated with emotion.

"Don't talk about it. Please . . . don't talk about it," she implored.

They lay for a long while, close and silent. The campfire burned until only a few glowing coals remained. If Bulldog or Jack came back to the camp they never knew it. Slater turned on his good side and lay with his head on her breast. His bandaged hand fumbled with the opening of her dress.

"Help me," he whispered huskily.

With trembling fingers, she opened her bodice and pressed his cheek to the soft skin of her breast. His lips kissed the smooth flesh while she brushed the dark hair back from his face and pressed her mouth to his forehead. It was so good to hold him. So wonderful to have the heavy burden lifted from her heart.

Long habits of concern are hard to forget, and she asked softly, "John Austin? Is he all right?"

"Fine," he murmured against her neck. "Kid has brains he hasn't used yet."

Laughter bubbled up inside her. She wanted to talk now. She wanted to tell him everything.

"Ellen said you could be hanged if anyone found out about us being together. She called it incest. I didn't know what it meant."

"She had it all figured out. True to form right up to the last."

"Her only thoughts at the last were for Travis." She shivered and tightened her arms protectively. "It was terrible to see her lying there, dying, and talking about Sam and my mother."

"Sam once said that Ellen was more devil than woman. I guess he knew what he was talking about."

Summer raised up suddenly, and Slater rolled over onto his back. She leaned over him so she could see his face.

"Slater," she said softly. Her fingers went over his lips, traced the scar that was familiar to them. "Slater, I've news to tell you. News that will make you understand why I had to leave you and why Jesse helped me." She kissed his lips, his scarred cheek. Her eyes smiled into his. "We've got to see a preacher and get a ring on my finger before I get any bigger." Her violet eyes searched his face. At first, there was nothing; then a smile that started at the corners of his lips spread into a broad grin. The forearm across her back gripped her tightly, and it was his turn to whisper.

"You're sure?"

"Positive!" Her eyes devoured his face.

"Don't that beat all?" He couldn't seem to stop grinning. When the shock had passed, he put an arm behind her head to pull her to him. "Damn these hands! I want to touch you, feel you."

Her laugh was a soft purr of pure happiness. "I'll touch you, feel you."

"We'll stop in Hamilton, love. That preacher will have to come out to the wagon. I'm marrying you tomorrow!"

"I don't have a new dress," she teased.

"You don't need one," he growled. "Hush your talking, woman, and lay here beside me . . . close to me. God, how I've missed you!"

"I'm afraid I'll hurt you."

"You'll hurt me a hell of a lot more if you don't. Come kiss me some more, sweetheart. Come kiss me and tell me you love me." He nudged her hand until it lay on his chest. "Touch me," he whispered, his heartbeat quickening.

She tremblingly traced the powerful lines of his chest, being careful to avoid his wounds, aware of that fast, deep heartbeat, hearing it accelerate as her fingers stroked the short black hair curling from his brown skin. Leaning her face against him, she let her lips drift down his body, the taste of warm, moist skin on her tongue and in her mouth. His body quivered and she became aware of the movement of his thigh against her. The heat of their bodies had become explosive, and she stopped her stroking hands.

"Don't stop!" His voice was muffled as his lips probed her warm white breast, and Summer felt herself shuddering as she faced a decision.

"We must! Darling, we must stop! Jack and . . . Bulldog. . . ."

For a moment, he lay still, breathing in rough gasps, his body seemed to shiver, then he drew back his head and smiled into her eyes. Wild, sweet hunger caused them to move together and their mouths clung in a long kiss. It was a while before either of them was calm enough to talk again.

"You're sure there's something there? Something of you and me?" Slater's bandaged hand gently nudged her flat stomach.

She laughed. It was so wonderful to laugh.

"I'm sure. Of course I'm sure. A few days ago, I hated the poor little thing. Now, I love it."

"Not more than me?" His lips were against her face, his tone anxious.

"Never more than you, darling." She slipped her arms around his neck and whispered in his ear. "I adored you when I was a little girl and I still do. You're my everything—my heart, my soul, my life. I love you beyond everything else in the world."

His lips crushed hers hungrily. "I want to love you!

Dear God, how I want to love you! These damn hands . . . it'll be so long. . . ."

"Not so long, darling," she whispered. "Only until tomorrow, when you fetch me home like you promised so long ago." She punctuated her words with soft, nibbling kisses. "We'll manage. You'll see. We'll manage just fine."